Playing with

Fuego

T0161797

KG MacGregor

Lambda Literary Award Winner

Bella
BOOKS

2012

Bella Books, Inc.
P.O. Box 10543
Tallahassee, FL 32302

Printed in the United States of America on acid-free paper
First published 2012

Editor: Katherine V. Forrest
Cover Designer: Kiaro Creative

ISBN 13: 978-1-59493-313-4

Other Bella Books by KG MacGregor

Malicious Pursuit
House on Sandstone
Mulligan
Just This Once
Sumter Point
Out of Love
Secrets So Deep
Worth Every Step
Sea Legs
Photographs of Claudia
Rhapsody

Shaken Series:
Without Warning
Aftershock
Small Packages
Mother Load

Acknowledgment

People often ask where I get my story ideas, and I can honestly say this one was inspired by the struggles I experienced as a white Southerner trying to find my way in Miami, Florida, one of the most culturally diverse communities in the world. It was only natural that I tell this story in first person. When I first moved there nearly twenty years ago, I was instantly caught up in the cosmopolitan excitement, and fascinated at being surrounded by so many beautiful people. Then I went through my phase when I wanted a machine gun mounted to the top of my car. Fortunately, that passed without bloodshed as I slowly came to recognize and appreciate all Miami had to offer. I left Florida last year for fresh digs in California, but with plenty of fondness for my years in the Magic City—proof positive that attitudes can be changed with greater understanding.

As always, I thank my editor and friend, Katherine V. Forrest, this time for helping me tackle a new point of view. Thanks and love also to my partner Jenny for her technical assistance, and for supporting my work in every way imaginable. To Karen Appleby, my glitch-finder, much appreciation. And once again, I salute all the staff at Bella Books for their hard work and professionalism, and kudos to Kiaro Creative for this dazzling cover.

About the Author

A former teacher and market research consultant, KG MacGregor holds a PhD in journalism from UNC-Chapel Hill. Infatuation with *Xena: Warrior Princess* fan fiction prompted her to try her own hand at storytelling in 2002. In 2005, she signed with Bella Books, which published the Golden Crown finalist *Just This Once*. Her sixth Bella novel, *Out of Love*, won the Lambda Literary Award for Women's Romance and the Golden Crown Award in Lesbian Romance. She picked up Goldies also for *Without Warning*, *Worth Every Step* and *Photographs of Claudia* (Contemporary Romance), and *Secrets So Deep* (Romantic Suspense).

Other honors include the Lifetime Achievement Award from the Royal Academy of Bards, the Alice B. Readers Appreciation Medal, and several Readers Choice Awards.

An avid supporter of queer literature, KG currently serves on the Board of Trustees for the Lambda Literary Foundation. She divides her time between Palm Springs and her native North Carolina mountains.

Contact KG through her website at *www.kgmacgregor.com*.

CHAPTER ONE

"Holy Jenko!"

Few things fire me up like a pair of cockroaches running in circles around my feet. There I was stomping and flailing about with the broom like a marionette, but it was all adrenaline. I just wanted to pulverize their gnarly innards and grind them into the concrete floor.

"You need to get over that woman!" That was our construction foreman Bo shouting at me from outside, where he was taking down the house's hurricane shutters.

To the untrained eye, yelling out my ex's name as an expletive probably seems a bit vindictive. That's because they don't know Emily Jenko like I do. Screaming her name helps squelch my lifelong impulse to swear, much like chewing gum keeps people from smoking and smoking keeps people from eating. Seriously, nothing says shit or fuck like a throaty "Jenko!"

"Palmetto bug or banana spider?" He took amusement from my aversion to Miami's crawly things.

"Bugs—plural—and I'm leaving their guts in here for you to clean up."

The kitchen flooded with light as he removed the last of the shutters with his power drill. The house didn't yet have new window frames, so the corrugated aluminum sheets we screw onto the outside every night are meant to discourage squatters. That works fine until some enterprising thief unscrews them and carries them off for what they'll fetch at the recycling center.

Other than his habit of laughing at my squeamishness over insects, Bo McConnell is one of the nicest guys I know. A towering African-American with more freckles than Howdy Doody, he respects women as only a father of three teenage daughters can. Underneath his ever-present Marlins baseball cap is a stripe of gray hair growing straight back from his forehead, which he blames on his girls. His soft hands belie three decades of construction work, but I think they suit his gentle soul.

Another reason I like Bo—and I'm fully aware this will make me sound like a xenophobe—is because he speaks flawless English, and without an accent. That's rare in Miami, where two-thirds of the population is Hispanic. It's not that I don't appreciate diversity. I just don't like being the one who's different.

There are only a handful of non-Hispanics like Bo and me at the Miami Home Foundation, a nonprofit builder funded by grants and donations from the community. Unlike Habitat for Humanity, which builds new dwellings on donated land, our mission is to renovate blighted homes to make them safe and attractive for families needing a hand up. Sometimes there's little difference between us and Habitat. We gutted this house all the way down to its frame and concrete foundation because vermin infestations and water damage from a leaky roof rendered the structure unrecoverable. Like Habitat, we employ a small construction staff during the week but rely also on unpaid weekend help. Recruiting all those volunteers—and then herding them on Saturdays—is my job. MBA in human resources, Dartmouth. On the days my job drives me crazy, I comfort myself with the fact that at least I have one, which is more than a lot of people in South Florida can say.

"It's a good day to paint...not so humid, nice little breeze. This feels more like March than May," Bo said, passing his drill through the window so I could lock it in the toolbox. Things of value have a way of walking off the jobsite here in Little Haiti, which is why even the toolbox is chained to an eyebolt in the floor. "What's our gang like today?"

"We've got the choir from the Morningside Church of Faith. Four men, eight women. Not too bad for a paint crew."

"Any linebackers?" That was our code for volunteers who look strong and fit. "I need that pile of extra blocks out back moved up to the curb for pickup tomorrow."

"Sorry. Maybe if we all pitch in for a half hour or so, it won't take too much out of anybody." The last thing we want is for one of our volunteers to keel over with a heart attack, so we're always careful not to give people more than they can handle.

While he went off to lug the five-gallon paint buckets out of the storage shed, I counted out a dozen T-shirts in various sizes and took them out to the end of the driveway, where the volunteers were talking excitedly and sharing coffee from a giant thermos. I always like how happy everyone is first thing in the morning. Church groups seem to stay that way throughout the day. It's usually the corporate types and teenagers who start groaning by the first break.

"Look, everyone. It's Daphne, from the training session." The woman attached to that exceedingly cheerful voice was Morningside's music minister, a curly-haired cherub with lines around her mouth and eyes, probably because she smiles all the time. If I were a churchgoing songbird, I wouldn't mind this jolly bunch, but I'm agnostic and can't carry a tune in a pickup truck.

Unlike the music minister, I suck at remembering names, but then I have a new crew of names and faces every week. A quick rundown of the sign-in sheet identified her as Diana.

"Good morning! I'm so excited to see you all here. We're going to have a fabulous day." Meryl Streep has nothing on me. "Daphne Maddox, volunteer coordinator for the Miami Home

Foundation. I'm sure you all remember me from the orientation last month. All right, let's see a show of hands. How many of you slept through that?"

That always brought a few chuckles, and helped me segue into a repeat of my safety spiel, a harrowing litany of things like tetanus, blindness and paralysis that could result from carelessness on the jobsite. Diana offered to pray for our deliverance, which seemed like a good idea.

As folks bowed their heads, I noticed a white Porsche Carrera creeping slowly past the house, its tinted windows shielding the driver from view. One thing about blighted homes is they tend to be in blighted neighborhoods, and it's all too common to see rich dudes in their sports cars and luxury SUVs trolling the streets of Little Haiti in search of a drug buy. Their brazen attitude always gets under my skin, but never more than when we have a church or youth group onsite. It pissed me off royally when the Porsche parked at the end of the row alongside vehicles belonging to our volunteers.

The driver made no move to exit, and when the choir members followed Bo around the side of the house for painting instructions, I considered calling the cops. It wouldn't be the first time they busted up some action on this street at our behest. Instead I decided to make a show of jotting down the license number, figuring whoever it was would get spooked and drive off.

Then the driver's door opened and a woman's leg emerged clad in skinny jeans and red high-topped sneakers, the designer variety, not the kind you actually wear when you want to sneak somewhere. Like any good lesbian brain, mine went to work on conjuring what the rest of her would look like but something was off about the context. If she was a drug buyer, she wasn't a very smart one. With everyone in the universe now holding a camera phone in their pocket, those guys never did more than crack the tinted window when they came by. Probably not a choir member either…just a gut feeling about rich camels not getting through a haystack in heaven, or whatever that saying was. And she definitely wasn't from the foundation because none of us could afford a hundred-thousand-dollar car.

As I got closer, I could hear her talking on the phone—Spanish, of course, because that's what nearly everyone in Miami speaks—and that's when I saw the familiar blue slip of paper in her hand. All the privileged, arrogant, entitled, pompous pieces fell into place. She wasn't a drug buyer, and she wasn't with the church or the foundation. She was here under court order to perform community service for a crime against society.

"If you want—"

She swung her other leg out and without even making eye contact held up a finger to shush me. Not a good idea.

I felt the blood running to my face and was already savoring the power I had to make this woman's life miserable. "If you want credit for today, you have ten seconds to hang up and get your butt over to the house. Otherwise just go on back to bed and we'll start this little game over again next Saturday."

I was already halfway back to the house when I heard her slam the door and scamper up behind me, but like a clueless twit, she continued to chatter away on the phone. I spun back around and whipped my hand across my throat as a sign for her to cut it.

She finally stuffed the phone into her back pocket, and by now was making eye contact, with a dark glare that must have rivaled my own—enormous brown eyes set between a deep V that bisected her perfectly sculpted eyebrows. Her angry look, no doubt, and I relished having put it there.

I shuffled the papers on my clipboard and thrust it into her hands. "Fill out the form and then come find me for your assignment."

Not that I had anything urgent to do. I just didn't want to dance from one foot to the other while she wrote, so I went into the house and pretended to sweep up squashed cockroaches while watching her through the window.

She stood about five-eight and had one of those slim figures that meant she could just go and pluck anything off the rack and have it fit perfectly. Makes me sick. Her long dark hair had tiny golden streaks all through it—like we don't know that's fake—and it was pulled back in a tight ponytail with two-hundred-dollar Jimmy Choo sunglasses perched on top.

"What do I put where it says Agency Number?" she called.

"I'll fill in that part," I answered gruffly, irritated to discover she had the sort of deep, husky voice I normally find very sexy. Not on this woman.

I stomped back down the front porch steps and snatched the clipboard from her hands.

"Follow me." I led her past the paint crews to the backyard and pushed the wheelbarrow over to the blocks Bo wanted moved. The whole pile was about the size of a pickup truck. "We need these brought around front and stacked at the end of the driveway. Two fifteen-minute breaks and a half hour for lunch. Cleanup starts at three and that gets you eight hours."

It was then I noticed her fingernails, finely manicured and painted a deep glossy burgundy, like she'd never done an honest day's work in her life. I felt a small pang of sympathy, enough to offer my work gloves, which she took without so much as a grunt of thanks. In fact, she'd stripped all the emotion from her face, as if she didn't want to give me the satisfaction of knowing how pissed off she was. Some people are too stubborn for their own good.

Maribel Tirado León, according to her paperwork. Thirty-three years old with an address on Brickell Bay Drive, one of the most upscale areas of Miami. No wonder I didn't like her. Most of our community service workers were drunk drivers but they usually got fifty hours and her court order said thirty-two. Probably winked at the judge.

Or more likely, the judge was her uncle or an old friend of the family, someone they all knew back in Cuba. That's how things work in Miami, and if you happen to be a fair-skinned, blue-eyed blonde from New England like me, whose command of Spanish goes only as far as *no hablo español*, forget it. Nearly every job in town requires you to be "bilingual," which means you can butcher English all you want but not Spanish.

So far, Maribel León was the walking, talking personification of everything I hate about Miami, but my list is long and she couldn't possibly hit all my hot buttons.

But then I watched her work, and over the course of the morning I developed a grudging respect as she whittled that pile of blocks down. No easy task because she had to balance them just right on the wheelbarrow, and it kept getting mired in the soft sand at the corner of the house. The second time it tipped over, I had to sweetly tell her of the No Cursing Rule we had on the jobsite. Good thing I hadn't thrown her in with the church choir.

At eleven thirty, another gang from the church showed up with a gigantic spread of sandwiches and salads, but Miss Attitude declined their kind offer to share. Instead, she spent the entire lunch break leaning against her car chattering on her cell phone. From the sour look on her face, she was complaining about me. I liked that.

While the choir gathered across the street under a shade tree, Bo slid down the wall and stretched his legs out alongside mine on the porch. "I don't know what you said to your community service worker, but I hope you've got a version that works on teenage girls."

"She needed a little attitude adjustment and I helped her get it."

"Looks like you made an impression. I don't think I've ever seen one of our reluctant volunteers work that hard. I had to tell her twice it was time to knock off for lunch."

I actually hadn't intended to make her move the whole pile of blocks by herself. That was a lot of work even for a linebacker, which she wasn't. But she seemed hell-bent to not complain or show any sign of weakness.

"I bet she'll be taking your name in vain tomorrow when she rolls out of bed."

As we got back to work, I had to admit I was feeling a lot less vindictive. She wasn't nearly the princess I'd thought she was, though I still doubted she'd ever done physical work like this before. She had muscles, though...the sinewy kind women got from working out with a personal trainer two or three times a week.

If anything dampened my impression about her, it was how she'd ended up here in the first place. Even the volunteers who goof off are still volunteers, the sort of people who give up a Saturday of their own accord out of kindness to others. Court-assigned workers never glow with pride and satisfaction the way our volunteers do after a day's work.

Miss Attitude wasn't glowing with anything but sweat, so much that her tight gray T-shirt was soaked and clinging to her slender back. I got a good look at it when she brought another load out to the curb.

By this time, I figured she'd learned her lesson—we weren't a bunch of pushovers—and Bo had left me feeling a tad guilty about how sore she'd be tomorrow. I started thinking if I pitched in to help, we could knock off the rest of the pile in an hour or so and she could finish up the day with something simple like pushing a broom through the house.

I was about to tell her that when Roberto Rodriguez pulled up in his building materials delivery truck and started chattering away with her in Spanish. "*Abadababababa* something-about-a-*baño abadababababa*.*"* Granted, I have a lot of trouble understanding Roberto's English but it pisses me off when these guys don't even try to talk to me at all.

"He wants to know how many bathrooms the house has," Maribel said, her deep, sexy voice quite businesslike.

"Uno," I answered pointedly, which was a huge mistake because he followed that up with about two hundred more words in Spanish, making me look utterly stupid because I had to look to Maribel to translate.

"He has two matching medicine cabinets but one of them is broken. He'll donate them if you'll write him a receipt for both."

One was all we needed anyway so that worked for me. "Tell him fine. I'll go get the receipt pad."

She was gone by the time I got back. Roberto jabbered a few more unintelligible words as I handed over the receipt, and then he drove off, leaving me to wrestle with getting the fifty-pound crate inside by myself. If I hadn't been such a jerk earlier, I could have just asked Maribel to lend me a hand. But I'd taken a lot of pleasure in making her day miserable and slapping on a sweet face now wouldn't change that.

I didn't even get the chance. The next time the wheelbarrow rolled around front, it was Bo who was pushing it.

"Need a hand with that, Daphne?"

"What happened to Miss Attitude?"

"Mari? Her hand was bleeding so I bandaged it for her and told her I'd finish up. She's out back holding a ladder for somebody."

Mari? How sweet. Not Mary, but *Mah-ri.* So sah-ri, Mah-ri. Bet it rolled right off her lips when she batted her eyes at Bo and got him falling all over himself to fix her little boo-boo. Where did these people get off feeling so special?

I let Bo carry in the crate by himself and took a moment to get a grip on why I was so annoyed, since I'd been planning to go help her finish up anyway. The fact he'd done it first meant he looked like a knight in shining armor and I looked like a total asshole.

Make that a total Jenko.

My gloves, though folded neatly beside what was left of the stack, were shredded from the day's work, and predictably stained with blood around one of the places that had worn through. In just the twenty minutes it took Bo and me to finish, I felt the start of a blister on my thumb in the same place. No wonder Maribel's—*Mari's*—hand was bleeding. I never meant for that to happen.

In fact, I never meant to make her whole day wretched either, at least not after I got over my initial hissy fit. Now that she was working with the others on the painting, she was all smiles and laughing about how she couldn't sing a note. She liked everyone here but me.

When Bo called for the afternoon break I caught up with her as she walked back over to her car. "Hey, uh…Maribel?"

"What now?" When she spun around, it was like she was shooting daggers from her eyes. Sure, I needed to fix the part of her Attitude that was my fault, but I wasn't going to kiss her butt to do it.

Nothing against her butt…no, I didn't need to go there.

"I, uh…I was looking at my notes and realized you didn't come to our orientation meeting last week. We usually require that for everybody, even the community service people."

"Yeah, I know. The clerk told me when I signed up but I'd already missed it. I figured I'd come to the next one."

"You didn't really miss a whole lot. It's just a basic rundown of safety rules, and I go over all of them again first thing every morning…which is kind of what you skipped by getting here late."

"It won't happen again," she said curtly and started to walk away.

"Wait, I wasn't trying to bust your chops. I was just going to say that I waive the orientation sometimes when it's obvious people know what they're doing. We give a couple of hours' credit for coming, and I can go ahead and put you down for it. That gives you eight hours so you can call it a day if you want."

"Seriously?" She gave me a sidelong look that I assumed was distrust. Better than contempt.

"Yeah, just try not to do anything careless next time you come." Like tearing the skin off your hands because you're too stubborn to let somebody know your gloves had worn out. "That would make me look bad."

"So I can go?" This time I got a smile, just big enough to show off an adorable dimple on her left cheek.

"Beat it. I'll see you next week." I was trying to sound friendly for a change but it came off more like a mom giving in to her kids. Not exactly the image I wanted to convey, especially since my thoughts of her were anything but childlike as I watched her backside twist away in those skinny jeans.

CHAPTER TWO

At least Emily got one thing right. Our south-facing balcony in Edgewater has one of the best views in Miami, especially on mornings like this one. From my lounge chair, I can see the cruise port, the Biscayne Bay and the high-rises of downtown and Brickell. Another skyscraping condo building is planned for the vacant lot beside us and it will cut off part of my view, but the real estate bust guarantees it won't go up anytime soon.

Also guaranteed is the fact I'm stuck here. Emily and I bought this prime corner unit on the fifteenth floor—two bedroom suites and a wraparound balcony—while the market was on its way up. Nearly half of the building's investors have defaulted since then, and our property values have tanked by forty percent.

Until a couple of years ago, Emily and I had both been on the hook for the loan. Then I did something incredibly stupid. She had stopped sending her half of the monthly payment, so I got her to sign a quit claim deed, turning over sole ownership to me. Sure, she forfeited her half of our sixty-thousand-dollar down payment, but she's now free and clear of the debt. I, on the other hand, owe a hundred thousand more than this place is worth.

Why do I have to ruin every single day by thinking about Emily Jenko first thing in the morning? I should be soaking in the sunrise from our balcony—*my* balcony. It was glorious, one of the few things about Miami I find worthy of its being called the Magic City.

Although I find the *Miami Herald* pretty magical too. I'd never been much of a newspaper reader, but some of the things that happen in this town are so outrageous, it's like reading *The Onion*. Half the time you can't tell what's real and what's parody.

Somebody wants to know why the same company gets all the vending machine contracts at the airport. I can answer that without reading another word—because their families were all friends back in Cuba. Or Puerto Rico. Or Colombia.

I peeked.

Surprise, surprise. They weren't friends after all. The Cuban contractor is the uncle of the county's procurement officer. Silly me not to think of nepotism.

You don't stand a chance in this town if you're not connected. I learned that the hard way when I made the final cut for assistant director of human resources at one of the cruise lines and lost out to a twenty-two-year-old Venezuelan guy fresh out of a college I'd never even heard of with a degree in international studies. International studies!

If I'd taken the job at the hotel chain in Boston, I'd be an assistant vice president by now. But no, I'd followed Emily, the love of my life, who picked a law firm in Miami because she was drawn to the glamour and sunshine. Then she realized the plum assignments at her firm went to the bilingual associates, no matter how many nights she burned the midnight oil at her desk.

At least that's where she'd told me she was. Turned out she and one of the other attorneys had found true love in the legal stacks and they left the firm together to hang out their own shingle in Sarasota. Emily was so very sorry, you know. She never meant for it to happen. Like I give a big fat Jenko.

The sliding glass door on the next unit banged open and I braced for the tirade that was sure to follow. It didn't take a psychic to know that when the door slid with such ferocity, Edith and Mordecai Osterhoff would soon be screaming at one another.

My neighbors were in their late seventies, a fiery combination of Long Island WASP and resettled German Jew. Edith is just about the staunchest liberal I've ever met, and Mordy isn't far behind…except when it comes to the Cubans. The retired head of a service workers union, he feels the same way I do about Miami being a banana republic. But where he's my simpatico, Edith is my conscience and his too.

"Because they don't give two shits about the workers," he growled at Edith. "They got their own union and it's called the Cuban Mafia."

Clearly, he'd read the same story I had.

"They aren't anything like the Mafia and you know it," Edith yelled back. She never backed down, and even seemed to enjoy these battles. "They came to America just like the Jews and worked hard to give their children a better life."

"The Jews didn't come over here and expect Americans to learn Hebrew. We melted into the pot with everybody else. They act like we're the ones who should accommodate them."

"Pipe down, old man. Daphne's going to think you're a bigot."

Even though we couldn't see each other through the wall that divided our balconies, they knew I sat out here every morning. Sometimes I thought they brought their bickering outside just to see whose side I'd take.

"I think I'm with Mordy on this one, Edith. Fifty years is a long time not to assimilate." Then out of nowhere, I got a mental image of Maribel León with her sweaty T-shirt and bandaged hand. "But I agree with you too. Our Cuban volunteers at the foundation work as hard as anybody."

Taking both sides wasn't acceptable to either of them and they began shouting over each other as though the loudest would win. When their respective diatribes wound down, I heard Mordy draw a deep conciliatory breath.

"Come over tonight, Daphne. Edith's making matzo ball soup."

"Since when?" she snapped.

"Be nice for a change. Daphne likes matzo ball soup."

"Fine, but you'll have to go to the store for parsley and eggs."

"Fifty-one years we've been married and you never noticed I go to the store every day."

"You only go to watch the women who stop in on their way home from the gym. All that spandex will make you blind."

No matter how much they fought, I knew they loved each other more than life itself. I'd seen it firsthand the night Mordy had collapsed during dinner at Roasters and Toasters on Miami Beach. Edith was practically in tears as we waited for the doctor at Mount Sinai to tell us it was only the flu. Then she began berating him for probably giving it to her when he took a bite of her corned beef sandwich. Three days later it turned out she was right.

For all my grumbling about the diversity in Miami, my life was richer for knowing Edith and Mordy. Now if only I could learn to appreciate the rest of the hodgepodge.

"I'll pick up a bottle of Manischewitz," I called. There was fine wine and there was the syrupy sweet concoction we always drink with dinner because it's kosher. "I have to go to work. You two try to behave yourselves."

On my way down the elevator opened on the fourteenth floor for Ronaldo García, the fortyish Brazilian man who lived directly below me. Even my lesbian eyes found him handsome. His crisp white shirts lit up his olive skin, piercing brown eyes and wavy dark hair slick with gel, and while I don't know Armani from Brooks Brothers, I'd bet my paycheck his suits were expensive, since they draped flawlessly from his slender body.

"*Bom dia*," he said, momentarily blinding me with his dazzling white teeth.

"Good morning." I stepped toward the back and tried not to inhale his cologne because it made me want to sneeze. Other than that, he was possibly perfect.

As handsome as Ronaldo was, I'd rather have run into his wife Tandra, who made me drool like a lecherous Neanderthal. She looked like a Maxim model with her long thin neck, four-inch stiletto heels and spandex dresses that barely covered her curvaceous backside. I even found her baby bump sexy as hell.

Maribel León would be smoking hot in spandex. She probably had a boyfriend as handsome as Ronaldo. Not a husband though. She struck me as too independent for that. Even in a Latin culture, I was willing to bet women like Mari called the shots.

Ever the gentleman, Ronaldo held the elevator door to allow me to exit first. I wish I could be friendlier but I'd never heard him speak a word of English and the few times I'd tried to interact, I'd gotten only a polite smile that suggested he didn't have a clue what I was saying. It was awkward.

At least Mari was bilingual. Even though she spoke with a slight accent—as most Cubans did—I had a feeling she was born right here in the good old US of A. Many of the Cubans of her generation had older family members who didn't speak English at all. The kids had grown up naturally bilingual because they spoke English in school and Spanish at home, and that's why they all had accents.

Wonder what Mari would think of my ten-year-old, formerly black Mustang, which I'd named Sally. Next to her Porsche, mine was a piece of Jenko. Pretty sporty when it was new, but the combination of salt on the snowy roads of New Hampshire and now the salt air in Miami had taken its toll on the paint job, leaving it a drab gray. I was stuck with it too.

"Fixated, Daphne?" Yes, I talk to myself all the time. When you live alone, you have to check every now and then to see if your voice works.

I'd been thinking about Mari way too much over the last few days. No matter how much I justified to myself coming down hard on her, I really didn't enjoy behaving like a jerk. Besides, I'm a well-educated human resources professional who knows you don't get your best work out of people by treating them like Jenko.

I pulled out of the garage, girding myself for my least favorite part of Miami, the commute to our office park out past the airport. At the very first stoplight, the driver behind me laid on his horn the split second the light turned green but I held my ground and counted. I know better than to assume the right of way, since cross traffic always continues like a conga line, with each car practically welded to the bumper of the car in front. Mordy calls it the Three Second Rule, meaning you have to wait that long before entering an intersection or risk getting broadsided.

A few blocks later I joined the quagmire inching west on the Dolphin Expressway. I can easily admit Boston traffic is worse, but no one comes close to Miami drivers on the Rude-O-Meter. I have a rule of my own, the Never Take Your Hands Off the Wheel Rule, which helps me fight the urge to flip off all the drivers who rush to the front of the Exit Only lane, only to cut back into traffic. Nine times out of ten they're talking on their cell phones because they're far too important to occupy themselves with such tedium as safe driving.

Forty-five minutes each way, thanks to the half million construction barrels that forced us down to only two lanes around Douglas Avenue and again at Bird Road. It's a wonder I don't drink all the time.

The first person to greet me was my boss, the foundation's executive director, Gisela Ruiz. "Happy Hump Day," she said, smiling smugly. Like most Colombians, she spoke English with a distinctive lilt.

I like Gisela, except when she rubs it in that Hump Day for me is Thursday, since I work Saturdays at the construction site. "At least I never have to face a Monday morning on the Dolphin."

As the public face of the foundation, she always dressed conservatively in a business suit and high-collared blouse, and wore her dark hair in a tight bun with large hoop earrings.

"You must be going out today," she said, eyeing my dress slacks and silk blazer. Most days, I wear casual chinos, saving my better clothes for when I have to meet with the public.

"I'm doing an orientation over a brown-bag lunch at Total Bank. They've got a dozen or so volunteers signed up for Saturday."

We were the only ones in the office at nine a.m. because— and this drives me absolutely berserk—everyone else was late. Everyone. Hispanic Time, they call it. They'd work through lunch and stay late to get their hours in, but forget calling a meeting in the morning because you never know when people are going to get there. Gisela lets it slide, writing it off to culture. Just another sign I'm not cut out to live in Miami.

My office was little more than a cubbyhole but at least it had a door and I didn't have to share it. It's not that I don't like the people I work with. I do, but some days their chatter seems endless, and of course it's all in Spanish. I can pick up a word here and there, enough to know I don't want to hear about what happened on such and such novella or that Macy's is having a sale on slingback *zapatos*. I spend a lot of time on the phone procuring both volunteers and donations of building materials, so I can get away with keeping my door closed without people thinking I'm antisocial.

My first task was to print out directions to Total Bank. When I saw the Brickell address, it too made me think of Mari, and her fancy condo building on Brickell Bay Drive. And that made me think of something I'd been meaning to ask Gisela, so I stuck my head in her office.

"Got a question for you."

"Shoot."

It was then I noticed the nameplate on her desk, Gisela Ruiz-Martino, and it occurred to me for the first time that I'd been calling Mari by the wrong name. The Spanish custom is to take both parents' surnames, the father's first and then the mother's, but to use only the first surname unless in a legal document…like court papers. That meant she was Mari Tirado, not Mari León.

"I've got this new community service worker at the jobsite, a woman. The weird thing is her paperwork says thirty-two hours, and I've never had anybody like that before."

"That is weird. She's not a drunk driver because fifty hours is the mandatory minimum by the state." She spun in her chair and began clicking on her keyboard. "We should be able to find out. Community service sentences are public record."

I gave her the name and went around her desk to look over her shoulder.

"Felony littering."

"Since when is littering a felony?"

"I don't know, but that's what it says. Adjudication withheld… so if she completes her community service, makes restitution and pays a fine, her record is expunged."

All of a sudden I didn't like Mari Tirado, and didn't care if she liked me. People who throw out their trash in public places are pigs. Self-centered, arrogant degenerates, which wasn't all that far from my first impression of her when she'd held up a finger as if to say, "Don't bother me, pissant. I'm on the phone with someone more important."

What did I care if she got a stupid little blister? I didn't care if her whole hand fell off. Well, maybe not something as bad as that. But she certainly didn't deserve having anyone feel sorry for her, and I wish I hadn't been suckered into waiving her orientation. I just played right into that game of hers, making her feel entitled.

Mari was in for a rude awakening on Saturday. If she thought hauling blocks was tough, wait till I sent her up on the roof with a hammer and a stack of shingles. In this heat, she'd melt after an hour.

CHAPTER THREE

I was on the porch counting out T-shirts when the familiar white Porsche rumbled to a stop in front of the house. Mari got out right away, this time dressed in carpenter jeans, brand-new workboots and a skintight pale yellow T-shirt. A green cotton ball cap with a University of Miami logo hid her face from the sun, and her long dark ponytail swung freely from the hole in the back.

"Well, well. Looks like someone got the fashion memo."

Bo looked up from the supplies he'd been sorting. "A woman like that looks good in just about anything."

Especially handcuffs, I think to myself. At least I hope I thought it to myself. It's not the sort of thing I meant to say out loud. Bo never cares what sorts of trouble our community service workers have gotten into, as long as they give it their all on the jobsite.

He went out to the driveway to meet up with the Total Bank volunteers while I waited for Mari, who marched straight up the steps and handed me a small brown bag from the hardware store.

"Sorry I ruined your gloves last week. I got you another pair."

"Thanks, but you didn't have to do that. I go through so many that I buy them in packs of a dozen." In other words, I work all the time the way she did last week. "You may want to hold on to these."

"Let me guess. They're delivering a new load of blocks and you want them carted around to the backyard." She never even cracked a smile and neither did I.

"The other volunteers are from Total Bank and they're hanging drywall today. I showed them a video at work on Thursday so they'd know how to do it and since you missed that, I figured I'd get you started up on the roof."

"The roof? I haven't been on a roof since I was a kid." She looked up dubiously, clearly thinking I had to be kidding. She was mistaken.

"Guess you won't be able to say that again, will you?"

Nailing shingles was pretty easy once you got the hang of it, but we couldn't let just any bozo walk around twelve feet above the ground.

"You're not afraid of heights, are you?" I had to ask.

She shook her head but I could tell she was not happy.

One of the things we generally try to do with our volunteers is instill confidence. Many of them come out because they enjoy do-it-yourself projects, but others just want to learn and feel good about their contribution. We present every single task— no matter how much skill it requires—as something an average person can do. I'm living proof it works because I didn't know the first thing about renovating when I started at the foundation and now I can do practically any job they give me, as long as it's not something that requires a license.

"You can do this. Come on. I'll get you started."

The first thing I did was tie a nail belt around her waist. She smelled good, the definition of which is no perfume, no talc and no hints of food fragrances from her shampoo. I've never understood why anyone would want their hair to smell like strawberries, herbs or almonds. Why not hot dogs or pickled beets? Because food doesn't belong in your hair.

As she filled the pockets with nails, I located a hammer and utility knife.

"Good choice on the carpenter pants, by the way." I slid the hammer through the loop on her thigh so it dangled by her knee. Then I dropped the closed knife into the narrow pocket on the other side. "Now all you need is water."

She'd brought her own reusable bottle, which I thought was pretty considerate for a convicted litterbug.

Once we scaled the ladder, I was glad to see Bo's work crew had already nailed the first course in place and added the chalk lines needed to keep the rows straight. The learning curve on laying shingles was steep enough without the detail work.

"We start at the edge and work our way up. Six nails for every shingle. Some builders think four's enough, but this is hurricane country. What you do up here could mean the difference between saving a house and losing it."

It always sounds really dramatic but we drive that point home with everyone so they'll understand how important their job is. Since Mari was nodding along seriously, I felt pretty sure she wouldn't try to take any shortcuts.

I demonstrated where the nails went and how to cut the first row of shingles so the flaps were staggered, and then stepped back to watch her work. Her first few swats with the hammer reminded me of my own a couple of years ago, when it took me thirty swings to drive a three-inch nail through a two-by-four. I can do it in half that now, but guys like Bo do it in four. Roofing nails are only an inch long, and I had a feeling Mari would get it down to four or five before the day was over. Her work last week left me with the impression she wanted to be good at everything she did.

When she reached for her fifth shingle, I headed toward the ladder. "It's going to get hot up here. Drink lots of water whether or not you feel like you need it, and make sure you yell for someone when you start down that ladder."

Realistically, I couldn't leave her up there for more than a couple of hours on account of the heat, but I didn't mind having her think I would. And just to keep an eye on her, I decided it was a good time to paint the eaves on that side of the house, which is a lot harder than nailing shingles because I have to look up and stretch my arm out, all while balancing ten feet above the ground on a ladder. What mattered was that my head was almost even with the roofline so I could watch her every move.

Jenko, this would have been a better job for Mari. All she had to do was scoot around on her butt. If I traded with her now, she'd figure out pretty quick this was harder than that, and she'd think I couldn't handle it. Righteous indignation was so complicated.

After about thirty minutes my neck was killing me.

"We ought to break for water soon."

"I'm good," she called, not even looking up. Show-off. She was near the end of her first row already. It was only a tiny fraction of what had yet to be done, but that's what made roofing so tedious. I had to admit, she'd made pretty decent progress for a novice, and her work looked good.

"At least let me fill your water bottle. This heat sneaks up on you."

I used my break not only to catch a drink but also to check on the paperwork for today's volunteers. I'd forgotten to get Mari to sign in, and by the time I got back up to the roof with her freshly filled water bottle and the clipboard, Bo was working behind her on row two. She'd probably called out to him to bring her a cold drink or come see about her poor little blister.

They barely acknowledged me, and I went back to work on the eaves, but within earshot so I could hear what sort of sob story she was peddling.

"You're pretty good at this," Bo told her.

"Believe it or not, I've actually had a little experience. I remember helping my uncle fix our neighbor's roof after Hurricane Andrew. All I did was hand him shingles but it was fun."

"I remember that time well. We all worked together for months to clean up—everybody all over the city. Where were you when it hit?"

"With *mi abuela*…at my grandmother's house in the Gables. Eight of us crammed into the pantry because it didn't have windows. I'll never forget how scared we all were…passing around the rosary and praying we'd see the morning."

"Tell me about it. I was living down at Homestead."

"You guys got hammered."

Right on cue, Bo sent six nails into a shingle with only twelve swings. "Fortunately I was renting. We lost half the roof, but the worst part was when somebody's pickup truck blew right into the living room."

"So many horrible stories, but we were lucky. And you're right about how we all came together afterward. It gave us a sense of community."

Yeah, and what did Mari do with that community? She dumped her trash on it. Felony littering! I looked it up—five hundred pounds of trash. She must have junked an old car in the Everglades or something. Those things take like a billion years to biodegrade.

Another forty minutes went by and I was ready to scream, not just at the cramping in my neck and arms, but at the Mister Rogers reminiscing going on between Bo and Mari. You'd think they were the only ones who'd ever faced adversity. I'd like to see either one of them dig out of one of those eight-foot snowdrifts like we had in New Hampshire!

Mari's magical spell finally broke and Bo remembered his twelve bankers working inside the house.

"I better get down and see about the drywall. Say, Daph… your neck's got to be killing you by now. Last time you did that, you went on about it for a month. Why don't you jump on up here and give Mari a hand with the roof?"

Nice going, Bo. Now Mari thinks I'm a whiner.

"I'll finish this side." Even if it killed me. My neck felt like I was wearing a tractor tire for a necklace.

As I stepped up on the roof to let Bo use the ladder, Mari's cell phone rang with one of those maddening salsa jingles. If I ever make it to hell, I'm sure they'll be blasting that out of every speaker.

She looked at the number then at me. "Is it okay if I get this?"

"Sure." I wasn't her jailer.

Her hushed tones weren't necessary since every word was in Spanish. For all I knew, she was plotting with someone to have me beaten up. Except I could tell she was pretty upset about something. Not angry…more like worried.

But then she hung up and went right back to work without a word.

I'd settled back on my perch at the top of the ladder, not three feet from where she was nailing shingles. The decent thing to do was ask if everything was okay, but it wasn't as if Mari and I were friends. By all accounts, she didn't even like me.

Not that I could blame her. As far as she knew, I was a slave-driving bitch who held a ridiculous grudge against her for getting to the site a few minutes late. It wasn't her fault the rest of us didn't have our watches set to Hispanic Time.

Okay, the real problem—Edith knew it and deep down so did I—is My Attitude, not hers. Miami isn't going to bend to suit me. The only people who survive here are the ones who realize that and go with the flow.

Okay, but the real problem—I know, I just said that—is going with the flow means going against my nature. That's what makes living here so difficult. I'm not the kind of person who runs around traffic to jump in front. Or the kind who keeps people waiting because I think my time is more important than theirs. Or blasts my own music on the beach because I don't give a Jenko what anyone else wants to hear.

I fight those things inside me because civil society means living by rules for the common good.

Edith felt the same way but said she understood how it got to be that way. A lot of Miami's Hispanics come from places where the roads have no stripes at all, and goods aren't plentiful. Pushing to the front of the line is what they did to survive. Those who waited meekly in the back didn't get any.

My conflict is internal. Doing things the Miami way throws me off-kilter.

I don't like having to shout over people at the deli counter, but that's what it takes if I want the clerk to notice me. But then every time I do it, I look around and see some other poor schmuck who's being ignored because she's politely waiting her turn. That kind of stuff makes me feel like a jerk.

Or when I run up on somebody's bumper to keep another car from turning in front of me, like it would kill me to be nice and let him in. By the time I get to work I'm all worked up, not from fighting with the traffic, but from wondering if anyone ever let that poor guy squeeze in.

I guess the bottom line here is if I want Miami to be a nicer place, I can start with myself.

"Say, Mari. We're going to break for lunch in about ten minutes. How about we look around for another job for this afternoon?"

"I don't mind this one," she answered, not even looking at me. "I like being up here and seeing it take shape."

Right, and we'll have to haul her off in an ambulance after she has heatstroke. I'd probably catch hell for that. "It's getting pretty hot up here."

"I'm used to the heat. I've lived here all my life."

Apparently, she also lived to be obstinate. And those pointed jabs about how we "outsiders" couldn't adapt wasn't going to win her any points with me. She could boil up here for all I cared. "Suit yourself."

"Wait." When she stood up to her full height, it was like looking up from the bottom of a totem pole. "I was just trying to say this was okay with me, but I'll do whatever job you want me to do. You're the boss."

Humility. I like that. And maybe a tiny bit of contrition.

"If you're okay with it, that's fine. Just don't pass out and fall off the roof. It leaves a stain on the driveway."

She almost smiled. Not quite though, because her dimple didn't show up. I didn't stare because I knew I'd smile back, and then she'd think I was kidding about the stain.

The lunch truck that canvassed construction sites pulled up out front and sounded its horn, which happened to be the first few bars of "La Cucaracha." It never made sense to me why a song about cockroaches made people want to eat.

I clutched my paintbrush and bucket in one hand and started down the ladder. "Wait till I get to the bottom and I'll hold the ladder for you," I told Mari.

Except my foot slipped off the next to last step and when I reached the ground, I did so with my ass. No big deal on the ass part, but now there was white paint all over my chest and legs, to say nothing of a stain on the driveway.

Mari whirled onto the ladder like it was a fireman's pole and was standing over me in three seconds flat. "Are you all right?"

"I'm okay." Jenko, I had paint in my mouth. Then I went to wipe it and realized it was all over my hand too. Which meant it was now all over my face.

The whole crew must have heard the commotion because they all came running. Even the Cockroach driver had stopped his truck and joined them.

I almost wished I'd broken something, and I even considered faking it just to keep them from laughing. But no, I was fine, other than feeling more humiliated than I ever had in my life. And that's without a mirror.

Mari still looked worried. "You want me to get a hose or something?"

I looked over at Bo hopefully, but his grim jaw gave away the bad news.

"That's too much paint," he said. "We can't wash it into the groundwater. I'll go get some rags and a drop cloth."

The only way to properly dispose of half a gallon of spilled latex paint is to scoop it up, let it dry and throw it out with the garbage. Then we'd have to scrub the driveway with soap and water.

Since I didn't have a change of clothes in the car, Bo would have to wrap me in something that would keep the paint from getting all over everything. In other words, I'd be driving home in a toga. Mother Jenko.

The paint coated me from the knees up, so when Bo got back, we tried to mop up the biggest globs with paper towels. Next came the drop cloth, which was covered with so much dried paint, dust and cobwebs that it was totally, totally Gross. I stood mostly still while he and Mari wrapped it around me, including a loop through my crotch that made me feel like I was wearing a giant diaper.

In a show of either mercy or boredom, the bankers had followed Cockroach back to his truck for lunch. Only Mari stuck around to gawk at the spectacle.

"You sure you aren't hurt? That was quite a fall."

"I'll probably have a bruise on my rear end, but it could have been a lot worse."

"You should have called somebody to hold the ladder."

It was all I could do not to parrot that back in a snippy voice. She was right, of course, but her observation was about as useful as a two-legged barstool.

Bo jumped in to save my sorry ass. "Sometimes we're the worst offenders. We get caught up watching everybody else and forget to pay attention to our own selves. I guarantee you Daphne would a whole lot rather see this happen to her than one of our volunteers."

Good thing he hadn't said community service workers.

"Or community service workers," he added. "You got everything you need?"

I wiped my hands one last time on the clean corner of a rag and dug my car keys out of my paint-covered pocket. "Make sure all the paperwork gets back to the office, will you?"

Just in case the whole sideshow wasn't enough, I discovered I could only walk in baby steps because the cloth was wrapped all the way down past my knees. I felt like a geisha.

In a ridiculous *coup de grâce*, Mari picked up my train and followed along like my freaking maid of honor.

"Daphne, if this was my fault, I'm really sorry."

"Your fault? Why would you think that?"

"I should have just come down when you told me to."

She had a point. If I hadn't been so distracted by thoughts of her dropping dead on the roof, I probably wouldn't have fallen in the first place. My conscientious concerns for her safety had caused this. I liked that.

But then it occurred to me that she might like it too. A little sweet revenge.

"It wasn't you at all. Got a little fleck of dust in my eye and I took my hand off the ladder at the wrong time. Just one of those things."

"Okay, well…I guess I'll see you next week."

I wasn't buying her phony concern. I knew she'd be laughing her butt off the second I drove away, and so would everybody else.

I would have if this had happened to her.

CHAPTER FOUR

Another Miami parking adventure, this one courtesy of the Four Seasons Hotel. There would have been plenty of room for everyone in the parking garage had the Jenko heads not taken up two spaces each for their Mercedes S80s or their Cadillac SUVs. One of them left just enough space for me to squeeze in and I made sure he'd have a hell of a time getting back into his car on the driver's side. That's what living in Miami does to you.

Fancy cocktail parties like this one were a rare treat. It was invitation only, a chance for us nonprofits to put our causes in front of the top brass from some of the biggest corporations in the county. Tonight's event, the Community-Business Partnership for a Better Miami, was sponsored by the Miami Dolphins, and

Gisela scored our tickets through her husband, who happens to be their orthopedic consultant. Yes, I hate how things are done in this town, but I don't mind it so much when we're the ones taking advantage of the connections.

This is the best part of my job at the foundation, getting the chance to rub shoulders with other business professionals. It's a given I'm on the lookout for other job opportunities—even Gisela knows that and accepts it for what it is—but my first priority is always to win support for our foundation. All the companies represented tonight want the image of being good corporate citizens, so they're ripe for our pleas. Gisela and I had put together a double-barreled pitch, where I gauge their interest in volunteering and she hits them up for money. More times than not this approach helps us come away with something beneficial for the foundation.

I slithered out between my car and the next, careful not to wipe either of the fenders with my slacks. I'd worn a dark green silk pantsuit, dressing it up with a scarf in hopes of appealing to the conservative values we found in most of our corporate sponsors. I'm not exactly a fashion plate. My goal is to look nice enough so they don't talk about me after I leave the room.

I got into the elevator with an older couple who were speaking Spanish, or maybe Italian or Portuguese. They reminded me of Ronaldo and Tandra, the couple whose condo was below mine, or rather what I thought they would look like in about twenty-five years. He was dapper with his silver hair and perfectly tailored pinstripe suit, and she, though easily in her fifties, had the lithe body and style of a teenager. Unlike my Latin neighbors, who always seem to be simmering with passion for one another, these two were clearly in the midst of an argument, and I held my breath waiting for the door to open so I could get the hell out of there before one of them hit the other.

Why are so many Hispanics such hotheads? And worse, why is it a license to act like a jackass?

"Oh, he's Venezuelan. That's just how they are." Or Argentinean, or Cuban. Fill in the blank with whatever. It all works.

I'd been to events at this hotel before so I knew my way to the seventh-floor lobby. Tonight's cocktail party was poolside, and I have to admit a rooftop pool on a balmy night in May does not suck. Too bad I don't get to see this side of Miami very often. But then I don't have five hundred dollars a night to stay in a place like this.

Gisela emerged from the crowd gathered around the open bar and took my hand. "There you are, Daphne. I was starting to wonder if you'd fallen into another paint bucket."

"You guys are all so funny," I answered drolly. They'd gotten a lot of mileage out of my weekend debacle. "The Brickell Bridge was stuck in the up position. Traffic was backed up all the way to Bayside."

"Did you bring the brochures?"

I had everything—brochures, business cards and nametags. "How do you want to do this?"

"You're not going to like it," she said, leaning back and wincing like she was afraid I'd hit her.

I hate it when she says that because she's always right. "I hate it when you say that because you're always right."

"The HR director from Mariner Cruise Lines is here. I was hoping you'd go make nice with her."

Just fabulous…the woman who'd passed me over for the international studies kid.

"We could really use their support, Daphne. And they're probably looking for a PR boost right now."

"Yeah, nothing spoils your corporate image like running aground on one of the world's most beautiful and endangered reefs." Especially on the heels of a fire that had forced two thousand passengers into lifeboats off Cozumel. I had a feeling they'd be making pledges all over the room tonight. "What about you?"

"Marco Padilla is here, and I happen to know he's a football fan. I plan to pull all the strings I can to land him on our Board of Directors."

One of the first exiles to leave Cuba, he was the head of a financial investment firm, and among the most powerful men in Miami. Getting his support could keep us solvent for years to come.

"Okay, I'll work my way over to Mariner Cruises, but first I see someone I need to talk to from American Airlines. We've been playing phone tag all week."

No, first I needed to pluck a glass of white wine off a cocktail tray. No way was I going to pass up a chance to drink something besides Manischewitz.

I'd never seen so many movers and shakers in one place before. If food poisoning were to hit this party tonight, the stock market would fall a thousand points. It was an honor to be invited to a function like this. Still, I was sure I'd enjoy it a lot more if I were the one being schmoozed.

By the time I reached the center of the pool deck, the woman I wanted to see had drifted off with someone else.

"Daphne Maddox, I know that name." The voice belonged to a man with very dark skin, small black eyes and an island cadence. Obviously, he had noticed my nametag.

"You must be Guillame Pierre." Our Haitian city commissioner, representing the district of our current jobsite. I'd been calling his office to line up some city volunteers, but no one ever responded. "It's nice to finally meet you. I've been trying to get in touch but you're so busy."

"A thousand pardons. I must apologize for not returning your calls, but this has worked out wonderfully. I much prefer having these discussions in person." He took my hand in both of his and stroked it tenderly.

I smiled as amiably as I could, considering I'd been warned not to believe a word he said. Pierre has a reputation for being a master manipulator, someone in City Hall who gets most of what he wants because he knows where all the bodies are buried. Gisela once told me he thought himself a ladies' man, and then she'd burst out laughing. No doubt she'd get a sadistic kick out of seeing him stroke my hand.

"I was calling to let you know we have two more renovations scheduled this year for your district. Perhaps you and some folks from your office would like to come out on a Saturday and work with us. It would be a wonderful opportunity to meet with your constituents."

"Oh, we're doing many things on behalf of the wonderful people in Little Haiti." He put his arm around my waist to steer me toward a cabana. "Perhaps we can relax away from this crowd while we discuss this in more detail."

Jenko. Jenko. Jenko.

My phone rang. It was Gisela. God bless her.

"Hello."

She said nothing. Just her evil laugh.

"No, it's quite all right. I was hoping you'd call."

Now she was shrieking hysterically. I'd bet a hundred bucks tears were rolling down her cheeks.

"Yes, this qualifies as an emergency. I'll let her know at once." I stepped out of Pierre's reach. "Sorry, I have to find my boss immediately and give her some news."

I found Gisela standing in a cluster of men that included her husband Jorge, and three other men, two of whom were members of the Dolphins. The third was Marco Padilla, the man she was hoping to sway to the foundation's board. In his early sixties, Padilla was an enormous man. Not like the muscled athletes standing next to him. More like a heart attack waiting to happen.

I smiled politely through the introductions before whispering to her, "I'm glad you had your eye on Pierre. What a sleaze."

"It was Marco who pointed out that he had cornered some poor, unsuspecting woman. I couldn't believe it when I saw it was you."

"I owe him one. And now I'm going to Plan B, which is to swim across the pool so I won't have to walk by Pierre again."

I cut a wide circle around the cabanas and slipped back into the crowd to find Irene Sanchez, Mariner Cruise's VP for human resources. Given the recent uproar over the reef accident and fire, I wasn't surprised to see her belt back a cocktail with gusto.

"Ms. Sanchez, nice to see you again."

Her puzzled look gave way to recognition. "Debbie!"

"Daphne. Daphne Maddox."

"I knew it was a D-something. How have you been?"

As I gave her the rundown on my job at the foundation, I couldn't help but notice how frazzled she was…bags under her eyes and very much in need of a visit to her hair colorist. Not that I could blame her. According to the *Herald*, the pending lawsuits against the cruise line had their stock in free fall, which meant the officers at her level were losing about a thousand dollars an hour.

After declining my request for volunteers—they were "spread too thin at the moment"—she made an offer of her own. "Any chance you'd still be interested in our HR department?"

"I thought you filled that position."

"Oh, we did. But we've grown so much over the past couple of years that we need more hands to deal with personnel issues."

Not true. The *Herald* article showed Mariner lagging the other cruise lines, and they'd just canceled their most recent order for a new ship. But the fact that they needed more HR staff meant something big was in the offing, like massive severance packages or transfer of benefits if they sold the company. My guess was anyone jumping on board now would be out of a job soon because Mariner Cruise Lines was going under, and I had a strong hunch the officers knew it.

"I appreciate your interest, Ms. Sanchez, but I'm really happy at the foundation." To say nothing of my aversion to sinking ships. Time to drop Mariner like a cast iron anchor.

As I eased myself away I spotted a familiar face, Carlos Moya, the owner and CEO of a national trucking chain. Carlos oozed with Latin charm, and sent us a dozen volunteers two or three times a year. I didn't need to press Carlos for more help, but I wanted to say hello and thank him for all he'd already done.

As I got closer, I saw he was engaged in serious conversation with a woman whose back was toward me. I didn't have to see her face to know she was hot. Tall and shapely, she wore a clinging skin-colored cocktail dress and stylish but reasonable two-inch heels. Her dark hair, accented with golden strands, hung freely about her shoulders.

"…and that's where the Iberican Fund comes in, Carlos. It's an extraordinary set of aggressive growth funds that outperformed last year's market by sixty percent. We've pulled back on bringing in new investors right now, but if you're really interested, I'll talk to Pepe. We'll have you and your wife out for dinner on the yacht."

I knew that voice. Come to think of it, I knew that hair… and that curvy behind was unmistakably the same one I'd seen in skinny jeans. I never forget a curvy behind.

"Hi, everyone."

Carlos lit up with a smile. Mari Tirado, not so much.

"Daphne, my favorite handyman…handywoman."

"Handyperson," I corrected, glancing at Mari for acknowledgment. She seemed to be checking the floor for a trapdoor.

"Excuse me," she said, hastily stepping away. "I need to catch someone before he leaves."

Carlos held a thumb and pinky to his ear in that universal talking-into-your-fingers gesture. "Call me, Mari. I'm interested."

I spent the next ten minutes making nice with Carlos, all the while wondering why Mari had taken off like her dress was on fire. Even more curious was why she was here at all. This was an invitation-only event for nonprofits and business executives from the top companies in Miami. Nonprofit staff didn't drive cars like hers or have "dinner on the yacht," so that meant she was someone important.

As I headed back toward Gisela, I spotted Mari sitting by herself on a wicker loveseat inside an open cabana. When I got closer, I saw she was on the phone, so I waited a few feet away where I knew she could see me.

This time she looked right at me and ended her call at once. The last thing I wanted was another confrontation like the icy ones we'd had at the house, but I couldn't get over her just walking off. One of us was going to have to be the grownup, and that was obviously me.

I said evenly, "I'll be the first to admit I don't understand much about Miami, but where I come from, people who know each other usually say hello."

She groaned and buried her face in her hands before straightening up and flipping her hair back over her shoulders. "Please tell me you didn't say anything to Carlos about me doing community service."

Of course. I should have realized she wanted to keep her brush with the courts on the down low. "Carlos has been very helpful to the foundation. He and I have much better things to talk about than you."

Though she was clearly relieved, she also appeared agitated. "Sorry…I just need to get my hours in and make this go away before anybody finds out about it. If I screw up, they'll yank my license."

I wanted to tell her actions have consequences, but since we left things last weekend in a pretty good place, I actually felt a little sorry for her. "I wouldn't worry about it too much. Even people who lose their license usually get waivers to drive to work."

She looked at me like I'd sprouted carrots out of my head. "Not my driver's license—my investment broker's license. For some reason, they frown on letting felons handle other people's money. Next time I break up with somebody, remind me to make sure her brother isn't a cop."

"Seriously. Give some people a badge and a gun and they—" She just said Her. As in breaking up with a Female Person. No way had I heard that right.

"It was either break up or kill her. Sometimes I wonder if I took the coward's way out."

It was a Her. Mari was a lesbian. *Oh, mi dios.*

She slid over and offered me half the loveseat, obviously not noticing she had rendered me mute. Cuban litterbug or not, being a lesbian put her in a whole different light. A bright, shining light.

I finally got my mouth to work. "What exactly did you do, Mari?"

"I had this girlfriend, Delores. She works with Morgan Stanley. We met at a seminar on estate planning and hit it off. We'd been living together for almost a year. Things were great until she committed the unforgivable sin."

"She cheated on you. Been there, done that."

"Worse. She stole one of my clients." She leaned back and crossed one of her gorgeous legs over the other one. "So I piled all her stuff onto her Jet Ski and dragged it on a trailer over to where she worked. Then I dumped the whole business behind her car in the parking garage."

I couldn't begin to count all the times I thought about doing something like that to Emily. So Mari wasn't a selfish pig after all. In my book, she was righteous. "And that got you felony littering."

"How did you know that? It wasn't on my paperwork."

Oops.

"I did a little research. I wasn't trying to be nosy but… okay, I was being nosy. Mostly we get drunk drivers and your sentence didn't match up, so I checked you out with the clerk of courts."

She looked away and shook her head with a laugh. "Figures."

"What?"

"I did a little research of my own. You realize, don't you, that property transactions are public record? Now I think I have a pretty good idea why you yelled Jenko when you fell off that ladder."

I could feel my face burning but getting upset about her invading my privacy would have been hypocritical in the extreme. "Why would you—"

"What I don't get, though, is why you discharged your ex's debt on the mortgage. You both should have walked away and let the bank eat it."

"I'll have you know I was raised to honor my debts." No matter how stupidly I acquired them.

"A mortgage isn't about honor. It's a business deal."

"Right, a deal in which I signed a contract that said I would pay."

"But the bank signed it too. They understood there was a risk involved in your loan, so they stuck a whole section in there spelling out what happens if you default. Basically, it says you don't pay—we take your house. So let them. That's business."

"And ruin my credit forever?"

"It's only temporary. First you buy a new car that will last you for seven or eight years and you take out a new lease on a rental apartment. By the time you need another loan, you'll have recovered."

"And I'll have kissed any new job prospects goodbye. Nobody gets hired these days without a credit check." The more Mari talked, the more she reminded me of yet another class of human beings that rubbed me the wrong way—people who did what they wanted and left the rest of us holding the bag. Except being a long-legged lesbian in a tight dress made her a lot more tolerable. "I just can't bring myself to do that. Walking away from our obligations is exactly what tanked all of our property values in the first place."

"Yes and no. The collapse came when more and more people found they couldn't make their payments once the adjustable rates kicked in, and they couldn't sell because so many other buyers were in the same boat trying to unload their houses. But the lenders weren't surprised by any of that. They knew a lot of these new homeowners were poor credit risks, but they'd already unloaded their loans onto other unsuspecting mortgage buyers without disclosing their lack of due diligence. That's like selling Ferraris at Ferrari prices when you know they have Chevrolet engines under the hood."

"Sounds like a pretty good racket if you're a banker."

"Exactly. And trust me, they didn't give a second thought to what they might be doing to your property value when they rubber stamped all those bad loans for your neighbors. So screw the banks. Do what's best for you."

"Is this the kind of advice you give your clients?"

"Always," she answered unflinchingly, "unless it's criminal. I'm a little more judicious about that."

"Good to know." We sat there smirking at one another until I kind of sort of smiled a little. "I'm sorry if we got off on the wrong foot at the worksite."

"If?"

"I have an issue with tardiness, okay?" She didn't need to know about my issues with Spanish speakers in America, flashy cars, prissy women on a construction site...or just Miami in general.

My phone went off again, a text message from Gisela telling me the Dolphins were interested in doing a media day on one of our upcoming projects.

"Duty calls."

She picked up her purse and eyed the exit. "Yeah, I should get out of here before somebody asks to see my invitation."

"You crashed the cocktail party?"

"Why don't you just announce it to everybody?" she whispered through clenched teeth. At least she hadn't shushed me this time. "I had an earlier meeting with someone in the bar and he asked me to join him."

"You mean Carlos Moya?"

"No, Marco Padilla. He's my uncle."

CHAPTER FIVE

I always like the days we put down the tile floor. Most of our big volunteer jobs—putting up block walls, painting, drywall—show off progress by the end of the day, but seeing the floor take shape gives the house an even more finished look, and the workers a sense of pride and accomplishment.

Not that we were wrapping up. We still had another week's work ahead, things like tiling the shower, attaching the baseboards, installing the appliances and working through the final punch list. We'd finish next Saturday by laying sod. That was backbreaking work, so I'd lined up a dozen teenagers from Jesuit Prep.

Saraphine Delacourt, the Haitian mother of three who owned the house, smiled and clasped her hands with the kind of excitement I usually reserve for getting out of jury duty. "It is so beautiful, so wonderful! God blesses me a thousand times with so many gracious hands."

Today's group was from the Doral Resort, and while none of them struck me as overtly religious, they all seemed fine with giving God credit for their work. It was hard not to be happy at bringing Saraphine such joy.

My overall experience with Miami's Haitian community was favorable, minus the creepy episode with Guillame Pierre. Like many of the city's immigrants, Haitians arrived on our shores in rickety boats and makeshift rafts, but they had a much tougher time with US Immigration officials than Cubans, who were automatically granted political asylum if they reached land. There were no such "wet feet-dry feet" provisions for Haitians, even those who claimed they were persecuted by their government.

Mordy and Edith, in a rare show of agreement, believed the unequal treatment was due to the fact Haitians were black, while the moneyed Cubans who came in the early exile waves were white. I find Haitians to be hardworking, community-minded people who want to get ahead in life as much as the next person. It makes me feel good to see someone like Saraphine get a hand up.

As nice a day as it was, there was a gaping hole where a certain community service worker should have been. Mari Tirado had found yet another way to irritate me. What I'd thought was a productive burying of our respective hatchets at the cocktail party had obviously been just a forgettable blip on her business radar, a way of making sure I didn't tell all her fancy clients she was a felon. I actually preferred that scenario to the notion that she'd assumed we were pals now and I would cut her some slack for not showing up.

Bo looked down from a ladder in the center of the living room, where he was tinkering with the wiring for a ceiling fan. "This is a good crew. We should finish the floor today."

I thought so too, especially since someone had already done the bathroom. That was the toughest part because the tiles had to be cut to encircle the toilet. Tricky stuff, best not left to amateurs.

"Maybe I'll pull a couple of folks out after lunch to paint the baseboards," he added.

"I can help with that. I'll go set everything up." I'd much rather work outside than slide around on the floor, even with my heavy-duty kneepads.

We were headed back to work after the morning break when Miss Slacker's Porsche pulled in. She popped out smiling like she didn't have a care in the world.

Before I could even get in a proper browbeating, Saraphine was off the porch and hugging her like a long-lost sister.

"What the Jenko?" I muttered under my breath, but not low enough to escape Bo's notice.

"Oh, that reminds me. Mari stopped by yesterday morning and said she had something she had to do today and that she'd be late. She wanted to get some hours in so she wouldn't get behind."

"She worked yesterday?"

"Yeah, she and Saraphine laid the bathroom floor. Took them about five hours. I've got her paperwork out in the truck."

All things considered, I was feeling pretty lucky I hadn't gone off half-cocked about Mari being late. That didn't mean I was happy about her thinking she could just show up whenever her busy schedule allowed. I'm the personnel coordinator and she should have come through me for permission to change her schedule. As a rule, we don't usually allow volunteers at the worksite on a weekday when there isn't anyone around to supervise them.

But I had to hand it to her for coming in a day earlier to bank the time.

And I was utterly annoyed that she and Saraphine were such lovey-dovey friends after just a few hours together. I'd spent five weeks working on this house and never gotten so much as a single hug. From Saraphine, I mean. Yes, I'm technically paid to be here, but it's not as if Mari was showing up out of the kindness of her heart. It takes a court order to get privileged people like her to come out.

"Hi, Daphne," she said, smiling all innocent-like. She had on her carpenter jeans again, and a thin, stretchy polo shirt that I could see through enough to know her bra had two perfect arcs of lace, one over each of her breasts.

"Hi, yourself." I realized I was grinning like a jack-o-lantern. Lace did that.

"Please tell me you've got something for me outside. I desperately need some fresh air."

"How about painting the baseboards?"

Her face fell.

"They're out back. It's easier to paint them first and nail them on afterward."

I'd laid several long strips of baseboard across two sawhorses, and she wiped them down with a rag while I stirred the paint.

"Long, smooth strokes so they won't look choppy," I said.

She caught on quickly and seemed to enjoy the work. Once I realized her uncle was one of the most important members of the Cuban exile community, it made perfect sense she'd want her criminal charges kept under the radar. There was no reason we couldn't do that, especially since she was doing such good work for us.

"By the way, you should have called me about coming in the other day. It was okay, but I'd feel pretty bad if there was a mix-up and you didn't get credit for your hours."

"I did call, but you were out of the office or something. I didn't see any point in leaving a message when it was just as easy to drive over here and ask Bo. He said it would be all right."

"Let me give you my card in case that happens again. It has my cell phone." How clever of me, unless of course she used it to switch her hours around and not come at all next week. "You and Saraphine sure got to be friends."

"Spending a few hours together in a tiny bathroom does that. We brainstormed some ideas for how she could save money for retirement."

"Saraphine?" She was a cashier at Publix Supermarket.

"I always tell my clients if they're going to dream at all, they might as well dream big."

"How does somebody with three kids save for retirement on her salary?"

"Anyone who makes money can save money. It just takes discipline and knowing the difference between what you need and what you can do without. She's got a job with benefits—not a lot but her employer matches her contribution. If she takes advantage of a few tricks here and there, she'll be able to get along just fine when she retires."

"Bet you didn't know you'd be networking for new clients on this job, did you?"

She gave me a little smile. Not a real one…more like one of those pained, indulgent looks that makes you feel bad without even knowing why. "Saraphine's quite a woman. Lost her brother and sister-and-law to AIDS and now she's raising their kids. I could send a few of my clients her way for lessons in character."

If she'd meant to shame me, it was a direct hit. I knew AIDS had devastated the Haitian community but knowing something in the abstract wasn't the same as actually knowing a person who'd been affected by it.

"It's good what the Miami Home Foundation did for her," she went on. "Getting this house fixed up gives her one less worry. You all should be proud of yourselves."

Maybe not all of us. I don't have anything to do with that part of the foundation. The board of directors has a selection committee that reviews applications and decides who's worthy of our help. I go out and sell the cause because that's my job. At the end of the day, I get to bask in the feeling of doing good in the world, which is supposed to make up for the fact my corporate counterparts who do the same kind of work get paid five times as much as I do.

At least I sleep well. I don't go to bed every night feeling like a slave to the almighty dollar, or in today's world, to the investors on Wall Street who don't care how you do business as long as you make a buck. Ergo, Mariner Cruise Lines stock was falling not because they had destroyed a fragile reef, but because bookings were down and their investors doubted they could turn it around.

I wondered if Mari caught the irony in what she said about the foundation relative to the sort of advice she gave her clients—that is, to do whatever was best for them, irrespective of how it affected others or even society at large. Or maybe she was implying that my intrinsic pride in doing good deeds is what's best for me. Social recognition is, after all, worth more to some people than money. Not her, necessarily. I saw the things she valued—the expensive sports car, the designer clothes and the high life of

Miami. What I didn't see was how she could reconcile such an extravagant lifestyle with concern for people like Saraphine and gratitude for people like me. Probably because having Mari's admiration wasn't the same as having her respect.

"How many coats are we supposed to do? That's your fourth."

Jenko. I was barely aware I was holding a paintbrush, let alone how long I'd been working on the same strip of wood. "Usually just two but this one had a few rough spots."

"Thought you'd be interested in knowing I came clean with Pepe...that's what we call my Uncle Marco. He saw us talking the other night and happened to mention he's thinking about joining your board. I didn't want him to be embarrassed if it came out later."

"How did he take it?"

"He wanted to spank me but couldn't figure out the best way to do that to a thirty-three-year-old. I told him not to worry, that just knowing he wanted to was punishment enough."

"You must be close to him." Close enough to influence his decision to join our board, I realized. Gisela would want me to tread carefully.

"He's more like a father than an uncle."

I'd always heard Cuban families were very tight-knit. "What about your real father?"

"Hardly knew him. He returned to Cuba not long after I was born."

"I thought the idea was to get out of Cuba and never go back...at least not as long as Castro was still there." Mordy said the Cubans would never go back no matter what, that they had it too good in Miami.

"My father didn't have any political convictions. He was fourteen years old when his family left and he didn't want to come to America, especially since my grandfather stayed behind to take care of their property. He was a successful construction engineer and they had a big house and several cars. That was the first wave and all the exiles thought the Castro regime would fall quickly and they'd be able to return."

"And fifty-some years later..."

"Exactly." Mari had no trouble talking and working at the same time, and even managed not to paint the same board over and over. "Mima—that's my grandmother—she says my father never accepted being in America, especially after my grandfather decided he didn't want to leave Cuba ever, even when Castro shut down his business and confiscated his property. Mima always thought it was because he had a mistress there. So when they opened the borders for the Mariel Boatlift in 1980, my father went back on his own. I was just a baby."

"He just left you and your mother all alone?"

"We weren't alone. Cubans have big families. We all lived with Mima, and there was Pepe—he took over as the man of the family—and the youngest brother, Felix." She snickered. "Felix is gay but no one is allowed to tell Mima."

"Oh, that's hilarious. So I take it they don't know you're gay either."

"They do, because I don't keep secrets very well. But it's not so bad if you're a woman. A Cuban man, he has to be macho."

The Cockroach Truck sounded out front. I would have skipped lunch just to keep talking but Mari pulled out her phone.

"I need to talk to Pepe's wife, Lucia. They're bringing Mima home from the hospital today. She's been there for the past three weeks."

That explained all the serious phone calls, which I'd assumed had been her talking to her friends about me. That makes me a world-class jerk.

When the break was over, Bo shuffled everyone around and I found myself indoors watching over a handful of Doral volunteers as they finished laying the floor. Mari was gone before I even had a chance to tell her goodbye. With the extra paperwork from Bo, she was at twenty-seven hours. Only five more to go.

Hour-wise, she hadn't really been on the site that long, but she was a long way from the crabby snoot that wheeled in late that first day.

Or maybe I was a long way from that crabby snoot. One thing was for sure—I misjudged her.

***

Mordy Osterhoff's last visit to a temple had been his bar mitzvah nearly sixty-five years ago. He didn't pray, nor read the Hebrew Bible. In fact, he'd pretty much renounced all belief in God and Abraham. But none of that stopped him from the traditions of the Sabbath, or his insistence on drinking only kosher wine.

"Suh-dah Slish-it," I said, knowing from the look on his face I had butchered it again.

"*Seudah Shlishit!*" he barked.

If I'd been the timid sort, I'd have been afraid of him despite the fact he was seventy-seven and slightly built. He was strong for his age, though, thanks to the fifty laps he swam each day in his obscenely bulging European swimsuit.

Mordy's main reason for going to the pool was to watch women in their bikinis.

Edith went to watch Mordy.

"Su-dah Schlischlit."

"Forget it. It's the Third Meal," Edith said. She was even less religious than Mordy but indulged him his Jewish customs by shutting down everything from sundown on Friday until Saturday night. No operating machinery or electronics of any kind. If they went to the pool, they walked down fifteen flights of stairs, and upon returning, waited for someone else to push the elevator button.

Most traditional Jewish families ate the Third Meal in late afternoon around three thirty or four. Mordy and Edith held off until four thirty on the days I came over because it's all I can do to get home from the jobsite and get showered in time. I have a standing invitation, but since I don't reciprocate that often, I only take them up on it about once a month. The meal is always the same. Salad, lox, sliced melon and matzo. And Mordy's beloved Manischewitz.

Marvin, their longhaired black and white tuxedo cat, lounged in his favorite place on a carpeted pedestal by the sliding glass door. He loved Edith, tolerated me and ignored Mordy.

"I had an interesting conversation today with one of our volunteers. Made me think of you, Mordy." I referred to Mari as a volunteer because it didn't seem right to single her out as a community service worker, especially since she'd soon have her record expunged. "A Cuban woman, a couple of years older than me, a first-generation American. Her parents came over as kids in the first wave. What was that…1960?"

"The Cuban Revolution started the year before but I think you're right. Most of the first wave came in 'sixty," Edith said.

She was a voracious reader, and I could always count on her to add details to anything, whether it was a movie, a news story or just some silly trivia that came up in one of our conversations.

We were suddenly interrupted by an announcement over the building's intercom, the only words of which I understood were "tow zone."

"Sounds like some idiot parked in the circle again," Mordy said. "Everyone thinks the rules apply to other people. They should just tow the jackass and be done with it."

Edith went into the hallway to hear the message more clearly, but came back shaking her head. "I wish they wouldn't use the intercom unless it's an emergency. It's only Javier who does that."

Javier was the doorman who never opened a door for anyone unless they were driving a Mercedes or Lexus. I begrudgingly tipped him every Christmas so he wouldn't let solicitors up to my apartment, but he was otherwise worthless.

"Anyway, this woman said her grandfather stayed behind to watch their property, just like your father did." Except while Mordy's father was trying to figure out how to move the money from his jewelry business to Belgium, he was picked up by the Germans and taken along with his brother to Bergen-Belsen, where it was assumed they perished.

"It wasn't the same. Castro wasn't herding people into the gas chambers."

Edith winked at me as she refilled his wineglass. "Some have estimated Fidel executed fifteen thousand or more."

"For their political views, not their ethnicity," he growled.

"A cleansing is a cleansing." She turned to me. "Mordy doesn't like it when anyone compares the Cubans to the Jews."

I lowered my head a little so he would look me in the eye. "I know, and I wasn't trying to goad you about it. Her family wasn't running for their lives like yours. The weird thing about it was that her father grew up here from the time he was about fourteen, but he missed Cuba, and when they opened the borders for the Mariel Boatlift, he went back and stayed. The only reason I thought of you was because it broke up her family, and she grew up without her father too. It must have been very hard."

"We do what we must."

"I know." I put my hand on top of his and stroked the rough, tanned skin. "I really appreciate how you've given me a window into history that I never got with books or movies. I understand the Holocaust so much better because of your stories and how you've lived your life. And now hearing this woman talk about growing up in the exile community here in Miami gave me a perspective I didn't have, and I thought of you. That's all I wanted to say."

CHAPTER SIX

Our last day at Saraphine's house. She and her children were itching to move back in, and we were just as excited to kick off our next project in Grapeland Heights out by the airport, but today was all about satisfaction and pride in a job well done.

Bo's crew had prepped the dirt and stacked seven pallets of sod at various places throughout the yard, at least saving us the task of having to truck it all from one corner to the other, one wheelbarrow-load at a time. Jobs like this took little training and even less supervision, which was good because we had no time to lose. Not with a crew that consisted of three teenage boys and nine no-shows.

Of all the groups that volunteered with us, youth were the most rewarding, as well as the most challenging and unreliable. I loved the message of hope they carried about the coming generation, but not their penchant for distraction and horseplay.

"Where's your hammer, homo?" one asked another as he pushed him playfully into the side of Bo's truck.

I resisted the urge to pinch his head off, especially when my mood got a favorable jolt from the sight of Mari's Porsche pulling in next to Mustang Sally.

The skinniest of the three teens, boasting several blots of supposedly flesh-toned acne medication on his forehead and chin, emitted a wolf whistle that changed octaves as Mari emerged from her car. "Some of that," he murmured.

As if.

When Mari joined us, it was all I could do not to wrap my arm possessively around her waist. Not that I possessed her. I just didn't want any of these peri-pubescent brats to think they could.

"Today's job is pretty simple. All these stacks of sod…we need to spread them out over the yard. Nothing really complicated about it, but I've done it many times and I can tell you it takes a lot of stamina. Your shoulders and legs are going to wake up very angry tomorrow. I was hoping a few more of your friends would join us, but if we keep at it and work hard, we should be able to finish right on time at three thirty."

"My dad's picking me up at eleven thirty," Pimple Boy said.

"Mine too," said Josh, the smallest of the three.

I whirled toward the third, practically daring him to speak.

"And I'm riding with Josh's dad so…"

Bunch of lazy Jenkos. But as much as I wanted to scream, I had only myself to blame. I should have realized the moment their faculty sponsor called to say something had come up for him on Saturday my leverage over the boys was up in smoke. Without their teacher to impress, they had no real motivation to even be here, let alone work. I was lucky these three had shown up.

And just in case all that wasn't enough, Mari's time was officially up at twelve thirty. That meant Bo and I would probably be here until well after dark getting the last patch down.

With two wheelbarrows, we broke into teams of three. I corralled Mari and Josh with the sole purpose of interrupting Pimple Boy's wet dream.

We started in the back corner of the yard with Josh handing me one square at a time to place, just as if we were laying tiles on a floor. Mari kept us supplied from the closest pallet.

"We leave a couple of inches between the squares because this is St. Augustine sod, the good stuff. It grows fast, so it'll thatch over these gaps in a few weeks." The rest of the story was the sod had been donated—left over from a city park project— and if we didn't space it out we wouldn't have enough to cover the yard.

After forty minutes of squatting, my thighs were on fire. And not in a good way, I noted, pushing away thoughts I didn't need to be having around a teenage boy. We rotated jobs and I took over the wheelbarrow part, which gave me an excellent view of Mari as she worked.

She looked just fine in her carpenter jeans and boots, but I'd been ruined forever by seeing her in that cocktail dress. Tanned legs that looked like they went all the way up. What I liked best about her outfit today was her white short-sleeved shirt, more like a V-neck than a Henley, since the buttons were undone all the way down to what looked like a sports bra. At one point she stopped for a long drink and the water dribbled onto her chest.

My entire kingdom for a cool breeze.

"Here you go, Josh. Why don't you handle the wheelbarrow for a while?"

I hadn't said a word about our usual morning break, and neither had Bo. We all stopped a couple of times for water but something told me if these kids ever sat down, we'd never get them up again.

Mari pulled off her hat and wiped her brow with her dirty forearm. "I should take a turn doing all the bending and twisting. Looks like a killer."

"I don't mind doing it again. You can hand them to me if you want." Fundamentally, I'm the same person who only four short weeks ago sent this woman on my very own version of the Bataan Death March just because she was a few minutes late. Now I'm volunteering to double down on the hardest job of the day so she won't have to. What was different?

I refused to believe it was because Mari was an attractive lesbian. Even though she triggered some of my more primitive instincts, I gave myself more credit than that. Emily Jenko was proof positive I can dislike an attractive lesbian.

The difference was Mari earned my respect over and over. She snapped out of her Oblivious Fog of Specialness the moment I signed her in on that first day. No more waltzing in late and not once had she complained or slacked off. I could add to that the fact her criminal transgression was bogus, and if we'd been friends at the time, I probably would have helped her do it.

"Today's your big day, Mari. I bet you'll be out celebrating tonight."

"The thought had crossed my mind."

"Party on South Beach?" Of course. She was exactly the sort of woman who got through the ropes at the most exclusive clubs.

She stood up and stretched backward with her hands bracing the small of her back. As she arched, the outline of her nipples was plainly visible. "I think tonight I'll settle for a long, hot, soapy bath."

Whereas I'd have to make do with a long, very cold shower.

"We've had a lot of…"—I couldn't exactly call her a volunteer, and I didn't want Josh to know she was doing community service— "workers come through here. You've been one of the best."

"What did you expect? You've watched my every move like you were afraid I'd try to escape over the back fence or something."

Oh, for Jenko's sake. That wasn't something I'd wanted her to notice. "It's your own fault for skipping the safety orientation. I was scared to death you'd cut your hand off or something."

"I've still got some time left to make that happen."

A horn blew from in front of the house and Pimple Boy announced with relief that his dad was here. The other boys called it a day as well and went out front to wait for their ride, leaving Bo, Mari and me standing over a yard that was barely half finished.

I was so hungry I could have eaten a school lunch. Instead I had about half a cup of crunchy peanut butter slathered on two thick slices of multigrain bread, and a bright green Granny Smith apple. A royal feast couldn't have tasted better.

Mari, as usual, spent her entire lunch break leaning against her car and talking on the phone. I don't even think she ate, but after her crack about me watching her all the time, I did everything I could not to stare.

"Sorry about the volunteers, Bo. A full house would have been nice today."

"I might be able to bribe a couple of my daughters into coming in tomorrow and helping me finish things up."

"Mari's time's up in about an hour, you know, and it'll be just us. But I'll work as late as you want me to."

His joints crackled as he pulled himself up. "Let's just see how much we can get done. We'll worry about the rest later."

Mari quickly joined us, somehow rejuvenated. "We ought to make good time now that we don't have those kids slowing us down, right?"

By her playful attitude, I figured she was already celebrating her departure. I was surprised when twelve thirty came and went without notice. If she was too distracted to check her own watch, I surely wasn't going to remind her.

"Mari!"

I looked up to see six teenagers rounding the corner, four boys and two girls. The fellows were dressed in baggy shorts and T-shirts with sneakers, while both girls reminded me of Mari on her first day—skinny jeans with ruffled tank tops. Obviously Hispanic.

"Chacho! You guys actually came."

"Because no one ever says no to Pepe," one of the girls said, trading cheek kisses with Mari.

"Come on over here and meet what's left of the crew." Mari introduced Bo and me as *los jefes*, the bosses. "Talia here is my niece, Chacho is my cousin—second or third, I can't ever remember—and all these other faces I've seen in Mima's kitchen at one time or another, but I don't think I'm related to any of them."

She took over the training as Bo and I watched, too overwhelmed with gratitude to even speak. It was like Teddy

Roosevelt had just ridden over the hill again, but this time carrying the Cuban flag.

I ended up in a trio with Chacho and one of his friends, enjoying arguably the easiest job of passing the squares to Chacho for placement. Best of all, we'd worked our way around to the shady side of the house.

"Sounds like everyone in your family tries to keep Pepe happy."

Chacho grinned, and for an instant, I saw a dimple that resembled Mari's.

"Pepe is like Papá Noel—Santa Claus—to people all over Miami, but especially family. He takes care of us. We all want to do our best and make him proud."

I remembered Mari's words about him wanting to spank her for getting arrested being punishment enough. "Your cousin sure thinks a lot of him."

"Mari? Pepe loves her. We all kid her that she's his favorite because she was the only girl until Talia was born. Everybody talks about how he took her with him all the time and whenever she cried he gave her whatever she wanted. He's the same way with Talia now. Both of them are spoiled."

I had no trouble imagining Mari as spoiled. Two weeks ago I might have sneered to think that, but here I was chuckling along with Chacho like a laugh track. It actually made me jealous to think of this family growing up so close and loving one another the way they did.

Not that my folks were Darth Vader and Joan Crawford. It's just that they were formal and didn't show a lot of emotion, whether they were happy, sad, angry or proud. I never felt unloved or anything awful like that but there were lots of times when I was with my friends and their families that I wondered what it would feel like to be hugged spontaneously just because.

By the time we reached the front yard, Mari, Talia and one of Chacho's friends were laying down the last corner. Bo and his crew were stringing sprinklers all over the yard to soak the ground before we left.

Mari and I stepped back to let the kids finish.

"You saved the day, Mari. Bo and I would have been stuck here till midnight if you hadn't called these guys."

"I knew Pepe would send them when I called him because he was really glad I was working off my hours here. He likes your boss, Mrs. Ruiz."

"And she likes him. She wants him on our board, so when I found out he was your uncle, I had to start being nice to you."

"And you didn't have much time." Oh, she was cute, especially when she smiled. "Lucky for you, I made it easy."

"Yes, you did," I said with as much sincerity as I could muster without going overboard and looking like I was just trying to curry favor with Pepe. "And any time you want to come out on a Saturday and grace us with your hard work and charming personality, we'll be happy to have you."

"Like I always tell my clients—dream big."

She pulled off her cap and loosened her hair, which was matted to her head from a day's worth of sweat. The rich black dirt from the sod was caked under her fingernails, in rings around her neck, and in the tiny crow's feet around her eyes. She was still gorgeous.

I was busy admiring that when I backed up a couple of steps to give the kids room to place the last squares of sod. My feet got tangled in one of Bo's hoses and I went sprawling backward onto my ass. Again.

"Are you okay?"

I gripped Mari's extended hand and pulled myself up. She had a way of sucking up so much of my brain that my legs forgot to work. At this rate, I'd kill myself in another month if she kept coming around to the jobsite.

"Good as new."

The water suddenly sprayed the very spot where we were standing and we leapt out of the way. From the faucet by the house, Bo rubbed his hands together with satisfaction.

"That's a wrap, guys. This one's ready for a family."

There were goofy, giddy grins all around as we congratulated ourselves. While the kids were pleased to get our thanks, it was obvious Mari's approval—and by extension, Pepe's—was more important. She hugged and kissed each of them as they climbed into their cars. I wouldn't mind if she did that to me.

"Mari, it's been a real pleasure," Bo said, shaking her hand. "Next time you want to break the law and end up out here with us, you just go right ahead."

"Thanks, but I think I'll take a pass on that."

Once Bo walked away, I started feeling awkward, like the last few minutes when you know something might happen but you aren't quite sure what you want it to be. I left Mari a few seconds to say something—see you around, thanks for the memories—and when she didn't, I decided just to stick with the official stuff.

"I'll get your paperwork off to the courthouse on Monday so you should hear from them later in the week. They're usually pretty good about following through right away."

"I appreciate it, Daphne. As much as I hate to admit it, it was kind of fun. If you guys didn't start your day at such a god-awful hour, I might even come around again sometime." She got into her car but didn't close the door. "But you know how I hate having to be at work so early."

"For you, I'll make an exception. Come back and see us anytime."

We were both just uttering pleasantries. There was little chance I'd ever see her again, unless her uncle came on the board and brought her along to one of our functions.

Just because two women were lesbians—single lesbians of pheromone-producing age—didn't mean they'd automatically be attracted to each other. Sure, I found Mari hot, but so did probably everyone else.

Even if I'd been the most charming person in Miami, it wouldn't have changed the fact I wasn't in her league.

CHAPTER SEVEN

I have as much right as the next person to walk around on South Beach. It doesn't matter—or at least it shouldn't matter—that most of these other women take their fashion cues from J-Lo, while I take mine from Hillary Clinton. I just have a different idea about what looks good on me versus what looks good on everyone else. I've never been one to wear skirts or dresses, and that isn't due only to my tendency to go ass over teakettle at the slightest bump on the sidewalk.

Nor is it because I don't consider myself feminine. It's not like guys go around wearing Capri pants and sandals with bows or sequins like I do. But I have neither the eye nor the clothes budget to shop for the sort of stylish things I find attractive on other women.

"I just love coming down here to people watch," Edith said as the three of us shouldered through the Labor Day crowd on Lincoln Road Mall.

There isn't much you can't see on South Beach, from a bare-chested bodybuilder walking a pair of Chihuahuas to a twenty-something woman in a bikini and sarong on the arm of a guy as old as Mordy. Or a toothless woman in an overcoat shouting profanities to no one in particular. Or a young African-American in a driving cap who had spray-painted himself bronze, standing perfectly still on an overturned box like a statue out of a civil rights museum. And lots of beautiful, olive-skinned Latin Americans.

And us. A fashion-challenged dyke with a short Jewish guy and his red-haired Amazon of a wife. What I find fascinating is we don't actually stick out, despite not looking like anyone else here. You have to be a lot more outlandish than us to get noticed on Miami Beach, and why would anyone look our way when there's so much else to choose from?

Not getting noticed suited all three of us until we'd stood five minutes waiting for acknowledgment by the maître d' at the Van Dyke Café.

"Hey, you see us standing here?" Mordy snapped. "What do you suppose we want?"

The indignant man never uttered a sound nor made eye contact, but he nonetheless led us down the sidewalk and dropped three menus at a pretty decent table.

As Edith and I tried to decide between pasta and Middle Eastern fare, Mordy craned his neck to follow the sight of an exotic woman in hot pants, thigh boots and a leather bustier, her surgically enhanced breasts motionless despite her steady gait.

"She's not interested in a dirty old man like you," Edith said drily. "You're stuck with me."

"For your information, you old biddy, I happen to know that woman. She's married to a man I used to work with at the union office."

I didn't believe that for a minute, but Mordy always had the ready answer when Edith caught his wandering eye. Had to be automatic after so many years together.

"First I catch you ogling other women. Then you lie about it. You have no shame. What do you think Daphne thinks of you?"

"Whoa! Leave me out of this. In fact, let's leave all of us out of it. We're here to celebrate the end of the summer and pay homage to working people. It's a happy occasion."

He scoffed across the table at his wife. "I told you Daphne didn't want to hear you bickering all the time."

"How can I bicker by myself?"

"Enough, you two!"

Tonight was our first outing in over a month while we waited for Edith's summer sinus infection to clear up. We'd walked the three blocks from our condo building to the Omni Station and picked up the Metro bus for a quick ride across the historic Venetian Causeway to Miami Beach. Even when we carried our beach chairs, made of lightweight canvas, it was easier than driving over and finding a place to park.

"Mojito, touch of bitters," I told the waiter.

Edith then ordered a scotch old-fashioned and we waited interminably for Mordy to determine which was their kosher wine. He settled on a sparkling rose, and when finally our drinks came, I proposed a toast.

"To surviving another brutal Miami August!" I couldn't say summer because the heat and humidity would be hanging over us for another two months at least, but there was something particularly vicious about August, especially Saturdays when I had to work on the jobsite.

"And to your raise," Mordy added, clinking his glass to mine again.

"I'll definitely drink to that." July had marked my fourth year at the foundation, a period during which I'd gone from volunteer coordinator to Gisela's right hand. She relied on me more than ever to represent us in the business and government community when she couldn't be there herself, and had rewarded me with a generous raise. Not that generous is all that large in the nonprofit world, but I can't complain about having a couple hundred extra dollars every month. I need to find a new car—or more likely, a reliable used one—preferably before Sally gives up the ghost on I-95 during rush hour.

The notion of car shopping always made me think of Mari Tirado, who advised me to buy something new to drive and sign an apartment lease as a prelude to walking away from my mortgage. I'd found myself thinking about her a lot at first after her community service stint last May, imagining how nice it would be if she called and asked to get together. But then she hadn't, and after three months I'd gotten the message I knew all along. Being lesbians was about the only thing we had in common, and it wasn't nearly enough.

"You'd never guess who called us the other day," Edith said.

Mordy grunted. "I thought we decided we weren't going to tell her."

"We have to tell her. Daphne's our friend."

This couldn't possibly be good, especially since I put together immediately who it had to be. "If it's who I think it is, I don't even want to know."

"You were too good for her," Mordy said, patting my hand.

"Why on earth would Emily call you?"

"She wanted to know how everyone was."

"I hope you told her I sold the place for half a million to a Peruvian billionaire and moved away."

"I did better than that. I told her you seemed happy."

Take that, Jenko. I hadn't actually thought about her much over the summer, not since I'd decided to break my habit of taking her name in vain because it meant she was popping into my head all day every day. But I can't honestly say I'm totally over Emily because the mention of her name still has the ability to stir something inside, even if it's only irritation.

"She's coming to Miami next week and asked if Mordy and I wanted to join her for dinner…and anyone else who wanted to come along."

"Seriously? I'd rather eat with Rush Limbaugh."

Mordy snorted. "Maybe we can get him too. I think he has a house up in West Palm."

"She also said she wasn't with that woman anymore. They broke up and the woman moved to Seattle."

That hit me harder than I would have liked. While it was satisfying to hear the grass wasn't greener with her co-worker after all, it also interested me to hear Emily was single again. The trouble with nostalgia, of course, is that it comes with blinders. Whereas my emotional side wanted to dwell on how we spent the first night in our new condo camping out on the bedroom floor, my rational side was yelling that she's the Devil's Spawn.

"I hope she stuck Emily with a big fat mortgage."

"Anyway…Mordy and I said we'd meet her at the Wynwood Kitchen and Bar." That was always Emily's favorite spot, a trendy place with great food that doubled as an art gallery. I hadn't been back since she left.

"I hope you have a fine time, but count me out." Even as I said it, I had an undeniable urge to be a fly on the wall for the evening. The thought of seeing Emily humbled and groveling actually made her more appealing than she'd been in a long time.

We paid the check and continued our walk down the outdoor mall to Drexel Avenue, where we cut over to the grassy area in front of the magnificent home of the New World Symphony. Already, hundreds of concertgoers dotted the lawn across from the towering wall that would soon display a live feed of the performance inside the state-of-the-art concert hall. These regular free Wallcasts not only brought the symphony to the masses, but also created a sense of community for all of us who mingled on the lawn to strains of classical music. I have to admit it's one of the coolest things about Miami.

Mordy had us pick up our chairs and move twice because the groups around us were boisterous, and he worried they'd talk and play around throughout the concert. We finally found what felt like the perfect place off to the side, where the only people near us were four Hispanic women—two couples, I realized by the way they were leaning against one another. They were lounging on a blanket and talking softly over a bottle of red wine they kept hidden on account of the local law against open containers.

A couple of years ago that might have been Emily and me with friends. If we had worked together on it, I really think we could have navigated this crazy town and made it home, eventually adapting to its Latin culture. There were plenty of Anglos in the crowd tonight, so it wasn't as if a pair of New Englanders could never fit in.

The idea of seeing her again for dinner was more intriguing than my initial reaction might have suggested. There really was something to the old saying that living well is the best revenge, and while I wasn't exactly dining every night on stone crab, I was a hell of a lot better off than she was, dumped on her butt in the Geriatric Capital of Florida. Proving to her in person she hadn't destroyed me had some appeal.

Who was I kidding? The fact that Emily was single again cast her in a whole new light, especially since she was the one reaching out. I hadn't forgotten we used to love each other or that we'd planned a life together for better or worse. I never expected worse would include a couple of years of her living with another woman, but it wasn't totally out of the question that I could get over it if she worked hard at regaining my trust. It was obvious she was still interested.

What am I, crazy? More like desperate and pathetic. Emily wasn't poking around back here in Miami because I'm her one true love. She was just looking for someone to break her fall and thought of me because I've been such a perfect patsy so far.

Excitement rumbled through the crowd as the wall—seven stories tall—lit up with the image of the conductor taking his place at the podium. In honor of Labor Day, tonight's performance kicked off with Aaron Copland's *Fanfare for the Common Man* before settling into the main program, an upbeat pairing of Haydn's *Surprise Symphony* and Vivaldi's *Four Seasons: Autumn*. Thanks to my parents' insistence on piping classical music throughout the house twelve hours a day for my entire life, I'm able to anticipate every note.

"Sorry we're late," a woman whispered nearby. The lesbians began to chatter excitedly at the new arrivals, alternating between Spanish and English—*Spanglish*, we call it—as if it were their own special language.

Mordy shushed them. "Zip it! We didn't come all the way out here to hear you."

I was too embarrassed even to look their way, but I couldn't argue with his results, since the group went stone quiet and stayed that way until the intermission.

"Sorry if we bothered you. I promise we'll be quiet through the second half." The husky voice sent my stomach into a spin.

"Mari?"

"Oh, wow! Daphne." She gave me the same look of trepidation as when I'd walked up on her with Carlos Moya at the cocktail party, and I realized she probably didn't want her friends to know how she knew me.

"I thought I'd run into you again at one of the Chamber of Commerce events. Business must be really good if you're too busy to drum up more."

She looked amazing in black tights with a sleeveless tunic and chain belt. Her hair draped around her shoulders the way it had at the Four Seasons affair.

"I'm staying busy enough. I guess you are too, at least that's what I hear from Pepe. He likes being on your board, by the way."

By now, the other girls had lost interest in our conversation, as had Edith and Mordy, all apparently satisfied we were work associates of some sort. I followed Mari as she stepped out of earshot.

"I got my record expunged, so I'm no longer a felon. Thanks for all that."

"I didn't do anything but sign your paperwork, but I'm glad things worked out."

She looked around me at Edith and Mordy. "Your folks?"

"My neighbors. They're great entertainment on a budget, even without the music." I returned her curiosity with a glance toward the person she had arrived with, a thin-faced woman wearing a midriff top that showed off a belly tattoo and navel ring. "Your girlfriend?"

She winced before cracking a smile that showed off her adorable dimple. "I wouldn't go that far."

"She's very pretty."

"So are leopards, but never turn your back on one."

I snarled and hissed like an angry cat, which made us both crack up.

"You're letting your hair grow," she said. "Looks nice."

"Thanks, just thought I'd try something different." That, and I'd moved professional hair care over into the Not Absolutely Necessary column until I resolved my car issue. A good cut was expensive, and a cheap one left me at the mercy of a mall salon where a novice stylist would smile and nod at whatever I said I wanted, and then proceed to cut my hair the only way he or she knew how.

"You come to these Wallcasts a lot?" she asked.

"Whenever I can. I'm sort of a classical music geek. How about you?" I hoped she was into it too, not just so we'd have something in common but because I had it fixed in my head from her ringtone that she liked the salsa music. Please let me be wrong.

"Not really. I like this though." She gestured to the crowd around us. "Any kind of music is better when I can just sit and relax with friends, especially if I don't have to get dressed up."

If she considered herself "not dressed up," I didn't even want to think what she thought of my baggy cotton fare. It's always been my view that one can never have too many pockets.

"It's nice inside too, though," she added. "The acoustics are out of this world."

"I've never been inside. I take that back. I went on a tour when they first opened, but I've never gone to a concert. It's on my list." My list of other things that were Not Absolutely Necessary, unfortunately. "Look, Mari. I know you were freaked out last May about people finding out you were doing community service. You don't have to worry about me telling anyone. As far as I'm concerned, that's all over and done with."

Translation: You don't have to avoid me if you'd ever like to use that cell phone number I gave you.

She looked back at the group of women and casually waved at Not Exactly Calling Her a Girlfriend. "I appreciate that, Daphne. At least the threat of losing my investor license isn't still hanging over my head, but I get embarrassed over losing my temper that way. My clients would think it was pretty reckless."

"And reckless isn't how anyone wants to describe their money manager."

"Exactly."

I told her about our current project in Liberty City, a renovation of a small Section 8 apartment complex. "That invitation's still open any time you want to join us. I could probably find some blocks for you to haul."

"And what about you? Are you keeping your feet on the ground, or are you still falling off and over things?"

"Oh, you're very funny. I bet you've been waiting to work that in for ten minutes."

"No, what's funny is how they still let you do the safety demonstrations. That would be like asking me to give driving lessons to fifteen-year-olds."

"Don't tell me you're one of those crazy Miami drivers." Of course she is. She's practically everything about this place that drives me nuts.

The crowd hummed as the conductor's image once again appeared on the wall.

"Guess I should get back to my friends. It was good to see you again."

The pleasure was mine. I wanted to ask her out. I wanted to kiss her, and then fly up to Boston together for a sunset wedding on the beach at Provincetown. Instead, I reminded her I had already tossed the ball into her court.

"I meant what I said, Mari. You're welcome to come around anytime. Or just give me a call. You still have my card, right?"

"I think it's with my court papers," she said, smirking. But then she kissed me on the cheek.

I barely heard a note after intermission, not even after Mari and her Not a Girlfriend quietly left, probably to go have sex.

CHAPTER EIGHT

To some Miamians, Liberty City is urban blight at its worst, a veritable Petri dish of crime and drugs, where hordes of dark people become riotous whenever the police shoot and kill one of their children. This was my eleventh project in Liberty City and I saw a different side, one in which neighbors step up for neighbors and people rejoice at having something shiny and new in the form of a safe and modernized home.

With over a hundred churches inside six square miles, this predominantly African-American community is easy pickings for volunteers. In fact, I have a waiting list of local groups that want to schedule a workday with us on our Section 8 project, but I have to balance their desire to help with our foundation's mission to give everyone in Miami's diverse community a stake in seeing all of our neighborhoods turned around. It's a good problem to have.

"How come you're still here?"

I nearly jumped out of my chair at Gisela's question, since I thought everyone had gone home already. I should have known better. She's always the first one in the office and the last to leave.

"Just trying to figure out how I can schedule a volunteer crew from the Miami-Dade Police Department onto our jobsite without alienating the whole community."

"If there's ever a group that needs to make a good showing in Liberty City, it's the police."

"I know, but we didn't cause their public relations problems, and I don't want to bring them in just to see the local kids go behind them and tear everything up. It's not like I'm up for a Nobel Peace Prize."

"Doesn't mean you won't get nominated, though."

She patted me on the shoulder and said goodnight.

I stuck around a few minutes longer watching the clock. I'd decided after all to meet Emily for dinner with Edith and Mordy at six, but my goal was to be a few minutes late to the WKB restaurant. I wanted her to sit there wondering if I'd changed my mind so she'd understand how the power had shifted between us. I now held all the cards.

While I'd managed to convince myself tonight was about getting that elusive thing called Closure, I also had a primal curiosity to see if she had any interest in groveling her way back, even if I ultimately decide it's not what I want. I'm not above forgiveness if something is still smoldering in the ruins of our relationship, but this time it has to be on my terms.

In my wildest dreams, I never thought the day would come when I could sit down with Emily and be civil. In the first place, she'd never been quick about admitting her mistakes, and I couldn't believe she was actually coming around, even under the laughable auspices of catching up with "friends." In the second place was how we'd left things after the property transfer. That whole affair had been acrimonious thanks to the fact she'd stiffed me for several months of mortgage payments despite promising to pay her half until we found a buyer.

So why am I even doing this? Because I'm lonely. I didn't even realize how much until the other night when I saw Mari Tirado out with her friends. I want a life like hers, and I've done nothing to get there. My only real friends outside of work are Edith and Mordy, and I haven't had a single date since Emily left.

Of course, none of that means anything unless Emily shows up tonight ready to admit all of the crap that happened between us was her fault. One hundred percent.

Rush hour traffic had thinned by the time I pulled onto the Dolphin Expressway, so much that my plan to arrive fashionably late required driving around downtown for a few minutes. What I hadn't counted on was a new set of construction barricades on Biscayne Boulevard that forced traffic into one lane, and I soon found myself even later than I'd intended. It was no surprise when my cell phone rang.

"I'm stuck in traffic," I said, not even checking to see who it was.

"Is this Daphne?"

The husky voice shocked me so much I forgot to keep up with the car in front, prompting an outrageous horn blast from behind.

"This is she."

"Mari Tirado. How are you doing?"

"Great…great." Pretty damn great, actually.

"Is this a bad time?"

There was no such thing as a bad time for Mari to call. "No, I'd much rather talk to you than kill someone with my car."

"That's you, always dangerous. I was wondering if you were doing anything tonight. I know it's short notice, but Pepe gave me a couple of tickets to the Arsht Center. The Hungarian Philharmonic is doing Mahler's *Fifth*."

"Oh, my God! That's one of the greatest symphonies ever. It sold out in like fifteen minutes."

"Think you can make it by six forty-five?"

I was eight blocks from home, only three minutes if I cut over to a side street at the next light. If I had to, I'd park the car and run.

We set our meeting place and I turned left in front of an oncoming BMW with what prosecutors would have called "callous disregard for human life." I was already home when I remembered my dinner plans.

"Edith, you guys go ahead without me. I'm not going to be able to make it."

I juggled the phone from one ear to the next, noting that getting undressed with one hand requires skills I haven't used in years. In my dream world, the practice I was getting right now would come in handy later tonight. But if I wasn't out the door in twelve minutes, nothing would ever happen at all.

There was a long silence before Edith answered. "I came outside because it's so loud in the restaurant. Is everything all right?"

"It's fine. Everything's fine. Edith, I have a date."

"With a woman?"

No, with a cockatoo. "Yes, the woman I was talking to the other night at the Wallcast." She and Mordy had urged me to ask her out, but I played it down, saying she was only someone I knew from work.

"I thought you said you weren't interested in her that way."

"I lied. She's taking me to Mahler."

"What should I tell Emily?"

I couldn't imagine sending a clearer message than the one she'd get from being stood up. "Just…to have a safe trip back to Sarasota."

A night out at the Arsht Center called for the most elegant thing in my closet. Now if only I knew what that was. Somewhere I had a pair of black silk pants that tapered at the ankle. They'd look nice with my highest heels, even if they were only an inch and a half tall. Now all I needed was something sparkly or fluffy or tiger-striped. Except I didn't own anything like that. The best I could do was a tight-fitting dark purple top, V-neck with three-quarter sleeves.

Wait! I had a sparkly belt somewhere, black with gaudy rhinestones. That left earrings. The dangly black ones…or the silver hoops…dangly black ones…silver hoops. I got it all put together with about three minutes to spare.

The concert hall sits only two blocks on the other side of the Omni so I spent that extra three minutes walking slower than usual. The last thing I wanted was to get there dripping sweat from racing through the sticky night.

I spotted Mari from behind as she stood talking on the phone just inside the door of the grand lobby. She wore another cocktail dress, this one a wraparound teal green number that looked like it was made for her. I entertained myself for a few seconds with the idea that she was telling someone about the exciting date she'd lined up for tonight, but then she turned and I saw that same look she'd worn when describing the investment instrument to Carlos Moya.

She dropped her phone in her purse and greeted me with a kiss on the cheek. I nearly swooned. I'm many things, but hard to please isn't among them.

"I'm really sorry about the late notice. I had to go all the way to the Gables to pick up the tickets and I didn't want to call until I had them in my hand. Then I started freaking out because US 1 was backed up to the Grove and I remembered how you hated it when people were late."

It was almost unfair that someone so hot had a voice that sexy too.

"I would have forgiven you for something this great."

She held out both hands to my ears and smiled. "This is an interesting look."

Son of a St. Bernard. Dangly black on one ear, silver hoop on the other. "Couldn't decide, but I drew the line at carrying two purses."

"I think it works." She presented the tickets. "Pepe did us right. You're not going to believe where these seats are."

Front row, box seats on the second mezzanine, stage left. Deep Joyful Sigh. According to the program, Mahler would come after the intermission. The prelude was described as a medley of Hungarian composers I'd never heard of, but it could have been salsa music for all I cared. Front row, box seats with Mari Tirado in a teal dress.

I was in such a state of bliss that I didn't even go berserk when dozens of people, including four others in our box, were seated by the ushers well into the first piece. Only in Miami did performance venues actually cater to the late-arriving crowd. Anywhere else they barred the door when the curtain went up.

Mari's low voice rumbled in my ear, sending shivers up my back. "Are you comfortable? Can you see everything?"

"I'm perfect. Everything is perfect." The music, the setting and especially the company.

As the violins softly swept into the second selection, my stomach loudly announced it was empty. The subject of eating had never even crossed my mind.

"Sounds like someone else skipped dinner to get here," Mari whispered.

"It was food or Mahler. Not even a contest." Anything that brought her lips that close to my ear was bearable. Except the gurgling continued, and as my luck would have it, seemed to be worse during the quieter passages.

When the lights went up for intermission, the man behind me tapped Mari on the shoulder and immediately launched into a conversation in Spanish, the only word of which I caught was Pepe. Apparently these seats were Pepe's season tickets, which meant most of the people sitting in the box were regular patrons, perhaps even friends of his. I tried to catch a word of the conversation, if only to reassure myself he wasn't complaining about my noisy stomach.

I was still in awe of the whole evening, so much that I didn't even bristle at hearing practically everyone around me speaking Spanish. Thanks to Mari, I have a newfound admiration for those who can transition between two languages so easily. She wasn't bilingual because she hadn't assimilated. She was born here, and as much a product of Miami culture as anyone could be. I'm the one who hasn't assimilated to Miami.

She wrapped up her conversation by kissing both the man and his wife on the cheek, another Cuban habit I was coming to appreciate. She then took my elbow and guided me to the exit. "Just making sure you don't fall out of the box. That would be hard to explain."

"Not really. If you ever have the urge to kill me, you can just push me over the railing. With my history, a jury would never convict."

"I'm taking a break from felonious behavior just now." There went that dimple again.

I couldn't believe this was the same woman who had once irritated me so much I had sentenced her to hard labor. Everything about her was fascinating, and I was rapidly rethinking every disparaging opinion I've ever had of Cubans in general, and her in particular.

"Let's find something to eat so we don't get thrown out by the usher."

Quite frankly, I didn't care about food at all, but the rumbling had to stop before Mahler. The best we could do was a small bag of something ironically labeled "gourmet" chips, and a couple of glasses of white wine.

"Mari, this is by far the most exciting event I've been to in years. I'm so glad you invited me."

"It's great you were able to make it at the last minute. When Pepe first called me, I turned him down because I didn't have any friends who were into this kind of thing. Then I remembered you liked it. A classical music geek, if I recall."

I was ridiculously pleased she had stored that detail about me, enough that I parked her use of the word friend on the back burner of my brain. "And you said this type of music really wasn't your thing, so I appreciate even more knowing you're suffering through this just for me."

"Now, now. I never said I was suffering. I'm not saying I'd want to sit through a concert like this every night, but it's good to do something civilized every now and then."

"A little *cultcha* never hurt anybody."

"I suppose not," she said with a chuckle. "I've always tried to cultivate a variety of friends so I won't get stuck doing the same things over and over."

Okay, that was the second time in the last thirty seconds she had used the F-word. Was she saying this wasn't a date?

"I get so tired of the club scene," she went on, oblivious to the spear she'd just thrown through my heart. "It's loud and pretentious, and you spend half the night fighting off guys whose greatest goal in life is to make it with a couple of lesbians. You know the kind I'm talking about."

"Oh, yeah." No, actually.

"So I'm perfectly happy for the chance to have a little *cultcha*."

The lights flashed and we headed back to our seats. Two friends, out for a casual evening of Mahler.

How fitting the symphony opened with a funeral march. I was dying inside. How could I have thought this was date? Exciting people like Mari don't date boring people like me.

Though I was painfully distracted by her crushing denial of our budding romance, I refused to let it dampen the thrill of an absolutely rapturous "Adagietto."As corny as it sounds, I actually felt tears stinging my eyes. The final movement, an uplifting rondo, gave me time to pull myself together.

When the concert ended I leapt to my feet and joined half the audience in thunderous applause. The other half—in one of the most detestable of Miami traditions—broke for the doors to beat the crowd. From the way Mari snatched up her purse and stepped into the aisle, it was clear she wanted to do the same thing but I wasn't going to let her get away with it.

"Mari, that was breathtaking."

"Very nice," she answered, smiling politely but still clearly eager to leave.

"Very nice? That's all you've got? You can't call something like that very nice." I lowered my voice to make it sound like hers but it came out more like a voice-over for a cemetery commercial. "It was exquisite."

"Exquisite! That's the word I wanted. I've never been so moved by a movement."

I turned away from her and continued to applaud, determined now to be the last one cheering. She eventually got the message, dropping her purse in her chair so she could clap along.

"I'm sorry if I rushed you," she said when I finally acquiesced to leave. "I should have realized you'd want to stay."

"It was so beautiful, Mari. I just hate to see people run out without giving the musicians their due. People in Miami always do that and it makes me feel embarrassed."

"You're right, absolutely right."

Here she was charming me again, all the more reason to be sorry this wasn't a date.

We followed the crowd onto the plaza at Biscayne Boulevard, where I braced myself for that awkward end-of-the-evening moment where Mari would blurt out a few pleasantries before kissing me on the cheek and walking off to hook up with one of her other "friends" for something more to her liking.

"Look, Mari…I know this wasn't your thing, but honestly, it was a night I won't forget for a long time. I'm really glad you thought of me."

"Too bad I didn't know about it sooner. We could have grabbed dinner or something. There are some nice restaurants not far from here in Wynwood."

Oh, that would have been precious—walking into WKB with Mari and tossing a friendly wave over to Emily. "Maybe there'll be another time, except now I owe you and I have no idea what you like."

"Monster truck rallies."

"That…would not have been…my guess." How could someone so cosmopolitan and—"You're lying through your teeth!"

"But I had you going for a second there, didn't I?"

"You're lucky there's a limit to my gullibility. If I'd surprised you with tickets, you would've had to go with me."

"And sit there to the bitter end."

"Until the very last car was pancaked." I like her a lot. I even like her as a friend, though I couldn't see myself fitting in with her South Beach party crowd. But I could sure handle being part of her rotation when she was looking for something a little different. It wouldn't hurt me to have someone around to keep me from taking myself so seriously. "What if we just do the dinner we missed tonight?"

"Works for me. You have my number now, right?"

I nodded, remembering I'd captured it on my cell phone.

"Thanks for meeting me. It was fun." She kissed me on the cheek again, and I caught her arm as she started to step away.

All that cheek kissing was nice but what I really wanted was a hug, and I didn't give her a chance to turn me down.

CHAPTER NINE

Marvin the cat makes me a nervous wreck every time Edith or Mordy open the sliding glass door. I have visions of him lunging for a bird or mosquito and plummeting fifteen floors, but Mordy always says he's far too lazy to jump as high as the railing on the balcony, let alone chase something. It's true I'd never seen him even run across the floor. I guess he's satisfied to have Edith do all the hunting and fishing for him, as long as he never misses a meal.

"She's changed her hair," Edith said, making a face that gave away what she thought of Emily's new 'do. "But it's not the same length on both sides. I don't think I could hold my head up straight if my hair was long on one side and short on the other."

Mordy chortled. "Should have left her hair the way it was and changed her personality instead."

Edith rolled up her magazine and smacked him. "Did no one ever teach you to keep your mouth shut if you couldn't say something nice?"

"There's nothing nice to say. She's a scumbag who walked all over Daphne and now she comes sniffing around because she got dumped on her ass."

Edith closed the sliding glass door and began lighting the candles throughout the living room in anticipation of nightfall, since it was Friday and they wouldn't turn on their lights again until tomorrow evening. "And what if they get back together someday, Mordy? Did you think about that? How's Daphne going to feel to know you think the person she loves is a scumbag?"

"Daphne isn't going to get back together with her. Emily's a whack job."

"Hello, everyone. I'm sitting right here. I can talk for myself." Although Mordy had done a pretty good job of summing things up. Emily lacked the one thing I value most in a person—integrity— and that was a deal breaker. But instead of running away from her as fast as I could, I was still drawn to her latest drama like a rubbernecker driving past an upside-down beer truck.

My night out with Mari had been loads of fun, but not the ride back down to earth after she'd made it clear we were just friends. With that being a dead end, I found myself back to entertaining Emily's renewed interest.

"My date last night sort of fizzled." I shared my humiliation over discovering it wasn't a date after all, but to save face with Mordy and Edith, I finished the morbid tale by saying I was still glad I went because Mahler was fantastic and Mari could turn out to be a friend. All that was true, as was the fact I wasn't ready to see Emily again just yet anyway. "I'm not going to put myself at her beck and call just because she happens to be in town. If she wants to see me, she can go out of her way a little bit."

"But you're open to seeing her again?" Edith asked.

It seemed Edith was cheerleading for our reconciliation, but I couldn't figure out why. Like Mordy, she knew all the sordid details about Emily's infidelities and mortgage arrears, but somehow came to a different conclusion. "What do you think I should do?"

"Tell her to take a hike," Mordy said.

"She asked *me*." She smacked him again, but gently. "I'm not saying this is what you *should* do, but I don't think you're happy by yourself, Daphne. A woman like you—young, pretty, full of life—shouldn't be spending so many nights at home alone. It's a waste. You and Emily used to go out all the time, but even when you stayed home, the two of you had fun. We could hear you talking and laughing on the balcony every night, and your lives just seemed so full. If there's a chance you can get that back, don't you think it's worth a try?"

I'd been thinking a lot about those good times. People always talk about nostalgia like it's something dreamy and warm. I never see it that way, at least not where Emily is concerned. I ache when I think of our best days, but not for yearning. I ache because I wonder if they were ever real, if Emily had felt love for me the way I had for her. I'd always thought so, at least right up until the end when she told me I'd been living in a false security for months, that she'd been thinking about leaving but didn't want to say anything until she was sure. Until she lined up her next move was more like it. How could I not have noticed that?

So the biggest hurdle for Emily and me getting back together isn't forgiveness. It's trust. If she could lead me on for months without me knowing, how could I believe anything she said or did?

"Tell her to take a hike," Mordy said again. "She's desperate now because she got dumped. You're not desperate. You can do better."

"I'm really glad we've had this little talk. Things are so much clearer now."

They'd probably fight about it later when I was gone but I knew no matter what I decided both of them would be in my corner. That was the beauty of our friendship, which had grown since Emily left for the simple reason that I spent more time with them now. In many ways, I'm closer to them now than to my own parents, and certainly more affectionate.

"Okay, give me a hug. I've got to work tomorrow."

"Are you coming for *Seudah Shlishit?*"

"Not this week, but thanks anyway. I may have to stay late tomorrow to help finish at the worksite." That was possible, but the main reason was Edith had me feeling like an old maid recluse. I needed to get out of the house for something more interesting, like maybe a stroll through the shops at Merrick Park over in Coral Gables.

Seeing Mari chat last night with Pepe's friends had prompted an unusual admission in my conversation with myself, and all day I'd been turning it over in my head to study its veracity. I really have no right to grouse about how the Cuban influx had changed Miami. I only got here four years ago and it was already their city. They didn't take anything from me.

Sure, people like Mordy griped about the effects, how the Jews who settled on Miami Beach after World War II were displaced in the 1990s by the Hispanic twenty-something professionals who drove up rents by turning it into a hip Latin nightspot and forcing the renovation of older buildings. They had lots of elderly friends who had grappled with that and ended up moving up the coast or to poorer neighborhoods well off the water. Mordy also had struggled to hold the service workers union together when their ranks split over loyalties to Anglo or Cuban leaders, and Edith grew so frustrated at how the City Commission shifted its focus to the Cuban community and its backdoor deals that she gave up on her civic activism.

I need to think. In the last couple of days I'd gone from cautious consideration of getting back together with Emily to "Emily Who?" to being cautious again. It was in the middle—that "Emily Who?" part—where I'd had the most fun. I could chalk that up to the thrill of being out with someone as engaging as Mari, but that struck me as simplistic. I might have felt the same way about going out with one of the Olsen twins just to avoid swallowing my pride and taking Emily back. That had to mean my subconscious mind was made up. I'd rather roll the dice than go back to someone who treated me like dirt just because she was a sure thing.

What I really needed was a network of friends like Mari has, people I can call up whenever I feel like going out. I'm certainly not going to meet anyone if I spend virtually every night at home or with my elderly neighbors.

So where are all the cool people at nine o'clock on a Friday night? I knew one way to find out—call a cool person and ask what she was doing.

This didn't have to be a big deal. If only someone could tell my stomach that.

I took my phone and a can of club soda out to the balcony and settled into my chaise lounge, taking advantage of the only time all week I have total privacy out here. Mordy and Edith never open their balcony door after sundown on Friday because it messes up their air conditioner setting, and they can't touch it again until tomorrow night.

There was only a slim chance Mari would even answer her phone, since being busy on a Friday night is part of what makes cool people cool. I was all ready to leave a message when she picked up.

"Whaddya know? It's the classical music geek. What's up?"

If Mari and I were going to be friends, I had to find a way not to buzz all over merely at the sound of her voice. "Just calling to say thanks again. I've been walking around all day with a huge smile on my face."

"Good for you. I guess that's better than a huge bruise on your butt."

"No, tomorrow is bruise day. I'm a little surprised you answered. I figured you'd be on your way out to some party on South Beach."

"I'm wasted. This whole week has been crazy. We've got this investment package—the Iberican Fund, we call it—for some of our premium clients, and word got out. Now everyone wants in on it. That's what you get when your whole philosophy is to make all your clients feel like premium clients."

"Now that you mention it, I remember when I walked up on you and Carlos Moya, you were telling him something about how you couldn't take on new investors but you'd try to work him in."

She chuckled. "That was different. Carlos really is a premium client."

"Okay, then you lost me."

"What I said to Carlos was all part of the sales pitch for the fund. The idea is to make my clients want in on something because it's a hot deal and available only to special people. As soon as they hear that, they want to be special too. Except now we're in trouble because word leaked out and everybody wants a piece of it."

"But that's a good thing, right?"

"Not for this one. We're limiting this to major investors. Hold on a second. This is going to be obnoxious." A blender roared in the background for several seconds. "Frozen daiquiri. I was getting desperate."

"Totally understand. Never get between me and a mojito." I never would have guessed Mari would be home alone on a Friday night like me. I wondered what the chances were that the rest of her weekend was free. "I promise not to keep you from your planned alcohol stupor, but I was serious about what I said last night about repaying your generosity with dinner. You probably already have plans tomorrow, but if not…"

"Oh, sorry. It's Mima's eighty-fifth birthday and it would take at least a Category Three to get any of us out of that. And Pepe left a message on my phone not to make any plans for Sunday, so this weekend's kaput."

If I were the insecure type, I probably would have jumped to conclusions over how she crossed off the whole weekend in advance, like maybe she was trying to head off a stalker or something. "It doesn't have to be a big production or anything. We can just meet for a bite somewhere whenever you're feeling caught up."

Mother of Mighty Mouse! Why had I said that? I just threw the ball back into her court. Now I'd have to sit around waiting another three months for her to call again.

"If we wait for me to be caught up, it may never happen. How come you're home on a Friday night?"

"How soon we forget. I have to be on the jobsite at seven thirty in the morning."

"Hmm…yuck. That reminds me, have you heard any more about how Saraphine Delacourt is doing?"

It took me a second to remember who that was. We'd worked on three different sites since Saraphine's house in Little Haiti. "I haven't, but that's not the kind of thing I keep up with. Someone in our office does, though, so I can find out if you want to know."

"I guess I could call her myself. I have her number somewhere. We talked a couple of times over the summer about her savings plan and I was just wondering how she was."

I felt a pang of something…sadness, loss. I couldn't put my finger on it exactly, but I wished Mari were interested in me for more than friendship. I was heartened to hear someone like her—someone who had "premium clients" paying her lots of money—ask how a low-income Haitian woman was getting along. That's the kind of person I want to marry.

"That was nice of you to help her out."

"It wasn't much. I'm surprised your foundation doesn't have a program in place to help people out with their finances. Between that and the renovations, you'd really be turning lives around… not that you aren't already. It would just give people more tools to go forward."

"I think it's a great idea. Unfortunately, those decisions get made above my pay grade."

"You like your job?"

What I liked was Mari being interested enough in me to ask questions, and then actually listen to the answers. If she'd wanted to blow me off, she could have done so by now.

"I like most of it. I didn't exactly train as a construction worker but some weeks that's my favorite part of what I do. It's certainly the least stressful. Probably not what my folks had in mind when they sprang for that Ivy League education."

"We all take our own path…well, except me. I did exactly what Pepe always wanted me to do, but at least it was something I liked."

"And I bet you're good at it." If a hundred-thousand-dollar sports car and a waterfront condo on Brickell were any indication. I doubted Pepe rained down luxury on his family without insisting they work for it.

As creepy as it was, I couldn't help wondering what she was wearing as she sat at home alone on a Friday night sipping a daiquiri. My fantasy involved a long white shirt with the sleeves rolled up…nothing underneath.

She told me how she majored in finance at the University of Miami after graduating from St. Theresa in Coral Gables. It's a familiar meme—just like Gisela's, in fact—that the well-to-do Hispanics send their kids to Catholic schools, then to UM, or The U, as it's called here.

"And what do you do besides work all the time?" I asked, fishing for an even better picture of who she was. "I know you sometimes go to classical concerts despite not being terribly interested in the music. About the only other thing I know is that you might have had a passing interest in Jet Skis at one time in your life, but something tells me you're over it."

"I'm way over it. I'm sure my ex is out there on the water every weekend and I wouldn't be able to resist the urge to drown her if I got the chance. I doubt they'd let me off with just community service for that one."

Nice to know other people are still bitter about their exes. Perfectly normal.

"What about you, Daphne? What kind of trouble do you get in?"

Dilemma: Embellish the details of my social life so I don't sound like a bore or tell the truth? It's an irrefutable fact my enormous mortgage payment leaves me little mad money, but I don't want to trigger Mari's "walk away" speech again. Not that her advice is bad. It makes financial sense, but it still feels wrong to me, and I don't want her to think I'm stupid for not doing it.

I must have pondered too long because she jumped back in to rescue me from having to answer. "That was just a figure of speech. You don't strike me as much of a troublemaker."

"Not all that much since Emily left. We had a few lesbian friends in town, but things aren't the same when you're not a couple anymore and everyone else is."

"Tell me about it. At least your ex moved away. Every time I go to a party, I'm always on edge about running into Delores. I know if I see her I'm going to throttle her. And at the risk of sounding like a third grader, it isn't just her that puts me off. It's every single one of my so-called friends who still speak to her all smiles like she's so nice. The woman had me *arrested*!" Her voice had gone ice cold. "It's my own fault for getting in so deep. I've outgrown most of those women anyway. At some point, we're supposed to quit playing in the sandbox. I need a better class of friends."

"You want friends who'd be sitting in the jail cell next to you talking about how much fun it was."

"Damn right!"

"All right, what the hell. I could use some excitement. Call me the next time you feel like making trouble."

I could do a lot worse than getting locked up with Mari Tirado.

CHAPTER TEN

Just because I never wear drawstring linen pants that flow like a long skirt doesn't mean I shouldn't. I have a bad habit of buying the same clothes over and over, and a worse habit of being the last one to surrender to a style change. The only thing set in fashion stone for me is no bright colors ever. I figure that's my subconscious talking, telling me not to call attention to myself because I never know what to wear.

Up until a few days ago when I went to the symphony, looking "just fine" was good enough. Now I find myself caught in a hopeless vortex of needing to look stylish but lacking the funds to do so—even if I had a clue what stylish meant.

The outfit I managed to cobble together from Marshall's and TJ Maxx—last year's overstocks—didn't suck terribly. Along with my beige pants, I bought a white camisole top and a navy blue overshirt that I could wear open. I got the idea from a mannequin at Neiman Marcus, where the pants alone cost three times as much as what I paid for the whole outfit at the discount stores.

I just wanted Mari to like it. I couldn't believe it when she called last night and said Pepe's plan for Sunday was a dinner cruise around the Biscayne Bay on their private yacht with some of their clients, and she wanted me to come along. My personal experience with yachts is that I see them sometimes from my balcony and wonder who all those bazillionaires are. Now I know.

After one last check to make sure my earrings matched this time, I started down to the lobby where she was supposed to pick me up "around seven o'clock." I had a feeling the window on that was up to half an hour, but I vowed to chill about it.

The elevator opened on fourteen for Ronaldo and Tandra, and their darling baby girl Isabel. It mattered not that the Garcías spoke so little English because the language around babies is universal.

"Isabel! Such a pretty girl." She was lively and bright, always riveted to my wide-eyed expressions and happy voice, and her parents beamed with pride. "You're so lucky...*suerte.*"

I know just enough Spanish to probably misuse it. But since they spoke Portuguese, not Spanish, I probably just called their baby a mushroom. I figured I could get away with a lot as long as I stayed with my wide eyes and happy voice.

It was only twenty after when Mari rolled up into the circle outside our lobby in her snazzy car. Two firsts for today—dinner on a yacht and riding in a Porsche.

"You look great. I can't believe you were worried about what to wear," said the woman wearing what appeared to be the actual outfit I'd seen on the mannequin at Neiman Marcus. She spun out of the parking circle and down a side street to Biscayne Boulevard, where she lurched into traffic after barely slowing at the stop sign.

"I take it this dinner tonight is actually a business meeting for you and Pepe."

"Yes and no. It's one of our important clients, Juan Olivo, and this is our way of thanking him for his business. But Juan is bringing one of his friends who might be interested in investing with Padilla Financial. Pepe wanted me to come because Juan and his partner are gay, and so is their friend. We just want everyone to feel comfortable. Are you okay with that?"

A prop. I could handle that. "Of course. Who am I supposed to be? Your girlfriend? Your date? Your hired escort?" If she said partner, I was going to insist we make it legal.

"I was hoping you'd be my date, but if you'd rather just be a friend who came along, that's fine too."

Flutter.

We'd gone only a few blocks when she whipped into the parking garage at Bayside. And I mean whipped. She's exactly the sort of Miami driver responsible for my Never Take Your Hands Off the Wheel Rule.

"I should be able to handle being your date. Will I need bail money?"

"Let's hope it doesn't come to that," she said, smiling in a way that obviously wasn't smiling. She parked and started to get out when I grabbed her arm, knowing I'd screwed up.

"I'm sorry, Mari. Forget I said that about the bail money. I don't want you to worry about me teasing you or blurting that out in front of people. It's forgotten. I won't bring it up again."

She nodded, and with the most earnest expression I'd seen on her yet, added, "And I'll try not to push you overboard, even though I could get away with it so easily with someone like you."

"Sounds like a deal."

"Oh, by the way…something I need to mention. I'm sure it's totally unnecessary to say this, but everything we talk about on the yacht tonight needs to stay confidential. People can be prickly about their finances."

"Of course." It would be gauche to brag about the three hundred bucks I had in savings.

We walked through the Bayside Marketplace and out to the docks, where we stepped aboard a yacht, smallish compared to some of the gargantuan vessels in neighboring slips, but plenty big. On its stern was the name *Mima's Dream*. The deck at the back held a dining table already set for eight and tended by a young Hispanic man in a white jacket and bow tie who introduced himself as Eddie. Mari ordered drinks for us and led me up a set of steep steps past the bridge to the upper deck, where Marco Padilla—Pepe—sat with an elegant older woman and three casually dressed men with perfect haircuts. Definitely gay.

Immediately, all the men sprang to their feet and Pepe made the introductions. Juan was the president of Banco Primero, a local bank that catered to Miami's Hispanic community. I'd reached out to them for volunteer work but had gotten no further than a loan officer, who said she didn't know who handled that sort of request. Meeting Juan theoretically gave me an avenue to follow up, but it didn't feel right to take advantage of Pepe's hospitality that way.

Juan's partner was Brian, a fair-haired Anglo like me. Their friend Michael—presumably the one whose business Pepe and Mari were courting—was balding but blue-eyed, which told me he probably wasn't Hispanic either.

Then there was Pepe's wife Lucia, who might have weighed a hundred pounds with bricks in her pockets, a stunning contrast to her portly husband. Apparently, she hadn't gotten the memo about casual dress, as she had on a flowing silk jumpsuit in pale orange, something I might have worn to a formal ball…assuming I ever went to such things.

I was introduced as Mari's friend Daphne, a director at one of Miami's most successful foundations. Technically true, since my title was Director of Community Relations, but more than a little aggrandizing.

Mari clarified our relationship for the guests by wrapping an arm around my waist as she steered me to a seat. Eddie soon appeared with our daiquiri and mojito and announced dinner would be ready in forty minutes.

Eight o'clock? Hispanics usually eat much later in the evening. I figured we'd eat around ten, but then it occurred to me our hosts were being hospitable, since not all of us have digestive systems that run on Hispanic Time.

In the meantime, taking in the sunset from the upper deck of a yacht with my gorgeous, rich friends, I was so, so overstimulated. Especially with Mari's arm around my waist.

One thing I appreciate about most bilingual Cubans is how they remember to speak English in the presence of those like Brian, Michael and me. Not that I understood any of what they were saying tonight. Financial lingo might as well be Spanish to me.

"…with the lowest residual security," Pepe explained. "Yes, they're load funds but they're heavily managed. Mari herself handles much of the research on the key performance indicators."

"Including site visits last year to eleven manufacturing and distribution centers throughout Latin America," she added.

"In other words, we don't base our investment decisions on earnings statements and corporate investment brochures. We verify it on the ground, and if the benefit cost ratios are found to be in decline, we pass. Iberican looks for rapid capital appreciation, and we're committed to ongoing review of assets. Our objective is…"

I could barely hear the motors of the modern yacht as we churned slowly underneath the MacArthur Causeway Bridge into the calm waters beside the old *Miami Herald* building, where I had an almost overpowering urge to shout, "I can see my house from here!" Then we turned out toward South Beach, past the small man-made islands that were home to Miami's mega-rich sports and media stars.

Mari leaned in, and with her voice barely above a whisper, said, "I promise we won't talk about this much longer. You doing okay?"

"I'm fantastic. Don't worry about me. Do whatever you need to do."

Michael was gawking at the waterfront mansions as much as I was. "Which one of those is yours?" he asked Pepe.

"I can only dream. For one of those, I'd have to charge much higher commissions." He hugged his wife. "And then there would be the matter of talking Lucia into leaving the Gables. I'd stand a better chance of convincing all of you to invest with Lehman Brothers."

I actually got that joke. Lehman was the brokerage firm that went under in the early days of the financial crisis. My father had lost a bundle with them, but fortunately his holdings were diversified. Pepe's remark made me wonder how the crash had impacted not only Padilla Financial as a firm, but Mari and Pepe personally. They sure didn't seem to be suffering, but then neither were any of the other investment survivors. It was just the poor schmucks like me whose meager wealth was tied up in tanking real estate.

Suddenly Pepe rose and clapped his hands. "Enough about business. Let's enjoy this beautiful evening."

He and Lucia led the men down a front staircase to the bow. Mari stayed put and so did I…especially since her hand was on my hip and I wouldn't have moved even for a cockroach.

"It gets crowded up there. We can go later. Sorry about all that investment talk."

"It's all right. I finally have an idea what you actually do for a living."

"The evil money changer."

"I have nothing against capitalism as long as it's fair."

"Fair is good. Our aim is to be the first investment firm on the bandwagon when a new or restructured business takes off. That's when risks pay the highest dividends, before other investors come on board."

"And why you hold certain investments back for just your premium clients."

"Exactly."

"So the people who already have the most money are the only ones who can make the most money."

"Technically true, but they also assume the highest risk because they can most afford to lose. By the time we bring our more conservative investors into the mix, the rapid growth has slowed but at least it's steady. That's a win-win."

Still, it's only a win for those with money to invest. What are the rest of us supposed to do while guys like Juan and Michael hoard all the money?

I forced a smile, noting with no small bit of irony that I had no business grousing about the One Percent while I was personally enjoying the fruits of their investments. Since they were kind enough to ask me along on this extravagant dinner cruise, I decided not to entertain any more rude thoughts about how any of them got their money or what they did with it.

"I take it you travel a lot, Mari," I said. As if she needed even more glamour in her life.

"Just a few times a year…mostly South America and the Caribbean."

"I had a job offer from Global Hotels in Boston that would have taken me back and forth to Europe every couple of months. Instead I followed Emily Jenko to Miami and wound up traveling to exciting places like Liberty City and Little Haiti."

She started to answer then snapped her mouth shut as she looked away.

"What?"

"Nothing."

"Something. What were you going to say?"

"I'm in the business of giving financial advice to people, and I sometimes do that when I shouldn't. This may be one of those times."

"I know, I know. You would advise me to walk away from my mortgage and go back to Boston."

"Still yes to the first, but I have no advice for what you should do about Boston. I was just going to suggest that you quit dwelling on a choice you already made. Whether it was right or wrong is irrelevant because you can't change your decision to come here. What matters is what you do now."

"I'm sure that's comforting for your investors after they've lost their entire nest egg."

"Except that wouldn't happen because I'd never let any of my clients put their whole nest egg in one place. But assuming they lost big…yes, it would still be my advice because I'm a financial planner. By definition, I plan for the future, not the past."

I wondered if her clients found her as confident and charming as I did, or if I was just under her Lesbian Spell. She made me want to go out and rob banks so I could give her all the money. Then she'd seek me out at cocktail parties the way she had Carlos

Moya, and I'd get to see her light up with a smile when I made a little telephone with my pinky and thumb.

"You need to call someone?" Mari asked.

Apparently I'd actually done that instead of just imagining it.

"No, I was just thinking your phone must ring off the hook if that's the sort of advice you give your clients. We'd all be better off if we didn't dwell on our mistakes."

"Absolutely." She slid her fingers along my forearm until they linked with mine. "I've been thinking about our conversation the other night, when I said I needed a better class of friends. That business at the concert...I wanted to cut out as soon as the performance was over and you insisted we stay. I should have realized I was insulting the performers, and I respect you for getting in my face about it."

I hadn't exactly gotten in her face.

Not that I had anything against her face.

"Anyway, that's a long way of saying I think you're pretty classy."

I could feel myself blushing, and for once, it wasn't because I'd said or done something stupid. "That's about the nicest thing anyone ever said about me, Mari."

There we were, alone on the sun deck with a fiery pink and blue sky in the background. Kissing her seemed like a really good idea.

Then Eddie appeared to tell us dinner was ready.

Mari held my hand all the way to the table, finally letting go so we could cross ourselves as Pepe offered a solemn grace. Finally, I got a payoff for those childhood catechism classes.

Dinner was a delicious mixed green salad with goat cheese and sweet guava vinaigrette, followed by roast pork tenderloin with seasoned rice. I had no idea where the food was coming from until Benito, a round man in a chef's jacket and toque, emerged from below to take a bow.

Juan, who had spent most of the evening talking finance with Pepe, directed his attention to me as Eddie cleared the dinner plates. "So you're the director of a foundation, Daphne? Which one?"

I was reluctant to correct him because I learned from Gisela that titles are very important in Hispanic business culture, and Pepe had seemingly gone out of his way to present me as more credentialed than I was. Nor was I comfortable with letting Juan think I ran the place, so I borrowed Pepe's words. "I'm one of the directors at the Miami Home Foundation. We use federal and community grants to renovate homes in blighted neighborhoods."

Michael snorted with unmistakable contempt. "Sounds like another one of those government giveaway programs. You let your house fall into ruin and we'll take other people's money and fix it for you."

Lovely. Mari and her uncle were schmoozing business from a Tea Party asshole. "We've been around for over thirty years, so that's enabled us to document the positive impact of our work, not only for the families that benefit directly, but also for the surrounding neighborhoods. Good housing grows the tax base, fosters business development, establishes a foundation for growing wealth among those who have traditionally struggled economically, and of course, improves the health and safety of people in ways that save public resources down the road." This is the case I make every time I approach a business or organization for volunteers. A simple act of generosity makes a huge difference to the big picture.

"I don't necessarily disagree with your results, but your underlying assumption is that we—and by that I mean taxpayers—should be renovating private homes. No matter how you slice it, that's a straight-up redistribution of wealth."

I looked to Pepe in hopes he'd steer the conversation elsewhere but he abruptly left the table to speak with Eddie. What I knew for certain was I didn't want to get into a back-and-forth with Pepe's investment prospect on the politics of urban development, especially when there was a growing likelihood I'd eventually say something to insult him. Deliberately.

Mari waded into the discussion instead. "I can't speak for the government, but Padilla Financial has been very glad to sponsor some of the Home Foundation's work."

"Which you do by choice," Michael said. "I have nothing against anyone who wants to give their money away, but when the government hands out *our* money like that, it's socialism."

The boat turned sharply and picked up speed, and Eddie finished clearing the table.

"Gentlemen, perhaps you'd like the bow for the trip home," Pepe offered, his hand sweeping toward the narrow passage on the deck.

Once they left, Lucia slid down to join Mari and me at the end of the table. "You'd think someone with as many Cuban friends as Michael would know better than to trivialize socialism and redistribution of wealth in the presence of a man who saw all of his family's property seized by a revolutionary."

Mari chuckled. "No Cuban cigar for Michael."

"Just a quick ride back to the dock," Lucia added. "We'll eat dessert after they're gone, and there will be twice as much flan for us."

As we chugged back toward Bayside, Mari and I climbed the ladder and found ourselves alone again on the sun deck. Not just alone, but sitting side by side with her arm around me. If I leaned into her shoulder, it would be almost like snuggling.

"Sorry about Michael. You handled him just fine."

"I hope I didn't screw up your business deal."

"Don't worry about it. There are some people you don't want to do business with and Michael's one of them. Answering to him down the road would be a serious headache because he'd be looking over our shoulder the whole time to make sure we didn't give any of his money to people who didn't deserve it. It's good we got to see that now."

The lights from the city danced off the water, causing Mari's dark eyes to sparkle. I really, really wanted to kiss her. Just one of those little casual smooches, where I might nibble on her bottom lip. No tongue, not on the first kiss…unless she kissed me back that way. I'd let her take the lead if that's what she wanted. Whatever I did, I needed to be discreet about it. The guys out on the bow were all turned the other way, but I didn't want to take any chances in case she was one of those people who—

She kissed me.

Okay, that worked too. Just a quick little smack on the lips like she'd been doing it all her life. Next thing I knew she'd scooted even closer and was looking out on the water with a smile that said she was very pleased with herself.

I was pleased with her too.

No longer in his white jacket and bow tie, Eddie hopped off the boat at the dock and fastened the moorings. By the time we got back down to the lower deck, Pepe was already shaking hands with the men as they stepped off.

Lucia appeared from below and presented us with a rolled up paper sack. "Eddie fixed our flan to go. Think that was a hint?"

And both of ours were in one bag. Think *that* was a hint?

I leaned into Lucia and we traded cheek kisses, and then I shook Pepe's hand. "Thank you both for a great evening."

"It will be more fun next time," Lucia said. "We'll make a day of it and go to Bimini."

Yachting over to Bimini with my new friends. "Wonderful."

The walk back to the car was quiet, which was okay with me because when I'm holding hands with someone for the first time, that's all I want to think about. Mari's hand was supple, with slender fingers that wove through mine like ivy on a trellis. Her polished nails brought to mind her first day on the jobsite when she'd worn through my work gloves until her hand bled. I squeezed it now in a silent apology. What an asshole I'd been.

We broke our grip long enough to get into her car and out of the garage, but joined again as she barreled up Biscayne Boulevard like she'd just robbed a bank.

"That was fast," I said when she came to a sudden stop in front of my building ten blocks later.

"Too fast?"

"If you mean the driving, yes. If you mean the end of our evening, yes to that too."

"Yeah, we got back to the marina sooner than I thought we would on account of Michael. We could always…"

"I'm off tomorrow."

She leaned against her door, crossed her arms and gave me the sexiest look I'd ever seen. And I do mean *ever*. "I have a spinning class at seven thirty."

"I have an alarm clock."

CHAPTER ELEVEN

I skipped the usual tour I give when someone stops by, where I show off the grand view from our balcony and all the modern conveniences of a moderately luxurious new building. By the time we stepped off the elevator, the bedroom was the only part of the house I wanted Mari to see.

Shoes were the first things to go, followed by my overshirt, which I tossed toward the loveseat that took up a whole corner of the room. What a fight that had been, with Emily arguing for a king-size bed that would have swamped the entire bedroom, and me wanting the queen so we could also create an intimate reading space where we could enjoy the gorgeous view.

Wrong on so many levels—not the loveseat part. I was absolutely right on that one. But it was way wrong to be thinking about my ex-girlfriend just as I was about to have sex for the first time in over two years. Was it also wrong for me to wish there was a camera on the ceiling that would let her watch me getting it on with somebody as hot as Mari?

Mari tossed her shirt on top of mine and I decided I'd spent enough brain cells on Emily Jenko for tonight. My introspection about the tragic end of our relationship was officially over.

I wrapped my arms around Mari's waist and pulled her to the bed, deciding I wanted to make love to her first in case the world ended in the middle of our romp and one of us didn't get a turn on top. She wrestled me for a moment as if she had the same goal in mind, but then I felt her surrender as she settled onto her back.

With our faces only inches apart, I looked into her eyes and held my gaze until she matched it. This was something I'd always done, a ritual to be sure we both were communicating the same feelings to one another. Oddly enough, the habit began as part of my sexual fantasies when I was only nine years old, years before my first intimate encounter. That's when I first heard that sexual relations were meant to be a form of communication without talking, what two adults—always a man and a woman, but I never imagined it that way—did to express their feelings of love. I coupled that with my father's advice to look someone in the eye when talking to them, so I never made love without making eye contact too.

Since I'd gone to Catholic school, I'd been taught that sexual relations also meant making lots of Catholic babies. By the time I reached puberty, most of my schoolgirl friends were light years ahead of me in sexual maturity because I had so many confusing questions that weren't being asked at all, let alone answered, so while they dreamed about sex as the ultimate expression of procreational love, I saw it as a chance to communicate other things. When they finally discovered sex could be even more fun if it had nothing to do with creating blessed zygotes, I was already there.

What I wanted to express by having sex with Mari was that I liked her and found her irresistibly sexy. No sweeping promises between us of unconditional, immeasurable love or expectations of forever and always. Unless of course that's what she has in mind. I'm wide open to that too, but for right now, I only need to know she likes me and finds me irresistibly sexy as well.

She was smiling with her eyes—at least that's how it looked to me. There was a certainty in her expression, like a mixture of confidence and daring, and it set a tone not of passion but adventure. We were here to have fun and I was more than okay with that.

Holding her eyes with mine until the last possible second, I lowered my mouth to hers. She let me lead the way, responding to the pressure of my lips, opening just enough to allow our tongues to touch, and moving her face with mine so we never broke contact. There was nothing tentative about any of it. We'd dispensed with all the questions about where this was going the moment she agreed to come upstairs.

This was all about enjoyment, and I happened to enjoy kissing very much. I always felt kissing was every bit as intimate as sexual touching, especially in the dark. In some ways it was even more expressive because it was something you did on purpose, as opposed to something driven by an out of control frenzy to reach a physical release.

Not that I have anything against having a physical release. I just haven't figured out how to think about somebody else while my body is exploding.

I could concentrate fully on how I felt about Mari as our lips played together like kittens in a box. I'd totally misjudged what kind of person she was, and now that I'd seen the truth of her through the actions of both her and her family, it was possible I'd also been wrong about the type of woman she was drawn to. Maybe she'd had enough of those sultry Latin ingénue types who helped themselves to your clients because it was their nature to act always in their own best interest, oblivious to how it affected others.

Mari might well have been waiting all this time for someone like me, a woman who had compassion for other people and honored her commitments. It was fun to play the field and have lots of sexy adventures, but the serious stuff you save not for the person who merely lights your fire but the one who shares your values.

Not that I have anything against fire lighting. It really had been a very long time since I'd enjoyed this kind of intimacy. Bouncing back into the sexual realm with someone like Mari was like eating bacon-wrapped chili peppers the first day after getting over the stomach flu.

And as much as I love kissing, I also love whatever comes next.

My knee had already worked its way between her thighs, and she made sure it stayed there by wrapping one of her legs around me. I found that very hot.

Also hot was the way she was breathing—deep, measured breaths that sounded almost like gasps. The best part was this little hitch she got once my hand started roaming across her stomach. I had a feeling that would only get better.

I tore myself away from her lips to pull off my camisole and then helped push hers upward and over her head. The glow of the city through the wide picture window cast enough light to pale my fantasies about what her breasts would look like. They were slightly fuller than I'd envisioned, but high and round with taut brown nipples that gave away her excitement.

Not that I have anything against full breasts. Hers were glorious and I couldn't wait to feel them collapse under mine when I crawled back on top of her.

But first was the matter of our pants. The excitement and curiosity surrounding the unveiling was amplified by the "does she or doesn't she?" matter of the pubic patch. In keeping with my resistance to fashion trends, I was the very last woman under thirty in my gym to surrender to the Sphinx. I kept insisting natural was better until Emily surprised me by getting herself a Brazilian for *my* birthday. I got my own the very next day and never looked back.

In the last couple of years, expensive personal grooming had come under tightening budget scrutiny, but I always found enough savings in generic groceries and toiletries to set aside sixty dollars a month for this essential gift to myself. The appeal went well beyond the intensity of a wet tongue on my smooth labia. I liked the way it looked and how soft it felt under my own touch, so much that I often went to sleep with—

Enough about me.

Mari's pants and ivory lace thong slid off her like quicksilver, revealing a lovely bare mons that glowed against her dark tan lines. Mercy!

I rolled the coverlet to the foot of the bed and nudged her back against the pillows. Then I shed my own pants and crawled onto her, moaning with bliss as our warm skin melded atop the cool sheets.

I wanted to tell her she felt magnificent, but we were now under a silent spell in which our bodies did all the talking. As my thigh pressed between her legs, she arched gently upward and threw her head back, allowing me to warm up my lips for the Big Event on her lovely neck. All the while her fingertips danced around the small of my back, occasionally dipping down to stroke the Y-shaped dimple at the base of my spine. I loved the tickling sensation and the boldness of her intimate touch, but I wasn't ready to turn my attention from her, not when every little thing I did caused that marvelous hitch in her breathing.

With a slight shift, I maneuvered back into position to kiss her, this time letting my fingers wander south to her breast. I struck a perfect rhythm to alternately tease both her tongue and nipple, and she soon began to squirm with want. That's when I lowered my head and took half her breast into my mouth.

She answered with a long hiss…no translation needed.

I pressed her breasts together and nestled my face between them, deciding this was where I wanted to sleep tonight much later when our bodies finally succumbed to fatigue. As I brushed my cheek against her pebbled nipple, I reached my hand between her legs and cupped her whole sex. The moist warmth turned to wet heat as she opened herself and I slid my fingers through her as if stirring honey.

I had to taste her.

She was ready for that, her lips swollen and glistening. As I lowered my mouth, I raised my eyes to look at her, but she was already lost. Her sharp intake of breath as my mouth fell upon her was all the proof I needed she was still there with me. I could have lavished that soft cleft with teasing licks and nibbles all night, but Mari climbed out of control right away. When her hand pressed against the back of my head to hold me in place, I knew her climax was imminent and I wanted all of her I could get. Without changing the strokes of my firm tongue against her clitoris, I slid two fingers inside her.

She cried out as her inner walls clutched my hand with spasms. "Oh, Daphne…"

It's always good to hear your own name called out in the heat of the moment.

I held my spot for nearly a minute while her waves receded. Then I went right back to work with my tongue, drawing a second, third and even a fourth climax until she tugged on my ear to say she'd had enough.

"I'm about to use your favorite word," Mari said, running her hand through my hair as I laid my head on her chest. "That was exquisite."

"It certainly was."

"My bones have gone to water. I couldn't move it I wanted to."

"You don't have to. Stay right here and go to sleep if that's how you feel." I didn't really mean that.

"Not a chance. I'm taking exactly three minutes to get the blood flow back out to my extremities, and then I'm going to show you all the mercy you showed me."

She was free to show me anything. I've never been the kind of girl to follow the very first kiss with a roll in the sack, but I'd been dealing with my attraction to Mari for so long, it felt like we'd been dating for weeks. Though I hardly knew her, what I did know made me trust her.

I was ready to start all over when she bumped me off her chest and onto my back.

"You have a gorgeous body," she said, trailing a finger from my throat through the valley of my breasts to my navel and back.

My brain couldn't form any words to answer, so I smiled and closed my eyes to concentrate on her touch. I've always been relatively happy with my physical self. It's my emotional and behavioral selves that need work, and I had high hopes Mari's calming presence would rub off on me in a good way.

"My name is Mari. That's M..." She traced an M just below my navel. "A...R..."—across my diaphragm—"and I." The last letter she drew from one of my nipples to the other, bringing both to hardened peaks.

"Now your address with the nine-digit zip code."

"Don't worry. I don't plan to leave any parts of you untouched."

She methodically delivered on her promise one inch at a time, starting with the tips of my fingers and working her way to my shoulders, leaving all the downy hairs on my arms standing in her wake.

"I like this spot right here," she said, gently pinching the pliable skin at the base of my earlobe. "I'm betting it has the same texture as one of your more private places."

Where Mari was concerned, I preferred not to have any private places. "Only one way to find out."

"All in good time." She nuzzled my neck until I turned my head for her, and then she nibbled gently on my earlobe. "What do you think about when you feel my teeth nipping at you here?"

I hoped this wasn't a character test, because I hadn't been dwelling on world peace. Nor did I want to tell her the truth—that I'd been listening to her breathe—because I didn't want her to become overly aware she was giving so much emotion away. "I'm really busy feeling. Don't ask me to think too."

"How good are you at feeling two things at once?" She returned her lips to my ear as her fingernails began gently scraping my nipple.

"It's..." I sucked in a breath through my teeth. "I'm very good."

"Lucky for you."

I caught her lips and pulled her into another deep kiss. She draped her leg over mine and continued lavishing attention on my breast, alternating between gentle caresses and sharp tweaks so I couldn't forget she was there no matter how many other hotspots were erupting. I considered reminding her that she hadn't finished writing all over me yet, but she didn't need any help, especially if her goal was to pluck me like a harp. Postponing the inevitable for a bit longer was a good idea anyway because I would probably explode the second she touched me, and I didn't have a clip full of climaxes just waiting to fire off. I'd be lucky to survive the first one.

The moment her hand left my breast I knew it was headed somewhere important. We both moaned when it got there, but that was the extent of our verbal communication from that point on. Everything else we said with our bodies, mine pushing upward as her fingers tickled my sex all too lightly, and hers sliding against me in what felt like a backbeat tempo. The effect of having her pull back as I pressed into her was maddening. It was also all that kept me from climaxing way too early.

She pressed her cheek next to mine, letting me hear every gasp, pant and sigh. It was thrilling to know she was as excited as I was, just as I'd been when she surrendered to me.

When her fingers dipped inside me and then back up to encircle my Screaming Clitoris, I felt the first hot vibration of my impending climax. I was barely aware that my hand was flicking her shoulder at the same speed and pressure I would have used had I been touching myself. She must have gotten my message, though, since she gave me exactly what I needed.

I drew a deep breath and held it, simultaneously clutching Mari's head to hold her close as my whole body shuddered with release.

The waves were still pulsing when she squirmed free of my grasp and lowered her face to my navel, clearly on her way to taste what she'd done to me.

"No, no…I can't. It's too sensitive." Even having her look at it was enough to send electric jolts through my whole body.

"So there isn't another one hiding in there?"

"One and done."

"For how long?"

"At least an hour."

Undaunted, she nuzzled my neck, letting her breasts sway across my abdomen. "Enough time to savor Benito's fabulous flan. Every bite is like an orgasm for your taste buds. I'm telling you, that man descended from epicurean royalty."

Fetching the flan from the living room where I'd dropped it required getting up, and getting up required moving. Flan couldn't possibly taste better than lying here with Mari felt.

Not that I have anything against eating in bed.

CHAPTER TWELVE

Mari's wealth management firm was in a canyon of office buildings and condos in the Brickell neighborhood, with its clean streets and broad, tree-lined sidewalks. The financial center of practically all of Latin America, it's home to dozens of international banks and foreign consulates. If Emily and I had shopped around before buying our place, I might have argued for something in this area, since it has restaurants and street-level retail in most of the buildings, and a supermarket within walking distance. Anything that keeps me out of my car is a plus.

Even getting here from my place was a breeze—a short walk to the Omni Station, then a twelve-minute ride on the Metromover, Miami's free downtown rail trolley that hums a few stories above rush hour traffic, and another short walk at the end. The only problem with walking around Miami is crossing streets, because Mordy's Three-Second Rule applies double to pedestrians. It's unwise to step into the intersection too soon, and once you do, you'd best quick-foot it to the other side.

I waited for a dark Chevy Suburban to pass, but instead it pulled against the curb at the corner into a No Parking zone. So typical. Drivers in Miami pay no attention to signs. It's beyond me why anyone would need such a massive vehicle in Miami in the first place, but apparently they're all the rage. There had been another one exactly like it parked in the circle at my condo, right under the Loading Zone Only sign.

Mari's office was on the twenty-fourth floor of One Brickell Square, a towering structure of white concrete and glass with marble floors throughout not only the lobby but the outdoor plaza as well. It was after six and most workers had gone for the day.

The mirrored walls of the elevator gave me one last chance to check my look. I'd gone home after work to change into something I hoped would pass for casual elegance, slacks with a plain silk blouse and a colorful silk corsage I'd gotten for Christmas two years ago from my Secret Santa at the foundation…someone with fashion sense. Mari was taking me to dinner across the street at Truluck's, and then giving me a tour of her condo. From the suggestive tone of our kazillion text messages over the last three days, I wasn't expecting to see any more of her place than she'd seen of mine a couple of nights ago.

Mari had described her wealth management firm as a boutique family business, which just happened to control more than two billion dollars in investments. She and Pepe oversaw the accounts with the help of five sales consultants, an accountant, three junior analysts—one of whom was Chacho's older brother—and three administrative assistants, including Talia's mom, who was Mari's sister-in-law. Another key player was Felix, her gay uncle, who served as the firm's legal counsel.

A receptionist, dressed as if she were on her way to a nightclub, met me at the door. All young Hispanic women seem to dress that way, probably knowing perfectly well how much pressure it puts on the rest of us.

"You must be Daphne," she said, her Spanish accent barely noticeable. Second generation, I'd guess. "Mari's in her office... next to last door on the left."

There wasn't another soul in the place, which made me feel bad for the poor woman working reception. She'd probably stayed late at Mari's request to show me in.

Mari was on the phone, but grinned and waved when she saw me. "Let me talk to Pepe. I bet he'll want to have you to dinner on the yacht one night. Does that sound like something you and your wife would enjoy?"

Ah, yes...dinner on the yacht with our friends. For Mari and Pepe, it was just another day at the office, while for me it had been a once-in-a-lifetime fantasy come true.

Beyond her desk was a gorgeous view of flickering lights from the luxury condos and hotels on Brickell Key. If I looked out on that all day, I'd never get anything done. Even the inside of her office was beautiful, with expensive furniture and not a single element of the décor out of place. Thirty-three years old and already sitting on top of the world.

"Hey, sweetie," she said when she dropped the phone. "Thanks for meeting me. Did you look around?"

"I saw enough. It looks like a great place to work." I was still playing back the mental tape of her calling me sweetie, and taking in the sight of her tight brown skirt, plunging ivory top and open-toed platform pumps.

"Come over here." She led me to the window and pointed to the building next door, soaring so high above us that its reflection twinkled in the bay. "That's where I live. I walk to work every day."

"Now you're just rubbing it in. I'd be downright cheerful all the time if I had your commute." I waited as she tidied her desk and collected her handbag. "Sounds like you and Pepe have lots of dinners on the yacht."

"Yeah, that's something he likes to do for all the Iberican investors. It reminds them how rich they are, so they don't balk when we tell them it costs five million to buy in."

"Five million dollars?"

"I know. It's not for average investors, just the ones who have serious cash. Most of our clients are institutions, like corporations, or pension funds and foundations. Pepe won't even let me invest because I can't afford it."

"I guess you won't be coming after my IRA."

She surprised me with a kiss, more intense than I would have expected in such a public place. "I don't care about your money, but I'm quite interested in your other assets."

Good thing.

"I never do business with my friends. They all want discounts and insider tips that would send me to jail. Besides, investing is risky, and friends don't like it when you lose their money."

The sound of a throat clearing startled me but Mari seemed nonplussed about holding me in her arms as the receptionist handed her a folded slip of paper.

"Sorry…I took a message." Her voice was decidedly apologetic, and I got the impression it was for the message itself rather than the intrusion. She didn't wait around for Mari's reaction.

Mari glanced at the note, rolled her eyes and dropped it into the wastebasket. "I know I said we'd eat at Truluck's but then I got a better idea. Hope you don't mind."

"You should know by now I'd skip dinner for the right distraction."

We walked out the main entrance and crossed the street to the mirrored SunTrust Bank building, where Truluck's occupied the ground floor.

"I thought we weren't going to eat here."

"We aren't." She went through her usual animated greeting of the hostess, who took her credit card and handed her a large paper bag. "I figured we'd eat in."

I like a girl who keeps secrets. And wears tight skirts.

One thing I truly adore about Hispanic women is their habit of walking arm in arm with other women. I'd see them all over South Beach or Bayside and wonder if they were lovers or just family or friends. So it was no surprise when Mari hooked her elbow with mine once we started down Brickell Bay Avenue to her condo building, the Plaza at Brickell. Whereas I considered my building moderately luxurious, her place was the whole enchilada. Or since we're in Miami, let's call it the whole *arepa*. The lobby looked like a grand ballroom, with marble floors, fountains and crystal chandeliers as big as my car. Mari pressed the button for the forty-ninth floor and I braced for having my ears pop.

Walking into her apartment was like stepping onto the cover of one of those urban home magazines, the kind that make you realize there's more to interior design than where to put the furniture. A single spot shone down from above the kitchen island, revealing one of the most elegant living spaces I'd seen in all of Miami. The brown and gray of her granite countertops set a muted tone for all her décor, which included a low-profile sectional sofa, wall-mounted electronics and a plush rug. Floor-to-ceiling glass formed the far wall, beyond which I could see the lights on the gantry cranes at the far end of the Port of Miami.

"This is incredible."

"Nice, isn't it? When I first went to work for Pepe about ten years ago, I'd look over here every day and dream about buying something in this building. Then one day at lunch I walked into the lobby and there happened to be a realtor standing there. Her appointment had stood her up, so she showed me this and I didn't even negotiate. Pepe could have killed me."

"You don't negotiate for your dreams. You just go get them."

"That's exactly what I told him." She set the bag on the counter. "Show yourself around while I get dinner ready. My cleaning lady came today, so I shouldn't have any embarrassing messes."

I wandered first into the near bedroom, obviously the one where Mari slept. Two entire walls of glass offered the same view as the living room, giving the impression of endless space. A king-sized bed draped in a gray coverlet and stacked with pillows dominated the suite, which included a walk-in closet as large as my guest room and a bathroom fit for a queen. It was all I could do not to riffle through her rack of designer clothes, but I didn't even try to resist counting the shoes—twenty-six pairs.

When I returned to the living room, Mari was nowhere in sight but the door out to the terrace was open. I walked past the dining table to what turned out to be a second bedroom suite, not quite as large as the other, but equally elegant because it had its own private terrace. What it didn't have was a bed. A futon— perfect for putting up guests you hope won't stay long—sat against one wall, but a desk, credenza and computer dominated this room.

"Mari, if I lived here, I'd never want to leave. It's gorgeous."

She came in from the terrace and waved me out. "You haven't even seen the best part."

Right she was. Nestled on the terrace was a bistro table draped in a white cloth, two chic place settings, a bottle of wine and a pair of flickering candles.

"Wow." I didn't dare say what I thought, which was that it was the most romantic scene anyone had ever set for me. I was more than happy to get romance from Mari, but I didn't want to read too much into it because we hadn't traded any words to that effect. All we had between us was one actual date and a night of hot sex. Really, really hot sex. For all I knew, dinner on the yacht or terrace was her idea of foreplay, not romance.

She'd probably be mortified to know how far *my* fantasies about her actually went. I joke in my head all the time about marrying every beautiful woman who gives me the time of day, all the while knowing that's my end game when I finally meet the right one. Not that I'm saying Mari's the right one, but if she is, that's where I expect romantic love to go. The moment she realizes she loves me madly and can't live without me, I'm sure I'll be ready.

"I assumed you liked stone crab," she said, pouring each of us a glass of Louis Jadot's Pouilly Fuisse, something I'd seen on menus but never ordered because it's out of my price range.

"Mari, this is wonderful, better than any restaurant could have been."

"Yeah, I probably should have cooked something, but I leave things like stone crab to the pros. I haven't eaten out here like this in a couple of years."

The math was easy on that one. It would have been right around the time Delores moved in. "I'd probably be out here every night, even if I was eating a Happy Meal by myself."

"What's not to love about it? Miami's the most beautiful place on earth."

I wouldn't go that far, but it was hard to argue from her perspective. It was a perfect night—eighty degrees with a balmy breeze, a half moon over Fisher Island, and no one else's music assaulting our ears. The only disturbance, if you could call it that, was the intermittent rumble of a low-flying jet on its way out of Miami International. For me, they have a certain cosmopolitan appeal, especially when they bank right toward South America. I picture exotic people like my neighbors Ronaldo and Tandra jetting back and forth to Rio or Buenos Aires.

"I've had some trouble adjusting to Miami, I have to admit. I feel like a total outsider most of the time."

Mari shook her head and leaned across the table to squirt lemon juice all over my cracked crab claws. "You do that to yourself. Miami opens its arms to everyone. All you have to do is walk in and make it yours."

"Which is a whole lot easier if A, you speak Spanish, and B, you have a boatload of cash."

"Have you tried to learn Spanish? They teach it practically everywhere."

I wanted to snap that I shouldn't have to learn another language to get along in America, but not at the expense of marring this perfect night. "I studied it in high school but I forgot most of what I learned. And even if I were fluent, there'd still be that little cash problem. I know I shouldn't complain because I'm better off than a lot of people in Miami, and I'm lucky enough to live in a good neighborhood."

"Even if you can't afford it," she added with a wink.

I thought she'd push me again to let the bank foreclose, but that single teasing jibe was all she had. We spent the next thirty minutes savoring stone crab and fresh greens salad, and then she cleared the table of all but the wine.

"When my family first came to Miami," she told me, "they lived together in a small house in Little Havana. Everyone found work, even my father and Pepe, and they were just kids. Fifteen years later, Mima owned a dozen convenience stores and a huge house in the Gables. They went from having everything in Cuba to having nothing here, and then having everything again. This is a land of opportunity for those who dream big."

I remembered her explaining how even Saraphine could build a comfortable nest egg for retirement, but that wouldn't work if she got sick or her company sold the supermarket chain to someone who didn't keep up her benefits. Mordy was right when he said the rules don't work for workers anymore.

So while I didn't want to sound argumentative, I didn't share her optimism. "I used to believe that too, but it's not as true as it was even ten years ago. The game's rigged now in favor of people who already have money. Don't take this the wrong way—I'm not judging you or what you do—but these people who make billions of dollars and then try to squirrel everything away in offshore accounts so they won't have to pay taxes are killing the rest of us."

"I'll give you that—some people are just plain greedy—but they aren't the only ones gaming the system. People of all income levels work off the books so they won't have to pay taxes. And we're all complicit. I saw you write a receipt to that guy from the hardware store for two bathroom cabinets when one of them was damaged. It was nice they donated but they got an extra tax break they didn't really deserve because you gave them credit for two and threw one away."

Moses on a moose! I couldn't believe she remembered that. "But I didn't do that for myself."

"I know. I'm only pointing out that hiding from the taxman is a widespread problem, something that's become normalized across all of society. It just shows up more among the rich because it's obscene to want tax breaks when you have more than you could ever spend."

"Do you think I'm a hypocrite?"

Mari reached across the table and squeezed my hand. "I'm not judging you either. I like how passionate you are, and we don't have to agree on every little thing. Like I told you, I think you're classy. You have no idea how refreshing it is to talk to someone who isn't totally wrapped up in herself."

A compliment for me and another dig at Delores, who must have been a real piece of work. To her other unpleasant traits, I'd have to add stupidity for letting someone like Mari get away. "I don't even know Delores and I think she's an idiot."

She huffed. "She's been calling me…wants to meet for dinner. That's what that message was at work."

"The one you threw in the trash?"

"Yeah, my friend Gladys—one of the girls I was with at the Wallcast—says she wants to smooth things over because we have all the same friends and it makes people uncomfortable. But then Clara thinks she wants to go out again, which is absurd. What, she thinks it's all okay now since I got my record expunged? That's insane."

Except there was something in her voice that sounded more like hurt than incredulity. I would have preferred foaming-at-the-mouth fury, especially after experiencing firsthand the siren's song of familiarity when Emily had called. If I could entertain the idea of taking a sleaze like Emily back, Mari could do the same with Delores.

Just as Mari had saved me from myself by asking me out to Mahler, I was obligated to return the favor. "Yeah, it's crazy to even think about it. Why would you want to give her another shot at your client list?"

"Exactly!"

"Okay, Mari. What are you not telling me?"

"Beg your pardon?"

I started counting her attributes off on my fingers. "You like romantic dinners on the terrace, intelligent conversation…and you help people like Saraphine when there's nothing in it for you. You're an incredible kisser, to say nothing of your other talents."

She rolled her eyes indulgently before draining her wineglass.

"I just don't understand how you can be single. There ought to be a dozen women out here trying to toss me over this railing."

"I could say all those things about you too, you know. And yet, here we are…the two of us, all alone and desperate." She poured another touch of wine in both glasses, and then corked the bottle. "I'll fess up if you will."

"You want me to spell out why Emily dumped me?" I could offer excuses and my elaborate rationale, but I own what I own. "I guess I stopped being fun. I tried really hard to like it here, but after she started working long hours, we quit doing all the things that make this a cool place to live. My whole life was driving to work in gridlock, fighting with people at the deli counter and coming home to eat dinner by myself. I complained…a lot."

"Sounds like you had a right to."

"I certainly thought so, but she said that's why she"—trotting out my dramatic voice—"sought comfort in the arms of another."

Mari huffed. "*Le ronca el mango.*"

"Mango?"

"It's a Cuban expression—literally speaking, it snores the mango. Mima says it all the time. Don't ask me why, but it's what you say when you think something's ridiculous. It's never your fault when your partner is unfaithful."

Snoring mangos means something is ridiculous…works for me. "She was probably right about the complaining. I'm sure it was a real drag to listen to it all the time, so I've tried not to be negative about everything, at least out loud. I don't want that to define who I am."

"That's one of the things I like about you, Daphne. You own up to your problems and try to fix them. Everyone should do that instead of blaming others. I still get mad at Delores for having me arrested, but I'm the one who lost her cool. I need to own up to that."

I have a special fondness for conversations that include things a beautiful woman likes about me. It's true I'm in a constant state of fixing myself, and I'm not above specifically fixing things to appeal to Mari. That said, learning to speak Spanish probably isn't on my list.

"What about you, Mari? What's your fatal flaw?"

"My fatal flaw…" She slowly twirled the stem of her wineglass. "I've been told I can be a bit…clingy."

"Clingy?"

"Apparently I don't give people enough space. I personally think being in a relationship is all about *sharing* space, but some people don't see it that way."

"Some people…you mean Delores."

"Let me give you an example. We both saw clients in the evenings sometimes. No big deal. But she used to get bent out of shape because I wanted her to call me if she wasn't coming home for dinner." She gestured at the table. "The last time I set a table like this out here, she didn't even get home until ten o'clock. No call, no text, and my calls kept going to voice mail. Then when she got home, she realized I'd been waiting for her. Instead of apologizing—what a concept—she gave me grief for expecting her to be here…said she didn't want to have to check in like a teenager with her parents."

I was unbelievably tempted to tell her she could cling to me all she wanted, and that I'd happily call and text her a dozen times a day to tell her exactly where I was. "It's just common courtesy."

"Right, but she said it felt like a leash. And to be honest, my girlfriend before Delores told me kind of the same thing, so there must be something to it. Maya said she was worried about losing herself, that she wasn't ready to be a single entity with someone else. She was only twenty-two, so that's reasonable, but still…I guess I just have a different view of relationships."

"I get what you're saying. When you're partners with somebody, you really do turn into one entity. You can't make decisions just for yourself anymore because you have to consider the other person, even if it's just dinner."

"Exactly, because when you don't, you start taking each other for granted."

"I don't know, Mari. As fatal flaws go, that one's not much to write home about. Tell me the truth. Do you sleep in your socks? Snore like a mango?"

That drew a laugh at first, then a serious tease from that deep, sexy voice that turned me into jelly. "I can't reveal everything at once. I'm like a present you have to unwrap slowly."

With that one simple declaration, I realized Mari Tirado was mine to lose. She liked me as much as I liked her, and despite all the things she had going for her, she was every bit as insecure about romance as the rest of us. We wanted the same thing—a loyal partner who was *truly* a partner. All that remained was ordering the invitations and planning the honeymoon.

"In that case…" I pulled her wrist closer to unfasten her bulky gold bracelet. "Why don't you pick out the room where you'd like to be unwrapped?"

CHAPTER THIRTEEN

Skirted leggings. Who even knew they made such a thing? It was the perfect cover for the skirt-averse like me, since it was actually a short, tight band of black spandex wrapped around brown tights that came to just below my knee. It looked especially good with my off-the-shoulder white Lycra top. Not actually me, but hip. That says a lot.

But this was absolutely the last outfit I was buying until next spring. Or until I won the lottery. Lucky for me, I'd scrounged it from the sale racks at Loehmann's, the mother of all discount stores. The only way I can pick up well-made expensive labels is after they've been shipped out and marked down at least sixty percent from when they were outrageous at Saks, Bloomingdale's or Nordstrom. Finding this outfit on the clearance rack meant it had lingered even longer. In a nutshell, that's why my fashion sense lags several seasons behind everyone else's.

Without my last-minute shopping spree, I'd have been forced to turn down what was probably my only chance ever at getting past the ropes into a trendy nightclub on South Beach. The DJ on Saturdays was the current boyfriend of Felix, Mari's gay uncle, and that was good enough to get us into the VIP section with whatever Hollywood or sports stars were in town this weekend.

But this hitting the stores for a new outfit every time we went out? That has to stop. My budget can't handle it, even at discount prices, and I could run out of fashion sense at a moment's notice and humiliate myself forever. Tonight, however, I was determined to have another brand-new experience of a lifetime.

Mari had promised to go with me next door to formally meet Edith and Mordy, who were feeling positively parental about making sure I didn't fall in with the wrong crowd or get my heart broken by someone who thought of me only as a plaything. I didn't tell them the plaything part didn't particularly bother me.

I had no delusions that Mari would sweep me off my feet and make me her princess. We were from two different worlds, and while it was true that she actually had swept me off my feet, I fully expected to find myself back on earth eventually. That could happen when I failed to dress with the appropriate flair or when I turned down an extravagant invitation because I couldn't afford it. Or it could happen anytime we were out together and ran into her Spanish-speaking friends. Any of those could awaken her to our stark differences.

Until that moment, I was happy to go with what we had. Mari and I were still getting along famously without ever having discussed the nature of our relationship. She wasn't that far removed from the Delores Disaster—which I could tell still bothered her—so I couldn't honestly expect her to get serious again anytime soon.

All that said, I was perfect for her, even if she hadn't realized that for herself. We fit together, not only in bed—where we'd spent a great deal of time over the past six days—but also in our temperaments. To me, that's what it really means to be compatible.

She deflected a lot of the anxiety and frustration I felt about Miami by unlocking many of the things that seem so foreign to me. It wasn't the yachts or trendy nightclubs, though it was nice she could give me those experiences. It was more the everyday things, and it had a profound effect on how I saw the whole city. We'd gone out Wednesday night to Versailles, the iconic restaurant on Calle Ocho—Southwest Eighth Street, the heart of Little Havana—where all the politicians stop by to schmooze the Cuban vote. My only other experience there—four years ago with Emily—drove home my feelings of "otherness." It took us fifteen minutes just to get through the English translations on the menu, and even then I ended up with something I hadn't meant to order and a waiter who treated me like I was an idiot. Things like that didn't happen when I was out with Mari, who not only handled all the translations, but also the social parlance that got us a great table and a waiter who fell all over himself to make us happy. I could learn to love just about any place where I was treated like that.

And what had I done for Mari? Nothing short of saving her life by pointing out that just because her car could go from zero to sixty in four and a half seconds didn't mean it should, especially when all three lanes of Dixie Highway are stacked up ahead. When that argument failed to sway her, I pulled out the big guns and told her she was scaring me.

For a second or two, I considered mixing and matching my earrings again to convince her I really had done it on purpose the first time, but then I decided that would dangerously undermine my already dubious fashion sense. The only way I could pull off blending in among style mavens was not to get noticed at all.

It was already nine thirty and I was starving. I understood finally why Hispanics eat dinner so late when Mari told me we weren't even going to the club until midnight because nothing ever happens before then.

When Mari knocked, I'd just put the finishing touches on my makeup, and had to admit I looked sort of okay. She was only twenty minutes late, and since I'd been persuaded to open my waiting window as much as forty-five minutes, I didn't even hold it against her.

"Hey, cutie." Seeing her smile as she eyed me up and down excited me as much as the idea of getting a wolf whistle from Olivia Wilde.

She wore a gorgeous open-back silver top that gathered at the neck over the sort of short black skirt I was afraid to wear. In her two-inch heels, her legs just went on and on. "You look stunning."

As we kissed, she slid her hands under my waistband to massage my behind. It wouldn't take much of that for me to chuck our plans for going out, but then she gave me a firm squeeze, disentangled and lapsed into what I'd come to know as her business voice.

"I just ran into one of my new clients in your elevator, Ronaldo García. I had no idea he lived in this building."

Finally, a chance to learn something about my mysterious neighbor. "I've tried to get to know him but I don't think he or his wife speak a word of English. What kind of work does he do?"

"He imports precious stones from Brazil, mostly emeralds. He's just getting his business off the ground."

"They're both so impeccable. And their baby is adorable."

"I haven't seen her, but having a family is what motivated him to start an investment account. He wants to bring his wife's mother to Miami to help take care of her."

"Wonder where he's planning to put her? Their apartment's just like mine—two bedrooms, two baths."

"Don't know. He hasn't said anything about buying something new. He's very frugal, though, and conservative with his portfolio."

"I guess that's what babies do to people." I'd be sorry to see Ronaldo and his family go, not because they were great friends, but because they were great neighbors. With my luck, they'd sell to a salsa band.

"Speaking of babies, my cousin's little one turns three on Tuesday and we're having a huge party at Mima's. I've been given orders to bring you."

"Orders from whom?"

"Lucia. She's managed to convince everyone you're a good influence on me, so don't go getting arrested between now and then."

Though she'd set me up for the perfect comeback, I stayed true to my vow not to tease her anymore about her littering arrest. Besides, I liked her thinking I was a good influence. "And what about you? Are you ready for me to meet the family?"

"Sure, it's no big deal."

That wasn't exactly what I wanted to hear. Introducing a new girlfriend to the family was an important ritual, because it was supposed to be a statement to everyone that This One was important enough to bring home. If it was no big deal, maybe it didn't matter to her what sort of impression I made, or what impression they made on me.

Stewing in silence over her flippancy was not how I wanted to spend my evening.

"If it's no big deal, then why should I even go?" I didn't mind that coming off as sharp, but I hadn't meant for it to sound whiny. "Don't you want your family and me to like each other?"

"Of course, and I'm sure you will, but that has nothing to do with why it's not a big deal. I was just saying that because I didn't want you to be nervous about anything. Our family is very close and some people aren't used to that. I know they're going to like you…"—she hooked her arms around my waist again and kissed me on the forehead—"because there's nothing not to like."

Good thing I'd shown a little restraint. What I thought was glib had actually been sweet. "They won't be upset I'm not Cuban?"

She loosened her hold in a pretty clear sign I'd struck a nerve. "Upset isn't the right word, but it's not anything to do with you. Mima doesn't speak very much English, so she'll be disappointed she can't talk with you."

That's the part I just didn't get—how someone who had spent fifty years in this country had gotten by without learning the language. The whole city of Miami had been turned on its head because of people like Mima.

"At least you're Catholic. That'll count for something."

"Raised Catholic," I corrected, since it had very little to do with my actual beliefs. "I'm more of a Recovering Catholic."

"I'm a Holiday Catholic myself. Good for Christmas and Easter but not much else. I've got all the rituals down though."

"Sounds like my neighbor Mordy. Six days a week he's agnostic. On the Sabbath, he becomes an Orthodox Jew."

"He's the one you want me to meet, right?"

"And his Irish wife, Edith. Let's do that so we can go eat before I fall over."

From the hallway outside their door, we could hear Edith and Mordy shouting at one another.

"Maybe we should come back another time," Mari said warily.

"Believe it or not, this is normal."

Edith answered my knock with a friendly smile. And she had a revolver in her hand.

"Edith, what's going on?"

"She's going to kill me," Mordy yelled from the living room. But instead of running for his life, he was sitting on the couch sipping Manischewitz. "She thinks I'm having an affair."

Edith laid the gun on the table and whispered, "Watch out for that. I can't remember if it's loaded or not."

Never a dull moment.

"Edith, you need to put it away before it goes off." Accidentally or on purpose.

"His girlfriend called here a little while ago and I answered. She tried to make out like it was a wrong number but I know better."

"Zilch! That's what you know because it's all there is to know," Mordy groused. "Did it ever occur to you the poor woman might have just dialed wrong? All it takes is one fat finger. You're paranoid."

"I'm with Mordy on this one."

"You always take his side," Edith said, her face falling as if I'd hurt her feelings. At least her voice had calmed from its menacing growl.

"If he'd been holding the gun, I'd be on your side."

Mari was still standing at the door as if afraid to move.

"My friend is going to think you don't love each other."

"That's silly. Why would I need a gun if I didn't love him? I'd just let him go off with his little slut and be done with him."

I blew my bangs upward to let Edith know I was exasperated, and then shook it off. If Mordy wasn't frightened enough to be hiding under the bed, I shouldn't be getting worked up about it either. "Okay, this is my friend Mari. Mari, these are the Osterhoffs, Edith and Mordy, who have been married for fifty-some years and would never actually do anything to hurt each other."

Mari smiled before nodding toward the balcony. "Whose cat is that?"

"Oh, my God!" My worst fear, other than perhaps seeing Edith shoot Mordy.

Marvin was crouched on the rail eyeing a magenta bougainvillea petal that wafted by the balcony on a gentle breeze. Before anyone could move, he leapt from the rail, and we listened in horror as his screech faded in the night.

***

"I can't believe it," Mari said solemnly, squeezing my knee as we drove across the Julia Tuttle Causeway. "Fifteen floors. If I hadn't seen it with my own eyes…"

Mari and I had rushed downstairs alone to save Mordy and Edith the anguish of retrieving the broken body of their beloved cat, only to find Marvin still chasing the errant flower. Best we could tell, a towering royal palm had broken his fall.

As they joyously celebrated his deliverance from doom, I sneaked out with Edith's gun and slid it under my bed. She could have it back—without bullets—when she'd calmed down.

"Where shall we have dinner?" I asked.

"YUCA?"

I shouldn't have been surprised. Everything about Mari screamed Young Urban Cuban American. It was also one of the priciest restaurants on Lincoln Road.

"How about something a little cheaper? I might want a little left over for a mojito at the club." To say nothing of groceries next week.

"Then how about you let me buy dinner? And if you want to buy me a daiquiri later, I won't stop you."

"Deal." I appreciated how quickly she settled that. It wasn't fair to make her live on my paltry budget but I have my pride. Still, if we were going to see each other on a regular basis, we had to work out the money thing. "But the issue is a little bigger than just dinner tonight. I'd like to take you out sometimes too, but I really can't afford the kind of places you like...certainly not the places you've taken me to."

She hit the brakes, slowing us dramatically. "Now you tell me! That's the whole reason I wanted to go out with you, so you could take me to extravagant places and pay the bill."

"Nice...you're going to make this even more humiliating by being a smart aleck."

"It's a nonissue," she said, taking my hand as she resumed a normal speed. "If anyone should feel bad about this, it's me, because I must have said or done something to make you think I care about that sort of thing."

Mari was very good at making me feel ashamed of myself. From the very beginning, I'd thought the worst about her instead of giving her the benefit of the doubt.

"No, you haven't. I'm sorry."

"If that sort of thing mattered to me, I'd go out with someone like Delores. What I care about is if you're someone I can trust."

"I am," I answered, fully chastised.

"I know. After what I went through, that's what I need to feel. This other thing...it's a difference we're not going to fix, so just let it go. Can you do that?"

All I could do was nod obediently. I would never bring up the subject of money again, even if all I needed was change for a dollar.

With the money issue settled, we enjoyed a leisurely dinner, and by the time we finished it was a quarter past twelve. We then took a short ride up Collins Avenue and valet parked at the Fontainebleau Hotel, home to LIV, one of the hottest nightclubs on the eastern seaboard. Mari took my hand and led me past a long line of people waiting behind the stuffed satin ropes.

"Antonio!" Mari greeted the doorman with her ritual kiss to the cheek. He was only a couple of inches taller than I, with a massive chest and arm muscles, and a shaved head.

"Good to see you, *chica*." He mumbled into a slender microphone that crossed his cheek and then pressed his finger to his ear. "Felix is on the right side just below the third skybox."

Bubbling with anticipation as Antonio fastened my wristband, I didn't dare turn back to see if anyone in the line was seething at our admittance. Everyone deserves the chance to feel special. Tonight was my turn.

Beyond the door was the most spectacular party space I'd ever seen, bursting with sound, energy and purple neon lights. I'd been to clubs in Boston, New York and Toronto, and it was clear to me LIV had been designed to make me forget all of them. The crowd on the dance floor wasn't near capacity, but one of the girls at work told me they held people in line because it revved them up for dancing and gave passersby the impression it was packed inside.

Mari pointed toward an elevated deck at the far end of the dance floor, where a man wearing a lime-green shirt with an ascot mixed the music. "That's Robbie T, Felix's boyfriend."

Theoretically, I know some DJs are considered better than others, but I have no idea why. What I do know is that only the best of the best work on the busiest night of the week in a club like this one. Accordingly, I replied, "He's amazing."

"I'll have to take your word for it. I don't know one from the other."

So much for that.

We squeezed between clusters of partygoers who were gathered on the risers for a better view of not only the dance floor but also the skyboxes, where the VIP celebrities would gather to be seen.

On the tier below the skyboxes were several sitting areas for small groups, modern U-shaped leather sofas surrounding sleek smoke-gray glass cocktail tables, all intended for private parties to be seen and envied. We flashed our wristbands to the bouncer and made our way to the corner.

"Mari!" A lean Hispanic man stood to welcome her with a kiss. He was dressed in a tight gray suit with a matching shirt and thin black tie. "I'm so excited you're here. And this is your lady?"

I like being her lady. "I'm Daphne. You must be Felix."

"That's me, the black sheep of the family. Not really…more like one of those dirty magazines you can't show to the little ones or the old people."

Mari butted in. "She's coming to Emilio's party on Tuesday if you need a beard for Mima."

"Only if you'll go with Robbie T…yeah, I didn't think so."

I learned that Felix was forty-four, the youngest of Mima's children. Besides his law practice, he played soccer in a city league and collected art.

"And every now and then, he collects artists," Mari said, gesturing toward Robbie T.

When the cocktail waitress came around, I tried to make good on my promise of buying drinks, including a dirty martini for Felix. With tip, it would have been a whopping sixty-five bucks—the down payment on my private jet—but while I was fumbling for bills, Mari reached past me and dropped her credit card on the tray. And before I could mount even a semblance of protest, she also dropped a kiss on my cheek. Case closed.

After our second drink, which was on top of the wine we'd had with dinner, Felix came back from talking to Robbie T and announced, "Next one's just for the *chicas*. Hope you brought your dancing shoes."

The energy on the floor was electrifying. Besides the dancers, there were dozens of others who lined the floor soaking up the club atmosphere, including one woman who seemed to be studying Mari and me. She was tall like Mari, attractive in an athletic sort of way…meaning she set off my gaydar. From where we were, I guessed she was Hispanic, since she had short dark hair and brown eyes. The way she was studying us, it occurred to me she might be Delores. That would suck. But then Mari looked her way several times without freaking out, so that left envy, and who could blame her? I'm out here with the hottest *chica* in Miami.

After thirty minutes of jumping up and down to a long, lively girl tune, the sum of my day hit me like a bus. Besides the buzz from the alcohol, the excitement of LIV and the emotionally draining episode with Marvin, Edith and her gun, I had also logged eight grueling hours on the jobsite. By the time Mari and I finally headed back to our corner, it was all I could do to walk.

"Look, it's Mari and Daphne!" It took me a second to recognize Juan and Brian, the men who'd brought their jerk wad friend Michael to dinner on the yacht.

The jerk wad himself, who was hidden by the others in the corner, his face lowered to the table, suddenly sprang up, sniffing hard as he attempted to wipe the white powder from his nose. "Our little social crusader."

Felix bustled back over, all smiles to realize we knew one another already.

I, on the other hand, was in a state of shock and ready to get the hell out of there before the cops came and dragged us off in handcuffs. When did I fall so far out of touch not to know people did cocaine in nightclubs as casually as they drank a margarita?

Mari's greeting to both men was a simple handshake, not the warm kiss she usually gave even her casual friends. I wasn't sure if she was reacting stiffly because of Michael's condescending reference or because she too had seen him snort a snootful.

Michael set his cocktail in the exact spot where his face had been, probably to cover any leftover evidence. I guess he got nervous all of a sudden that a Pollyanna like me might not take kindly to his brazen drug use.

"Felix, we're going to head out," Mari said suddenly. "Daphne's had a long day and I have work to catch up on tomorrow. Thanks for getting us in."

I echoed her appreciation and we left hand in hand.

"Was it all right that we left? I didn't know Felix was friends with that creep. I just wasn't in the mood to listen to him tonight."

"Are you kidding?" The look on her face when I told her about the coke was one of total shock, which I was glad about.

It might have been a deal breaker had she blown that off as no big deal. The very idea that a cokehead had ridiculed me for my nonprofit work was absurd.

"I really do have work to catch up on tomorrow," she said as we climbed into her car. "A couple of my portfolios are out of balance and I have to figure out where I screwed up before I meet with my clients on Wednesday. If you'll let me stay the night we can have a couple of hours together in the morning. I promise I'll make it worth your while."

"You'd better. I have a gun under my bed."

As we pulled out, I caught a glimpse of the woman who had been watching us inside. Her eyes continued to follow us as she strode briskly across the valet circle and climbed into—what else—an enormous black SUV parked in the fire lane.

CHAPTER FOURTEEN

A flower vendor met me as I stepped off the Metromover platform and I didn't hesitate to trade him a five-dollar bill for a colorful array of tulips, lilies and roses wrapped in cellophane. Though I'd already met several members of Mari's Cuban family, I was still nervous about the birthday party. Mari hadn't exactly said so, but I had a feeling Mima's opinion carried a lot of weight with everyone, so I wanted to make a good impression.

I'd taken the Metro mover to Brickell so Mari wouldn't have to deal with downtown traffic, and the whole time I was riding, I was looking below to see if the SUV happened to be there. The fact that I'd seen so many in such a short span of time was clearly a coincidence, and my paranoia a delusion of grandeur that I was important enough to follow.

I dialed Mari as soon as I saw her Porsche turn the corner. "I see you. Do you see me?"

Her Porsche came to a halt at the curb with the window down. "How much for a hand job?"

"I'll give you twenty."

We both had changed into jeans from our work clothes, and I filled mine out pretty fine if I had to say so myself.

Mari nodded toward my wrapped gift. "I hope you didn't spend a lot. There are twenty-two of us and we compare notes."

"Fine, I'll be sure to get you all a cheap book about dinosaurs. *Los Dinosaurios*. Is that okay?"

"Perfect. What if he asks you to read to him?"

"I can muddle along when I see it written down. My working knowledge is limited though. I know how to ask for important things, though, like *vino blanco*, and *el baño*."

"Let's hope you never need more than white wine and a bathroom."

We pulled into a wide circular driveway in front of a two-story Mediterranean-style house, yellow with white trim and a red tile roof. The yard was brightly lit, landscaped with fan palms and towering birds of paradise. At least a dozen cars, including several luxury vehicles, spilled over onto the lawn.

"Welcome to Mima's. Pepe and Lucia moved back in here with her a few years ago, but it will always be Mima's to our family."

"Is this where you rode out Hurricane Andrew?"

"The pantry off the kitchen."

The house was teeming with people, including several small children who ran screeching from room to room. All the random chatter was in Spanish until Chacho, Mari's cousin who had helped lay the sod at Saraphine's house, stopped chasing the little ones to greet us. "Hey, I remember you!"

"Daphne," I reminded him.

"*La jefa*." He grinned at Mari. "Pepe told us you had a new girlfriend, but he didn't say who it was."

Mari nodded. "I gave her your phone number so she can call you and Talia whenever her work crew bails on her."

Her deadpan delivery left Chacho speechless.

We walked through the elegant home, with its intricate crown molding and terra-cotta tile floors. Gorgeous Caribbean art and overstuffed furniture with abundant pillows gave the place a comfortable, homey feel. Mari introduced me to one face after another, mostly Hispanic names I'd never remember.

From Mari's descriptions of her beloved Mima, I expected a spry woman who doled out sweets to the little ones on the sly. Instead, we reached the kitchen to find an elderly woman in a wheelchair, singing to a small boy who was sitting on her lap.

"That's Mima and Emilio, the birthday boy," Mari said softly, obviously not wanting to disturb the precious scene.

Emilio sang the last few words with her, clapped his hands and scooted off her lap to run after the other children.

"Mima?" Mari kissed her grandmother and spoke to her in Spanish. When she spun the chair in my direction, I realized the woman had suffered a stroke that paralyzed the left side of her face and body. "*Mi novia*, Daphne."

Her Girlfriend. I liked that a lot.

"It's very nice to meet you." With Mari translating, I was able to tell her what a lovely home she had, one that was full of beautiful things and many people who loved each other.

It was interesting to me that Mari had talked so much about Mima and never mentioned her condition. I guess I wouldn't have either, not if I wanted to believe she'd get better.

I stuck close to Mari's side and met still more family members, including her mother, Estrella. Without ever seeing Mari's father, I knew she looked just like him, because she and her mother could not have been more different. Estrella was a couple of inches shorter than I was and several pounds heavier, with bold facial features and wavy hair. I learned she was technically still married to Mari's father, who was in Cuba, but lived with her longtime boyfriend Cesar about an hour north of here in Coral Springs.

I wouldn't exactly call Mari's demeanor toward her mother cool, but it didn't compare to the warmth she seemed to share with Pepe and Lucia, or the love she showed for Mima. According to Mari, Estrella didn't normally attend events such as these, not surprising since this was, after all, her estranged husband's family.

It was hard not to wonder how she felt about Pepe taking over her family after her husband left.

By the time we circled back to the living room, Felix had arrived…without Robbie T, of course. It was too bad he couldn't find acceptance with his family, but the cultural expectations for Hispanic men are difficult to overcome. I was glad for the familiar face.

"Ladies, good to see you again."

"I have a bone to pick with you," Mari said, steering him by the elbow into the corner. No doubt, she was ranting about Michael's behavior at the club and her concerns that Felix could suffer from the fallout.

I waved across the room to Pepe and Lucia, who were working the room with smiles and hugs.

"Wow, I didn't expect that," Mari said when she returned. "Felix said Pepe called him and asked him to show Michael a good time at the club. He's brought Michael on as a client after all."

"I thought he wasn't going to do that."

"So did I. Can you excuse me for a minute while I talk to him?"

I found a stool in the corner from where I had a great view of most of the action. Mima's caretaker had wheeled her into the dining room so she could watch the party, and Felix was having his turn at her knee.

Mari and Pepe weren't being festive at all. On the contrary, they seemed to be having angry words until Pepe threw up his hand dismissively and stormed into the kitchen. Mari glared after him for several seconds, and then shook it off before returning to my side.

"From here, that looked like it didn't go well."

"I don't know what's up with him. It's fine if he changed his mind about Michael. He doesn't have to answer to me about that, but I've been sending him e-mails for the past three days so I can make sense of what's going on with a couple of my clients' portfolios, and he hasn't gotten back to me about any of them. And he doesn't want to talk about it tonight because it's a birthday party, not a business meeting. I've never seen him be so rude. I told him if he'd just answer my e-mail, I wouldn't have to keep bothering him."

It was hard to imagine Pepe being anything but polite, especially to the niece everyone said was his favorite. Whatever was bugging him obviously didn't last. Before long he was calling the family together to cheer on Emilio as he opened his presents.

When he got to the dinosaur book, Mari urged me closer to talk to him.

"Do you like dinosaurs?" I asked.

He nodded as he studied the writing inside. "*Es español o inglès?*"

"It's both. Spanish on this side and English over here." I pointed to the facing pages, and decided to try one of the few Spanish phrases I remembered from high school, in honor of his birthday. "*Cuàntos anos tienes, Emilio?*"

His curious look, combined with a few giggles from some of the teenagers in the room, had me rethinking what I'd said. Spanish speakers don't ask how old you are, but how many years you have.

"*Dígale uno solamente*," Talia said, snickering.

"Only one?" What had I asked? *Cuàntos*…how many. *Anos*… oh, no. I could feel my face heating up, and from the laughter that grew around the room, I was now sporting a deep red blush.

Even Mima was laughing.

The word for years was *años*, not *anos*…which probably meant I'd just asked a three-year-old how many assholes he had.

"*Oh, mi dios.*" I buried my face in my hands and then peeked through my fingers at Mari, who was smiling and shaking her head. There was no way out of this but to laugh along. When someone asked about my most embarrassing moment, this would be the story I would tell for years to come.

"I'm sorry I laughed at you but that was hilarious."

"I probably scarred poor Emilio for life."

"Maybe so, but the rest of us can't wait to post it on Facebook." She gave me a sympathetic hug before breaking into giggles again with Talia.

While they were cutting Emilio's gigantic chocolate birthday cake, I retreated to a chair in the corner of the dining room, where I was soon joined by Lucia.

"I hope you don't feel embarrassed, Daphne. We all made silly mistakes when we learned English."

"That poor child. Did you see the look on his face?"

She laughed and gave me a hug. "You were a good sport. I'm so glad Pepe insisted on Mari bringing you to our dinner on the yacht. You're a breath of fresh air."

I smiled. Not a real smile. The kind you stick on your face and hold so people won't know you're thinking a Great Big WTF. I remember Mari describing how she'd followed Pepe's plan to go to UM, to become an investment manager and join his business, but I never would have dreamed he had dominion over her dating life as well. Had she also reported back on the status of her "conquest"?

When I thought about the sequence of events, it didn't take long to put all the pieces together. Mari had probably mentioned the bit about taking me to the symphony...or maybe Pepe had heard it from one of his friends who shared the box at the Arsht Center. He thought it would be good PR to have somebody from a nonprofit center on hand to help schmooze his clients—until he realized they were right-wingers. Then he put on a big show of pretending he didn't like their politics when it was probably mine he didn't agree with, since he'd taken on Michael as a client after all.

Or maybe he figured I'd be a good influence on Mari after Delores. Whatever. And all he had to do was insist. Nobody says no to Pepe.

What. Ever.

Mima's caretaker rolled her wheelchair next to me, said something to her in Spanish and left the room. I'd been ready to storm out but doing that now would be rude.

"Would you like some cake?" I caught myself acting like an idiot, enunciating slowly in a loud voice like Mima was hard of hearing. I stood up and pointed to it and she nodded.

I wanted the night to be over so I could go home, slam my door a few times and drink a whole bottle of something. Mari Tirado had a lot of nerve.

When I got back with the cake, I realized I didn't know what I was doing. I handed Mima the plate, which she took with her good hand.

The caretaker returned with a linen napkin and tucked it around the collar of her dress. "If you'd like to help, you can hold the plate up close to her mouth."

"Of course." I didn't mind helping at all. In fact, it gave me a chance to calm down a little. I wasn't looking forward to the scathing conversation Mari and I would have on the way home, and I especially dreaded the outcome. If Mari was seeing me only to please Pepe…that was so twisted I didn't even want to think about it.

Mari joined us and knelt on the floor next to her grandmother. "Mima, *te gusta*?"

"*Sí.*"

Of course she likes it. What's not to like about chocolate cake?

I didn't understand the rest of what they said, but when Mima finished her cake, Mari kissed her and said goodbye.

"Are you ready to go?" she asked. So innocent.

I made the rounds to say goodnight and laughed along as everyone got in a last chuckle over what I'd always call my Anus Debacle. Then I walked out to the car silently and waited for Mari to open the door.

"Is everything okay?"

I didn't know where to start, so I didn't.

"Please don't be mad. They were only teasing. Everyone likes you, I promise."

"Big deal. It only matters what Pepe thinks."

"What?" She turned in her seat to face me, making me wish I hadn't started it. I just wanted to go home. "What's this about Pepe?"

"Lucia told me you only brought me onto the yacht because Pepe insisted. Is that why you're telling Mima I'm your girlfriend? Because it's what Pepe wants?"

Her face twisted with confusion until she did the worst thing she possibly could have done. She laughed.

"Don't even!" Now I know why Edith had gone for her gun. "Well, is it true?"

"Technically, yes. I told him—listen to me." She reached for my hand and when I tried to pull away, she gripped it even tighter.

"I told him I didn't want to invite you if it was going to be just another boring business dinner. I wanted you to have a good time, so I said I'd rather wait until we could relax and enjoy it. He was very excited to hear I wanted to ask you out, and he *insisted* I invite you. In fact, he promised to get the business discussions out of the way early so we could have a good time. So yes, he insisted."

I had two choices, neither good. I could assume she was a squirmy liar and be furious, or I could believe her and feel foolish. Since I'd already set the lifetime bar on idiocy with Emilio, I decided foolish was not much of a leap.

"Do you feel better now?"

"I do."

"Good, because there's something else I want to say." She still had my hand and raised it to her face to kiss my palm. "That was so sweet when you helped Mima with her cake."

"Oh...it was no big deal."

"It was to me, because it made me realize I've fallen in love with you."

I experienced a shudder deep in the pit of my stomach, the kind that happens only after a profound surge of emotion or when your airplane drops unexpectedly. "Then I guess you've finally caught up with me, because I think I fell in love with you that day back in Little Haiti when you told me you'd been helping Saraphine figure out how to save for retirement. I thought that was the coolest thing I'd ever heard, and it showed me what a good person you were."

"And when were you planning on telling me this?"

"Verbal communication is so yesterday. I thought I'd show you instead."

The compact seating in the Carrera didn't lend itself to all I wanted to show her, but by the time her tongue wrapped around mine, I hardly cared that the gearshift was prying my ribs apart.

CHAPTER FIFTEEN

What I need is a really good curse word, something that evokes the vilest, most offensive thoughts possible so I can project them *from* myself instead of feeling as if they're being heaped upon me.

"Sorry I'm late." I slid into a chair at the far end of the conference table from Gisela. I was particularly sorry today because it was a full staff meeting, which meant I'd kept everyone waiting. I hate when they do that to me, and since they all know it, I was sure they were taking a lot of pleasure in my obvious frustration.

Being late for work was the least of my worries. I'd arrived in a very expensive taxi after having my car towed to a shop in a strange neighborhood just past the airport. The mechanic, who spoke very little English, didn't have time to look at it, but after I signed a statement agreeing to pay up to two hundred dollars for repairs, he promised to call my cell phone with a diagnosis. At least that's what I'd thought he said.

"No problem, Daphne. I was just getting to the volunteer report."

I had my papers ready and rattled off all the relevant numbers. We had a steady stream of volunteers to tap through the end of October, but things were looking bleak for the holiday months, especially since our next project was slated for Allapattah, a mixed neighborhood of mostly Caribbean and Central American immigrants, many of whom preferred living under the radar of law enforcement, the tax man and immigration officials.

"I'm planning a corporate push through the Chamber of Commerce, and I'll revisit some of the groups that volunteered with us last year and see if they want to keep their streak going."

One by one, the various departments checked in with their updates and the meeting was adjourned. None too soon, since I had a phone message from the mechanic.

"This is Daphne Maddox, the woman with the black Mustang. Did you find the problem?"

*"Abbadabba...abbadabba...*fuel pump."

"Do you have the part?"

"No, but I get today."

"But it will be under two hundred dollars, right?"

*"Si...*yes."

"Okay, go ahead and replace it."

Good thing, because that's about all I had to last till next payday. Thirty-one years old, living on my own and working in a professional position. And still eating ramen noodles three times a week.

Gisela came into my small office and closed the door, a move that got my attention, since it was standard protocol for personnel issues. Surely she wasn't going to ream me out for being late for the first time in four years.

"Tough morning, Daphne?"

"The worst. My car gave out on the other side of Bird Road and I had to have it towed. They should have it fixed this afternoon." I knocked on the veneer desk, since it was the closest thing to wood in the room.

"I can give you a lift after work if you need one."

"That'd be great." So if she wasn't mad at me, why was the door closed?

"Something very strange happened after our board meeting last night, and I wanted to make sure you weren't...how should I put this...feeling any undue pressure." She leaned against the door and folded her arms, staring down at the floor pensively. "Marco Padilla wants my support with the board to manage our foundation's investments, which are in the millions. I found his request...frankly, alarming, and I wouldn't be surprised if the chairman asks for his resignation should he formally propose such a thing. It's a blatant conflict of interest. Then he told me you were in a relationship with his niece, who is a partner at his firm, as if that might influence my decision."

Surely she didn't think my seeing Mari posed a conflict for the foundation, not when her own husband worked for the chairman of our board.

"Gisela, with all due respect, I can't imagine why anyone would have a problem with me seeing Mari Tirado. I didn't even meet her through Marco Padilla. She's the woman we looked up last spring who was doing community service for felony littering."

If her burst of laughter was any indication, she didn't have a problem at all. "You sure can pick 'em."

"I'll have you know she picked me."

Her jovial smile faded. "Which is all the more reason for us to talk about this."

"You don't think Mari's using me to influence you?" As much as I hated the thought, it sure cast Pepe's insistence I come along on the yacht in a whole new light. At least Mari's words and actions had settled any questions about her feelings for me.

"Surely not, but I want you to be aware in case it ever comes up that such an arrangement is out of the question. If she asks to speak to you about the foundation's investments, just tell her it's off limits."

That night on the yacht, I'd been so impressed with Pepe's business ethics because of the way he'd shunned Michael's millions over a difference in values. Not only had he flip-flopped on that, he'd clearly stepped over a line by approaching Gisela for the foundation's investments. I didn't want to think he was acting sleazy, but when it quacks like a *pato*…

***

Over the past few weeks, I'd enjoyed so many wonderful things about this Magic City with Mari that I'd totally forgotten just how much I hate it!

My rude reminder came courtesy of Bird Road Auto Center.

From the privacy of my bathroom, I glared at my angry reflection in the mirror, amazed that Carlos the Mechanic hadn't been the least bit intimidated by this look. "Did I not specifically ask him if a new fuel pump was covered under the two hundred dollars?"

Carlos had called his ten-year-old son over to explain in English how the pump itself was what he said was under two hundred dollars, and I'd agreed for him to go ahead and get the part. The labor, he said, was another one-eighty and the towing an extra fifty. Obviously, it was my fault I couldn't understand his atrocious English, and also that I now had the equivalent of two months' of groceries floating on my credit card at eighteen percent interest.

It was easily the worst day I'd had in months. Years, actually, since Emily's leaving had been a blessing in disguise. I was even a little glad Mari was seeing a client in Ft. Lauderdale tonight because she didn't deserve to be subjected to my bad mood. Besides the issue with my car, I had stewed all afternoon over Gisela's news about Pepe's business proposition, wondering if I should say something to Mari to get Pepe to back off. I wouldn't want to see either of them embarrassed, and a request from the chairman for Pepe's resignation could have that effect. But then just before I left for the day, Gisela came back into my office to say she'd called him and explained the difficulties, and he'd assured her he understood.

"At least one thing went right today."

What I needed now was a long soak in a hot tub with a trashy book. In absence of such a book, I settled for a copy of Edith's AARP magazine, which she'd given me because of a story on senior volunteering. From there, I was drawn to a depressing article about how much a single woman needed to save for retirement. At the rate I was saving, I'd have to work till I was ninety.

A booming voice from the intercom speaker in the hallway startled me so much I dropped the magazine in the tepid water. Whatever Javier said was entirely in Spanish—*abbadabba… abbadabba*—probably another scolding for someone to move their car out of the circle before it was towed. Edith was right about needing a rule to limit intercom use to emergencies, especially at night.

I dressed in baggy cargo shorts and a T-shirt so I could sit out on the balcony for a while before turning in, hoping there was a breeze to keep the mosquitoes away. When I slid the door open, I was hit by the unmistakable smell of something burning.

"What the—"

Several floors down, directly below Edith and Mordy's apartment, thick black smoke poured from the balcony. Two enormous fire trucks, horns blasting and lights flashing, converged on the street below from opposite directions, scattering those who had already run from the building.

That's when it struck me what Javier had said. *Abbadabba fuego*…fire! The building was burning down around us and it never occurred to him to have someone make the announcement in English so we *Americans* could get out.

I banged on the Osterhoffs' door until Mordy appeared. "There's a fire on one of the floors right under us. We have to get out now!"

"*Zayin b'ayin!*" His favorite Hebrew phrase, something about a dick in your eye.

With me carrying their indifferent cat Marvin, we headed for the stairwell and found it gray with smoke. I pulled my T-shirt up over my face and tucked Marvin underneath next to my bare stomach so we wouldn't keel over from smoke inhalation.

One floor below, we ran into Ronaldo García, who apparently had returned to his apartment to retrieve a pouch. "*Medicina para Isabel*." Medicine for the baby. He took Edith's arm and walked with her the rest of the way. The Perfect Man.

Hundreds of people from our building and those nearby had gathered on the street to watch as the fire crews brought the blaze under control. Edith chatted with some of her friends from the pool and came back to report that a woman had left a candle unattended and it was caught by billowing drapes.

"Idiot," Mordy grumbled. "She could have killed us all."

I was still fuming about the fact that Javier had warned everyone only in Spanish. If I'd been listening carefully, I might have caught enough of what he said to know there was a problem, especially since I noticed the sign by the elevator every single day—*En caso de fuego*…in case of fire…*no use el ascensor*…do not use the elevator. But it was unconscionable we didn't even have a system for emergencies that all of us could understand, and from the grumbling of the other residents, I wasn't the only one who thought so. Our homeowners association would have to remedy that.

When the fire marshal finally cleared us to go back inside, the elevator on our wing was so packed I offered to take Marvin up by the stairs. He got heavier at every floor but at least he remained true to his nature, calm and compliant. Mordy would have said he was too lazy to squirm.

To my delight, their door was propped open when I reached the hall and I dropped my furry load inside, where he immediately collapsed as though exhausted from being carried up fifteen flights of stairs. My arms and legs were burning with fatigue.

"I'm glad this day's almost over," I groaned. "It started out horrible and stayed that way."

Mordy chortled. "You think you had a bad day, you should ask Edith about hers."

"Mordecai Osterhoff! We agreed we wouldn't tell anyone."

"You agreed. Besides, this is Daphne. We've got no secrets from her."

As much as I wished that weren't the case, it was essentially true, thanks to our adjoining balconies and their penchant for arguing outside.

"Edith had a little run-in with the boys in blue today."

"It was a misunderstanding!"

"I'll say." Now that he'd opened the can of worms, he took his usual seat on the couch, smirking at Edith's discomfort.

"I went over to Target this morning. Marvin won't eat anything but Fancy Feast and they have it cheaper than anybody in town. Mordy said he was going to the pool."

"Which I did," he interjected.

"Except on my way home from the store, I saw him leaving in a car with another woman. I got so mad…"

I instantly regretted giving Edith back her gun, even though I'd watched her remove all the bullets. "Please tell me you didn't—"

"I yelled at them but they wouldn't stop, so I followed them up Biscayne all the way to the stoplight by Walgreen's. I swear it was just a little tap on the bumper."

"You rammed their car?" Obviously, I had underestimated her ability to surprise.

"Just a little scratch…but when they got out I saw it wasn't Mordy after all."

Mordy hooted hysterically. "That's what you get, you crazy woman!"

"Edith! What did you do?"

"What do you think I did? I lied. I told the policeman it was just an accident…that a bee flew in the car. I wrote the woman a check for four hundred dollars right there on the spot and he let me off with a warning. Four hundred dollars for a stupid little scratch!"

"With intent to maim," Mordy added. "You're lucky you aren't in jail."

At Edith's urging, I followed her out to the balcony where we could talk privately.

"What's wrong with me, Daphne? It's like I'm turning into a paranoid lunatic all of a sudden. I could have sworn that was Mordy in the car, but when that man got out, they didn't look anything alike. He was tall and handsome…how could I possibly have thought that was Mordy?"

Adding today's events to the fact she had threatened Mordy with a loaded gun over a likely wrong number definitely suggested something was wrong. "Edith, when was the last time you saw your doctor?"

"I'm seventy-six. All my doctors are on speed dial."

"But I bet you haven't talked to any of them about this, have you?"

"Do you think I'm crazy? Mordy does."

"I think you should have some tests done. There could be a simple explanation." I sure hoped it was simple. It had never even dawned on me that Edith might have something seriously wrong with her that was causing her outrageous behavior.

As I let myself into my apartment, I was overcome with sadness at the thought of Edith being ill. I'd be devastated if anything happened to either her or Mordy. Hell, I'd even been distraught when Marvin had taken his header off the rail.

My relaxing bath seemed like a lifetime ago. Sweaty from climbing fifteen floors and covered with cat fur, I peeled off my clothes and stepped into the shower for my third cleansing on this grubby day.

I'd been glad earlier Mari was busy with a client tonight, but now I found myself wishing she were here. The fire episode had me too wound up to sleep, and all I could think about was my awful day. I just wanted Mari to hold me…or I could hold her. Either one worked. I didn't even need sex.

Not that I have anything against sex.

I now had something I'd been missing. I had Somebody. Mari and I were in that great space where we were finding out all the special things about each other and doing things we both enjoyed. She might not be ready for being around me on a day like this.

Then again, if she were here it wouldn't have been such an awful day.

And even if it was an awful day, I didn't have to be such a jerk about it. That reminded me again of Emily's parting shot about me being miserable to live with because I complained all the time, the one I'd told Mari about over a romantic dinner on her terrace.

Miami's not so bad when you have Somebody. I wasn't miserable when we first arrived, not when Emily and I were making an adventure out of finding our way around. There were plenty of fun things to do, but the grind of everyday life wore us down—the traffic, the relentless heat and humidity, the economic divide, to say nothing of the language and cultural differences. I came home every night feeling like I'd been away at war, and soon we stopped doing those fun things that made living here bearable. Now that I was seeing Mari and getting out on the town again, I needed to let all our great times offset days like this one.

I wondered if she was home yet and how her meeting had gone. Quarter to eleven…hard to imagine she was still with her client, which meant she probably could have called by now but for whatever reason had decided not to. I wasn't going to get all insecure and possessive, but it was deflating. How do you ignore somebody you're supposedly falling in love with?

Like I needed something else to worry about tonight. Why couldn't I just text her? Say I hoped her meeting well and I was going to bed. Nothing clingy about that.

Except I spent the next hour looking all over my apartment, my car and the lawn outside for my phone.

CHAPTER SIXTEEN

There were few things I hated as much as admitting my mother was right about something. Always treat everyone with kindness, she'd said, because someday you may need their kindness in return.

Carlos, the Spanish-speaking mechanic, wanted nothing to do with me today. He hadn't seen my phone and he didn't have time to look for it.

The last time I remembered using it was talking to Mari yesterday right here at my desk as I ate lunch. I'd turned my office upside down, and couldn't shake the unwelcome thought that someone from the night cleaning crew had found it on the floor and taken it. What other explanation could there be?

After wasting almost an hour of my morning, I came to grips with knowing I should call my provider to suspend my service. There would probably be a fee for that, to say nothing of how much I'd have to lay out for a new phone if this one never turned up, but I couldn't just sit by idly while someone racked up thousands of dollars in calls to Costa Rica.

The phone on my desk buzzed. "A call from Banco Primero."

Odd, it had been ages since I reached out to them for volunteers. But Pepe's client Juan was the CEO, so maybe he was having his people reach out to me. Something told me he didn't share Michael's values, and perhaps this was his way of letting me know.

"This is Daphne Maddox."

With a marked Hispanic accent, the woman on the other end of the phone introduced herself as a loan officer. Something about a package…asset relief…and a request to verify my social security number.

"Excuse me, but what's this about?"

"You applied to refinance your condominium mortgage, yes?"

I had, but not with Banco Primero. "Do you have my loan application?"

"Yes, it has been transferred to me, but I need to confirm the information."

No way was I going to argue with that. Banks trade paper all the time and I don't care if it ends up at the First Bank of Cuba as long as it gets processed and approved. I rattled off all my personal information, including the cell phone number I hoped I could keep after the temporary suspension of my service.

A lost cell phone seemed trivial compared to something as big as getting my refinance application through.

"Daphne?" It was Rosa Moran, our part-time information technology specialist. She had the widest eyes and brightest smile I'd ever seen on anyone, which always amazed me, since about ninety percent of her job was fixing technical problems for grouchy people like me. "Guess what I found in the breakroom last night after everyone had gone?"

My beloved phone!

"Oh, my God! I think I love you." I hugged her with the same joy Edith had shown Mari and me when we brought Marvin back alive from his skydiving adventure. "I didn't even miss it until late last night and I've been going crazy ever since."

"Yeah, sorry about that. I couldn't call you because…well, I had your phone. I meant to leave it in your desk drawer before I left but then I got home and found it in my pocket. I charged it for you, so it's all set to go."

Six missed calls, all from Mari. And two voice mails.

"I noticed something weird though. Is there any reason somebody might be tapping your phone?"

"Tapping my phone? You mean like listening to my calls?"

"Or tracking your location…retrieving your voice mails. Things like that."

She took my phone and rubbed her finger along the back. "Your battery is really hot, which it shouldn't be, because you haven't been using it. Plus, I powered it down last night because it rang a couple of times and I figured you'd want those to go to voice mail. But then it turned itself back on. I noticed the backlight kept coming on and it would stay on for several minutes. That happens sometimes with a software download, but not ten times in one night. It was like someone was using it and if it wasn't you…"

I couldn't imagine anyone would find my phone messages interesting enough to hack. "That is weird. My life's about as exciting as the US tax code. It had to have been software upgrades."

"Just thought I'd mention it."

"I appreciate it. And I really appreciate you finding it and bringing it back."

I hugged her again, and when she was gone, sat down to savor my messages. I had missed Mari's offer to stop by on her way home last night, but it would have been right in the middle of the chaos so it was probably for the best. I was especially touched by her message from earlier this morning, in which she wondered if I was okay and even raised the fear that I might be mad at her for something. I'd entertained those same doubts about her before realizing I'd lost my phone.

She answered on the first ring. "There you are! I was beginning to wonder if you'd lost my number."

"No, just my phone." I told her all about my misadventures from the day before—the fuel pump, the repair bill, the fire and the phone. "But today's a new day and it's off to a great start already. Except Rosa, our IT person, says there's something weird going on with my phone. They must be doing upgrades or something."

"What do you mean weird?"

I told her about the battery heating up and the backlights coming on when I wasn't using it.

"Mine's been doing the same thing lately, so it must be like you said, software upgrades."

"Do I get to see you tonight?"

"I'd say that all depends on whether or not you can get the blindfold off."

***

I pulled into the garage of the Plaza at Brickell, embarrassed at driving my ancient Sally among the residents' expensive cars. Mari would say that's my hang-up, and that no one cares what I drive as long as I drive it fast enough. Then she'd encourage me to trade it in on something new that would last me through a bankruptcy.

To my great annoyance, a car was already parked next to Mari's Porsche in her guest space, a silver Mercedes SLK. Mari had warned me about this. Some visitors park wherever they want, she said, knowing full well a tow truck can't navigate the sharp turns and concrete pillars. I managed to find an unmarked visitor space at the far end of the garage, and resisted the urge to accidentally write something obscene in lipstick on the windshield of the SLK.

As I rode the elevator to the forty-ninth floor, I thought about Mari's exercise regimen of climbing these stairs three times a week. I'd almost passed out last night climbing a third as high, but then I'd been carrying a fifteen-pound sack of purring fur. After feeling firsthand what stair climbing had done for Mari's butt muscles, there was no denying its merits and I was tempted to make it part of my routine.

Since I hadn't seen Mari last night, I was ready to jump her bones the second she opened the door. Instead she met me in the hallway, pulling the door behind her so it was open only a crack.

"I have company...Delores is here."

Not something I wanted to hear. Ever.

"She stopped by out of the blue. I kind of had a feeling she would because I haven't returned any of her calls."

Didn't want to hear that either, since it meant Mari had practically baited her into showing up instead of just calling her back and telling her to piss up a rope.

"What does she want?" I distinctly remembered her saying one of her friends from the Wallcast thought Delores wanted to go out with her again.

"Just to talk, she says. Apparently she got a conscience all of a sudden and feels bad about what she did."

I felt bad about what she was doing now, and regretted my restraint with the lipstick. "I should go then."

"I'm sorry, Daphne, but I need to get this over with so she'll leave me alone." She had the decency to look as though she felt guilty. "I asked her to walk over to Truluck's for dinner because I don't want her here. I promise I'll tell her not to come back again."

"You don't have to promise me anything. We're all adults." The words were mature but the tone left a lot to be desired. I was irritated and not very good at hiding it. Especially since she'd apparently made dinner plans with Delores without even asking me if she could break our date. Surely it had occurred to her that pulling me into the room and dipping me for a passionate kiss would send Delores an unmistakable message to get lost.

Unless that wasn't the message she wanted to send.

Until now, I'd never realized I had a jealous streak. Emily's tryst had left me so hurt and angry that I never even considered trying to win her back. But Mari...I wanted Mari. I didn't want her wrestling with nostalgic memories of nights she'd shared with Delores, or second-guessing how easily she'd given up their dreams when she dumped all her junk on the Jet Ski.

"Look, Daphne. I haven't even spoken to her once since I kicked her out. There could be a lot at stake for me here. I know for a fact she downloaded files on at least a dozen of my clients, and if we can just have one civil conversation, I might be able to convince her to come clean. I feel like it's my only chance. I have to try."

Either it was true or she was the best actor in the world, because her plaintive voice left me no choice but to believe her. That didn't mean I had to like it.

"Fine," I grunted. "I'm sure I can find something else to do tonight."

"Please don't be mad." She tugged both of my wrists until I was in a full embrace. "I thought I made it pretty clear the other night that I'm crazy about you."

No fair. "Can I help it if I want you to prove it every night?"

She covered my pouty lips with her smug ones and pressed her hips into mine. Funny how arousal trumps irritation. Every time.

"Do you want me to call you later?" she asked when we came up for air.

I could show a little understanding given the circumstances, but I was too proud to let her think I'd be waiting by the phone all night. "No, that's all right. I'd rather have you on a night when I can get your undivided attention."

"I promise to give it to you."

She kissed me again and I left feeling like I'd made the best of a bad situation. I even managed to walk past the SLK without kicking out one of the headlights.

By the time I reached my building my mood had mildly improved. The sight of Edith's caved-in front bumper cracked me up as I pulled into my marked space. It wasn't until I got out that I noticed the vehicle next to hers—a black Chevy Suburban like the one I'd been seeing all over Miami. Paranoia or not, that was an incredible coincidence.

A woman's hand caught the elevator door as it started to close, a strong hand with a sure grip. The rest of her looked equally confident—obviously Hispanic, tall and straight with smart black slacks, a crisp blue shirt and a gray blazer—the whole of which set off my gaydar like a four-alarm fire. The moment I realized that, I recalled where I'd seen her before...at LIV, where she'd been watching Mari and me dance, and where she'd gotten into the black SUV.

My floor was already lit up and she pressed sixteen, which had me wracking my brain to figure out which one of my neighbors up there entertained lesbian friends at night.

But then she got off when I did and all the hairs on the back of my neck stood up.

"Daphne Maddox?"

"Who's asking?"

She unbuttoned her blazer—revealing a badge and gun that were clipped to her waist. "Special Agent Elena Diaz, of the United States Internal Revenue Service."

CHAPTER SEVENTEEN

Emily Jenko was behind this. I'd bet a whole paycheck on it.

I took every imaginable tax deduction allowed but I could justify each one and I'd even saved the damn receipts! I had to, because my father was a CPA and he'd done my taxes since I was sixteen, when I'd started working summers at the recreation center. I didn't have any income other than my salary at the foundation, though Dad had gifted me the maximum contribution to a Roth IRA for the last few years. That couldn't have been illegal or he wouldn't have done it.

"May I come in?"

"What's this about?"

"I'd rather talk inside if you don't mind."

It wasn't as if I had a whole lot of choice. Screwing around with the IRS is in the same category of Stupid as joking about a bomb in your underpants on your way through airport security.

That didn't mean I had to fix her tea. I closed the door and stood my ground in the entryway. "Okay, now tell me what this is about."

It's pretty hard to intimidate someone who's carrying a gun. She walked right past me into the living room, looking around as if she intended to buy the place.

Not that I have anything against selling.

"How well do you know Maribel Tirado León?"

Color me shocked. "Why do you ask?"

She continued to look around, never once making eye contact. "Could I trouble you for a glass of water?"

Cooperate with the IRS…cooperate with the IRS…cooperate with the IRS.

I was tempted to fill the glass directly from the tap because Miami water was absolutely undrinkable, but hearing my father's mantra in my head, I fetched a bottle from the refrigerator. "Mari Tirado is a personal friend."

"Does she manage any of your personal investments?"

"If she did, wouldn't you already know that?" *Cooperate with the IRS.* "I don't really make enough to invest in the market… other than a small Roth IRA."

"Has she given you any gifts of significant value?" Her tone was deceptively casual, as though her interest was only curiosity, not investigative.

I knew better. "No."

"You recently applied for federal mortgage relief. Your home is very nice, by the way."

My refinance package! That's what this was about. No, why would she be asking about Mari?

"What does my mortgage have to do with anything? Why are you here?" I'd cooperated so far, and it was high time she answered a question or two. "Are you allowed to come into my house and just ask me all these questions? Don't you need a warrant or something?"

I wanted to swallow my whole head when she pulled a folded blue document from inside her jacket.

"I have one, an arrest warrant issued this afternoon by the US District Court. But I'd rather not have to execute it, Ms. Maddox. It might be possible for me to clear this up without taking you into custody and that would certainly be my preference. I assume it would be yours as well."

My mouth was quite dry, which made it difficult to gulp. I was hers and she knew it. "Yes, I applied to refinance, but that was over a year ago. Every time I call, they tell me it's still being processed. I finally heard from somebody today, but she just wanted to verify the information."

She stood there nodding along, which made it seem like she wanted to hear more, so I gave her the B-version of how I'd gotten over my head with the mortgage. The A-version, which I share only with people I know well, includes the part about Emily being a deadbeat cheat, but I saw no reason to communicate my personal woes to the IRS.

"According to the bank's latest filings with the Treasury Department, your package has been expedited by Banco Primero. It seems they've approved not only a reduced interest rate, but thanks to a special provision of the TARP funds, they've forgiven more than a hundred thousand dollars off the principal. Was that something you expected?"

If I'd heard her correctly, it was raining Glory Hallelujahs. "I remember checking the box on the application to request a reassessment, but from what I've been reading, they don't usually do that for people who have full-time jobs and keep up with their payments." I'd looked for every loophole I could find to qualify for assistance, but nothing I'd said or done had been illegal. "I still don't see why you're—"

"Did you ask anyone for assistance in negotiating these new terms?"

I didn't know for sure that Juan had intervened on my behalf, so I didn't want to say anything that might get him in trouble.

"I got help last year from one of the banks I work with to fill out the forms." I described my job as a volunteer coordinator, and how it brought me into contact with several banks in Miami. "But I haven't been to see anyone else since I sent them in. Did I do something wrong?"

I suddenly realized we'd both sat down at my dining table.

"Are you saying you weren't aware of actions by anyone advocating for new terms?"

"No."

"Did you ever mention your mortgage situation to Maribel Tirado?"

Why did she keep coming back to Mari? I felt like I was marching deeper and deeper into some sort of trap she would spring the second I admitted something, and I had no idea what she was fishing for. However, I'd seen enough TV shows to know I should stop helping her hang me. "What exactly does your warrant allege that I did?"

She unfolded the document and spun it around on the table so I could see it. With a hand that sported an enormous class ring from Georgetown, she pointed to a line just below my name.

"Conspiracy to commit securities fraud? What does that even mean?" I'd already told her I didn't have any investments.

"The moment your mortgage terms were submitted to the US Treasury for approval, you became the beneficiary of a suspected criminal enterprise involving securities fraud."

"But all I did was—" Never the brightest bulb in the pack when it came to finances, I tried putting the pieces together. "I don't get what any of this has to do with Mari Tirado. I didn't even know her when I filled out those refinance papers."

Up until that point, the agent had been all business, showing no discernible emotion, but the look on her face now was almost apologetic, like she really hated having to break bad news. "We have reason to believe she and her uncle, Marco Padilla, facilitated your recent mortgage action."

So that was it. Mari talked to Pepe, and Pepe talked to Juan. Suddenly my application got transferred to Banco Primero.

"I don't know anything about that." Actually, I know what everyone else knows, that peddling influence is the Cuban way of doing business. Everyone on the outside grouses about the ethics of their favoritism, but the IRS does more than grouse. Apparently it's illegal when it involves Treasury funds. I'd had a few dreamy thoughts of spending the rest of my life with Mari, but not behind bars. "Look, Agent…"

"Diaz."

"Agent Diaz, I don't have any idea what's going on, but I can promise you I haven't done anything wrong, and I haven't asked anyone else to do it for me. I talked to Mari a long time ago about how hard it was to make payments, but all she told me was to walk away from my loan, just to let the bank foreclose. I'm sure this is a misunderstanding. She might have asked around for information, but she never would have asked anyone to do something illegal."

In fact, despite being part of a prominent, wealthy Cuban family, Mari had never struck me as the kind of person who would pull strings behind the scenes. I'd seen her business ethics up close with people like Saraphine and Michael, and the fact she didn't press her friends for business made her one of the most principled money handlers I knew. There's no way she'd use her influence like that, if she even had it to use.

"You indicated earlier you didn't have any investments other than your IRA. Are you aware Ms. Tirado's firm has established an account in your name in the Cayman Islands, an account that holds over six million dollars?"

Holy Mother of Maddoff! "Why would they even...? That doesn't make any sense."

"We think they're using you to hide profits from their investors."

"No, there's some mistake." Mari wasn't like that, and neither was Pepe. They were decent, hardworking people who appreciated American values.

"I'm sorry, Daphne. There's no mistake. The account is registered in your name with this address, and they provided a photocopy of your passport, which they needed for the Cayman bank authorities. We assume they got that from your mortgage application."

If it wasn't a mistake...it meant Mari wasn't in love with me. She was using me to hide assets from the IRS.

The realization crawled over me like the jaws of a python. I was torn between wanting to cry and wanting to throw furniture off the balcony. Instead I managed to keep my cool in front of the IRS agent so she wouldn't know how humiliated I was.

"I have no knowledge of an account like that. If someone opened it in my name, it's a fraud."

She tucked the warrant back into her jacket and stood as if ready to leave. "I believe you. We were pretty sure you weren't directly involved, but I needed to know for certain. I apologize for the heavy hand."

How about an apology for the pounding in my head or the searing lump in the back of my throat?

"So what do I do now? Sign an affidavit or something that says the money isn't mine?" I doubt she'd endorse what I had in mind, which was to go back over to Mari's with Edith's gun and wave it in her face until she peed in her pants.

The possibility of emptying that offshore account also had a lot of appeal.

Agent Diaz folded her arms and took a couple of measured steps toward the balcony. "I was hoping you'd be willing to do a bit more."

"Like what?"

She dragged her chair around to my side of the table and sat facing me, her legs apart and her elbows on her knees. I used to strike that same pose knowing it would prompt my mother to yell at me to sit like a lady.

"We've been building our case against Padilla Financial for almost a year. They're using an investment instrument called the Iberican Fund, which I assume you heard all about it when you accompanied the family on their yacht."

"Right…a bunch of companies in Latin America on the verge of taking off."

"The fund looks and sounds perfectly legitimate. In fact, most of the manufacturing and distribution companies listed in the prospectus are receiving investment funds from Padilla and doing very well. But one of them—a company that doesn't appear in the formal filings with the SEC—exists in name only. It's a shell company in the Caymans. Up until last week, that account was holding investor funds that were being used to augment payouts. Are you familiar with the term 'Ponzi scheme'?"

Son of a Pharaoh. "It's like a pyramid, right?"

"Exactly. As long as Padilla Financial keeps taking on more investors, they have plenty of cash to pay out earnings."

I remembered Pepe describing the Iberican Fund in detail to Michael. Mari said she'd traveled to several of the businesses and confirmed their potential for growth. Why would she do that if the whole thing was bogus?

"Right now, the fund appears successful because investors are getting dividends. Somewhere down the road, however, that shell company is going to quote-unquote 'fail,' and the investors will take a loss. They'll be upset…sure, but they'll chalk it up to market forces, especially since they enjoyed such high earnings in the beginning. The beauty of this particular scheme—and I've got to hand it to them, it's clever—is their clients probably won't lose a dime in the long run. They may even make a little but not the margins they hoped for. All the real earnings on the investments to the legitimate companies go to Padilla Financial, and they aren't being taxed at all because they're going into accounts like yours that will never be withdrawn because you don't even know they exist. We're talking millions."

Even I understood how clever that was, and deep down I felt better about knowing no one was actually losing money.

"Our securities investigator thinks the recent transfer of funds into your account and others means that so-called company is about to go under."

"But why are they using me? That doesn't make any sense, and neither does meddling in my mortgage." I also wanted to ask if my write-down was still legal. After a personal blow like this, it would be really nice if I came out on the other side of this with a debt I could manage.

"My guess is they needed to hide their funds under names that can't be easily traced back to Padilla Financial."

"Except you traced it."

Diaz nodded, but tipped her head as if barely conceding the point. "Only because we happened to be monitoring you after you took that dinner cruise aboard their yacht. According to our source, that's where it appears they're doing most of their business, away from telephones and places that can be bugged."

So there was a source, someone on the inside of Padilla Financial leaking details to the IRS.

Now it was my turn to get up and stomp around. This wasn't my mess but I was in it up to my eyeballs whether I liked it or not. Walking away from my mortgage—even at a lower rate and principal—and leaving town for good were looking better all the time.

"You still haven't told me what you want me to do."

"We haven't finalized our plan at this point. We're working another angle, but you might be the only chance we have to get exactly what we need for prosecution, which is an invitation to dinner on their yacht. That would involve you setting up a meeting with Mari and a friend of yours"—she pointed a finger to her chest—"who wants to invest. I'll contact you when we're ready."

I wondered if Special Agent Diaz would feel special right now if I threw up on her shoes. I suddenly remembered the conversation with Rosa about my phone, which made me think of all the sexy texts Mari and I had sent each other in the past week. "You've been bugging my phone, haven't you?"

She didn't have to answer. At least she had the decency to look marginally ashamed of herself. They knew all along I wasn't part of this, but went through the whole charade with the arrest warrant so they could blackmail me into working with them. While it pissed me off plenty to be manipulated like that, it didn't hold a candle to how I felt about Mari.

I was glad for the chance to help bury her.

"I'm sure I don't have to tell you that everything we discussed tonight is confidential. If you reveal the contents of our discussion to anyone, you could be charged with obstruction of justice, which carries a possible prison term of five years." Diaz buttoned her jacket as she stood, effectively hiding her gun.

"I'm not going to say anything."

"I know, but I was still obligated to tell you that. I can only imagine how you're feeling right now...used, betrayed. I know you'll be tempted to confront Ms. Tirado about this, but you mustn't do that. Trust me, we'll handle this, and they'll pay for it. You're one of the victims here, and I'm truly sorry for what they've done to you. I'll contact you soon about how and when we need to do this."

When the agent left, I watched her through the peephole until she disappeared onto the elevator. She had seemed genuinely regretful, but I didn't doubt for a minute she meant every word about me going to prison if I tipped Mari off.

Not that I would. The hardest part for me would be keeping up the pretense of being nice to her long enough to follow through with their plan of introducing her to Agent Diaz. I never dreamed anyone could treat me worse than Emily had, but boy, was I ever wrong. At least I knew Emily had loved me once, and that deep down she felt guilty for leaving the way she had. Only a month ago, I'd considered forgiving her, and writing all of it off to her being confused about infatuation and lust versus real love.

But Mari wasn't confused about anything. She was just the best liar I'd ever met.

Greed was something I understood, at least conceptually. People who worked in finance did it because—*news flash*—they liked making money. The more, the better. These days, it wasn't good enough to make a few hundred thousand a year through intelligent, *honest* work. Not when your peers were making millions by bilking their clients and betting against their own investments.

What I couldn't fathom was how Mari could give lip service to her oh-so-lofty principles when it came to things like doing business with her friends, but she had no qualms about leading me to believe she had genuine feelings for me, especially after sharing something as intimate as sex. I just couldn't wrap my brain around that. I had to think at least some of it was real. No one could be that diabolical, but I'd seen with Emily how someone could twist things around in their head in order to justify their behavior. Mari had probably convinced herself she liked me well enough to have casual sex, but there was no way she was "in love" with me.

And, as of right now, the feeling was mutual.

CHAPTER EIGHTEEN

Some days the Miami River smells like dead fish. It's even worse when hot, sticky air hangs over Allapattah like a cellophane blanket. Welcome to November in Miami.

Bo's future son-in-law, a patrol officer with the Miami-Dade Police Department, spearheaded our volunteer crew of cops today. All eight of them were nailing shingles on the roof like old pros, each trying to out-macho the others with his construction prowess. They hardly needed supervision, which left Bo and me free to caulk around the doors, windows and tiles inside.

Despite the heat, humidity and fishy odor, I needed a day of mindless, physical work. No way could I have handled a job where I had to think, not with the IRS agent's words still playing in my head. A whole night of tossing and turning had left me drained. None of the scenarios I'd imagined could legitimately explain how this had happened. I wanted to believe Mari was innocent. I just couldn't, not with that mysterious bank account out there.

I'd drawn the last bead of caulk around the bathroom door when my cell phone chimed to announce a text message. It had to be Mari because that's how we communicated when we knew the other one was working. I still hadn't decided how to handle her, or even if I should try. As angry as I was, it made more sense to avoid her altogether until it was time to introduce her to my supposed friend.

Except the text wasn't from Mari. It was from Agent Diaz, who said she was out front and needed to talk.

"I'm calling a break, Bo. I'll let the guys up on the roof know."

The black SUV that had been following me for days was parked across the street and two doors down beneath a Poinciana tree that littered the curb with leaves, pods and red, feathery flowers. If they were trying to be inconspicuous, it wasn't working, particularly since all of our volunteers were police officers and knew exactly which vehicles belonged to federal law enforcement. I yelled up at them to take a break and strolled down the street as casually as I could.

Diaz was behind the wheel wearing aviator shades and a tight black polo shirt, her elbow resting casually out the window. If anyone saw her—and by anyone, I mean all eight of our police volunteers—they'd make her as a dyke first and a cop second. At least that would partially satisfy their curiosity about why I was going to see her, because they'd think we had something going on.

She gestured for me to get in on the passenger side. It was only then I realized there was a man in the backseat, twenty-something and kind of goofy-looking, with a dark tan and shaggy blond hair. Obviously one of my Nordic cousins. I wondered if he felt as out of place in Miami as I did.

"Daphne, this is Henry Smith, my colleague. He'll be my partner in the field."

I could only manage a nod in his direction. What was I supposed to say? Pleased to meet you? I wasn't. I wish I'd never met any of them, Mari included.

"Our other angle didn't play out so we've decided to go ahead with our plan to set up a business meeting with Ms. Tirado."

I wasn't particularly interested in their plan. "How did you know I'd be here? Let me guess. You're still tracking my phone."

A grunt was her only reply but it spoke volumes. I wanted this over with. The idea of federal agents following me everywhere I went was infuriating, especially since they knew I hadn't done anything wrong. They'd probably doubled down on their surveillance since last night in case I tried to get in touch with Mari.

"What if Mari isn't involved? This could all be her uncle's doing. She may not know anything about it." That was the only explanation that gave me any comfort at all, especially if Pepe was doing all this behind her back.

"She has access to all the books, Daphne. I know you don't want to believe she'd do it, but looking at companies' financial records is our specialty. One person can't hide something this big. It can only happen with her knowledge and consent."

No, I didn't want to believe it, but it was pretty hard to make sense of how Mari could manage all her accounts and not know where the money was going. Besides, she'd said herself that she'd done all the research on those companies, so she had to know one of them was bogus. Still…the fact she'd been confused about a couple of her clients' portfolios and traded angry words with Pepe gave me the faintest glimmer of hope he was keeping her in the dark.

"Daphne, the only piece we're missing in our investigation is a detailed description of the Iberican Fund from the horse's mouth. We have to record their sales pitch so we can show they're misleading investors on where their money goes. All I need is for you to introduce her to me as a friend of yours who wants to invest. Can you set up a lunch meeting?"

"Mari and I never meet for lunch. We're in different parts of town, and she usually hooks up with clients for lunch." To say nothing of the fact that Mari knew one meal in a Miami restaurant would tank my lunch budget for the week.

"Restaurants aren't so good anyway," Blondie said, tapping Diaz on the shoulder. "Too much white noise."

"It won't matter. The goal is to get a private meeting on the yacht because that's where the real business gets done. That's the one we have to record."

"But only if I can get close enough," he added. "Anything outside of three hundred feet just isn't reliable."

"I got it, Henry!" Diaz snapped.

"Just sayin'."

Touchy. Sounded like they'd had a few glitches in the past.

"Can you just call her and say you have a friend who's not happy with her broker?"

That probably wouldn't work, not as long as Mari had a policy of not doing business with friends. I understood that now, since her friends would go ballistic watching her drive around in a Porsche she bought with their commissions while they ended up with zilch.

"If I tell her you're my friend, she probably won't give you the time of day, at least not as far as money is concerned."

"Why not?"

"She doesn't hit her friends up for business. She says it makes things messy if they lose money. And friends always expect her to give them discounts and insider tips."

"Would she do it as a favor to you?"

That was hard to answer, since the Mari I knew was rigid about her principles. That said, the Mari I knew wasn't even the real Mari. She and Pepe had put on a big show of turning down Michael's business only to chase it later. "If she could use me to hide millions of dollars in a secret account, she might use one of my friends if it was to her advantage. But we just talked about this a few days ago. Won't it make her suspicious if I suddenly bring somebody around?"

The two agents exchanged grim looks, and Diaz sighed with frustration.

"Maybe we should just go with the straight-up business approach instead of bringing Ms. Maddox into the picture,"

Blondie said. "The fewer people involved, the less risk of something going wrong."

Diaz banged a fist on the steering wheel, and then ran a hand through her short brown hair. "Then we're going to need another opening. I can't just call her out of the Yellow Pages."

I had no clue what they meant by a straight-up business approach, but I liked the idea of leaving me out of it. Getting revenge on Mari didn't matter as much as getting out of this mess completely.

"How does she usually pick up clients?"

"Referrals, I think." Michael had come to Pepe through his friend Juan. "The best way to get to Mari is probably through someone who already has an account with her. That's what they usually do...get their clients to bring in friends to invest."

Diaz shook her head. "It's too risky to reach out to one of her investors. Once they find out their money's tied up in a racket, they'll get spooked and try to pull it all out. We won't be able to stop them if they do. You have to be the one who makes the referral. What if I pretended to be somebody you met through work? Think she'd go for that?"

"What, you want me to call her out of the blue and say I ran into someone with five million dollars who wants to invest?" As if there were lots of millionaires in a place like Allapattah.

"Five million?"

"Yeah, that's the minimum to buy into the Iberican Fund." It occurred to me it didn't look good for me to know so much about Mari's business dealings, but I wasn't interested in sticking my neck out for something that wasn't going to work. "Wait a minute. I know how you can get to her. There's a Chamber of Commerce cocktail party Monday night. That's just two days from now."

"Will both of you be there?"

"Yeah, but why would you even need me? Mari goes to those things to network. You could just walk up and talk to her."

"I need you because you give me an entrée, and she'll pay attention because she thinks it matters to you. The last thing I'd want would be for her to get distracted by someone else and walk away. We'd never get our foot back in the door."

"Going to be tough to get good sound with that many people around," Blondie said. "Get her off to the side if you can."

"We really need your help to do this, Daphne." It was the same apologetic tone Diaz had used the night before. "Our chances of pulling it off are a whole lot better if you're there to lend us credibility. It'll be a piece of cake. You and I can just act like we're talking about something else and when she walks over, that's it. You make the introduction, let us talk for a couple of minutes, and when she takes the bait, you excuse yourself and step away."

"And what if she doesn't take your bait?"

"Let us worry about that. We're pretty good at what we do."

I could believe that of Diaz, but Blondie looked like he'd be better at surfing than investigating.

She patted my arm awkwardly, as if she wasn't comfortable with touchy-feely stuff but wanted to give off at least a hint of compassion. "We'll make all the arrangements to be there. Just go to the cocktail party on Monday like usual, and I'll find you. I promise it'll all be over for you as soon as we get our meeting. We might even get it all on tape at the party. Oh, and one other thing…"

"I know, I can't say anything to Mari or you'll lock me up for five years." I whirled my finger around in a whoop-de-doo gesture that was even more satisfying than flipping a bird. "What if this is all a mistake? Did you ever stop to think how many lives you'd be ruining if you were wrong?"

"There's no mistake. I wasn't going to tell you this…but we found another Caymans account like yours—in the name of Mr. and Mrs. Mordecai Osterhoff. Mari used you to get to them too."

She might as well have hit me upside the head with a two-by-four. It was bad enough they'd involved me in their scam, but dragging Edith and Mordy into it was so far over the line I couldn't wait to help put them in jail. And now I knew it had to be Mari because Pepe didn't even know the Osterhoffs.

Walking back to the house, I spun a few ideas about how I was going to get through the next few days without having to deal with Mari. This called for something contagious, like hepatitis A or meningitis. I could overcome my symptoms long enough to get to the Chamber meeting, and then have a relapse immediately after. By the time Mari figured out I was faking, she'd be in jail.

"What'd you do, Daphne?" It was Nick Johnson, a beefy patrol officer who had lifted so many dumbbells he couldn't even straighten his arms. His eyes followed the SUV as it vanished around the corner.

I couldn't think fast enough but Bo was there to save the day. "They're always coming by asking about drug dealers."

Johnson nodded pensively. "Right, I bet you see a lot of that in the kind of neighborhoods you work."

"All the time," I said, hustling back inside so I wouldn't have to answer any more questions.

I had to come up with a dreaded disease. Otherwise I might need Edith's gun after all. I could tell Mari I'd gotten a nasty stomach virus from a woman at work. That would get me out of doing anything tonight and tomorrow. With the right makeup I could even manage to look peaked on Monday and complain that I needed a few more days to shake it. By then, Diaz would have her in jail.

I didn't have to fake how bad I felt. It made me physically sick to think Mari had been using me. Pepe wouldn't have gone to his friend and fixed my mortgage on his own. No, Mari's fingerprints were all over that, so they'd have to be connected to the Caymans account too, especially since Edith and Mordy had an account there too.

Unless all those things really were unrelated.

Okay, so maybe Mari had mentioned my mortgage problem, and Pepe followed up with his banker friend. Through that he got access to my passport and couldn't resist an easy opportunity to hide the firm's money. Maybe Pepe's shenanigans were the reason Mari couldn't reconcile her portfolios.

Mari knew all about my personal issues with Emily because she'd looked me up online. Pepe could have done the same thing with Edith and Mordy, especially if Mari had told everyone the story of their first meeting. And why wouldn't she mention something as dramatic as Edith waving a gun around or Marvin surviving a fifteen-floor fall?

But how had he gotten their passports to open the account? Probably faked them, since he'd faked everything else. Or he could have gotten hold of their original mortgage application, since he was friends with all the bankers.

I didn't want it to be Mari. I'd done these sorts of mental gymnastics before back when I didn't want to think Emily would cheat on me. She never had to make excuses because I made them for her all the way up until the undeniable truth was staring me in the face.

Now I was making them for Mari, but I didn't have that nagging feeling that I was fooling myself. It couldn't be her. She just wasn't like that.

The Cockroach Truck sounded its horn, and my stomach growled in response.

Our roofing crew had already congregated around the truck by the time I walked out, and Bo was laying out from his cooler the feast his wife had prepared. I'd been so absorbed in last night's drama that I never even thought about packing lunch, and since I'd skipped breakfast, it was Cockroach Truck or nothing.

"You forget your lunch?" Bo asked as he tucked a clean checkered napkin around his collar to keep food off his filthy T-shirt. "I've got more here than I can eat in a week."

"I've seen you eat, Bo. Two sandwiches, potato salad, deviled eggs and…what's that, banana pudding? That's just a snack for you."

He chuckled. "Maybe I should have said more than I ought to eat in a week."

"I'll grab something from the truck."

The instant I stepped off the porch, I caught sight of Mari's white sports car pulling into the space along the curb where Diaz had been parked only a couple of hours ago. The same rush of adrenaline I got from cockroaches surged through me and I wanted to dash back inside.

Grinning and animated, Mari hopped out of her car and waved me over. It was hard to believe someone could hide such deceit behind a cheery face like that.

"I have a surprise for you," she said, opening a Styrofoam dish to reveal a steaming pile of chicken and yellow rice. "*Arroz con pollo* from Versailles. I met Chacho and Talia for a late breakfast and thought about you slaving away over here."

The fact she may have betrayed me did nothing to diminish the wonderful smell wafting up from her offering, and my stomach made the decision to put my doubt and hostility on hold long enough to eat. "This looks fantastic."

"I knew you'd like it. I had to break all your traffic rules to get over here before you ate something else." She presented me with a plastic fork and urged me to sit on the warm hood of her car.

As the first savory bite woke up all my taste buds, it occurred to me I'd never told her exactly where I was working. That meant she was somehow following me too, which was almost as unnerving as having the IRS watching my every move. "How'd you know where to find me?"

"Never underestimate my ingenuity when it comes to tracking you down." She leaned on the fender next to me, leaving enough space between us to squelch the lesbian fantasies of our volunteers. "I called Pepe from the restaurant and got him to call Gisela. She gave you up."

Plausible, but it was still unsettling, especially since it was a team effort between Mari and Pepe.

"Look, I'm sorry about last night…that business with Delores. There was something weird about the whole thing, like it was business, not personal."

I found that comforting, not weird.

"I tried to talk to her about the files she had taken, and she finally said she was sorry for stealing my client. She wanted to make it all up to me by introducing me to one of her clients. I told her forget it. I don't want to be friends, associates…nothing. If I never see her again, it'll be too soon."

It was Delores! She was the other angle Diaz was working, and I was willing to bet the farm she was the IRS's source for this whole thing too. Diaz said she'd been investigating Mari for nearly a year, which was right around the time Delores got dumped. Vindictive harpy!

I was ready to spill my guts when that bit about five years in prison popped back into my head. Instead, I tried to make reassuring small talk, anything that kept us off the subject of her business dealings. "It's good to get a clean break. You don't need to be surrounding yourself with people who bring you down." Or set you up to get arrested…like I was doing.

"All this time I've tried to put that Delores mess behind me, and the whole time I was wishing I could smooth things over so I'd never have to worry about who showed up at what party or what they were saying behind my back. Now I realize I don't care about any of it. Let people gossip if that's what they want. I have a wonderful family and enough true friends to fill my life." She leaned sideways and nudged my shoulder. "And I have you."

I shoved a forkful of rice into my mouth so I wouldn't have to answer, but since common courtesy called for some kind of response, I nudged her back.

"I've made some stupid mistakes over the past couple of years, but I'm ready to get my life back on track. I was lying there in bed last night and started thinking about Saraphine. Remember her?"

I couldn't eat fast enough to avoid talking altogether. "The woman in Little Haiti?"

"Yeah, remember how I said your foundation needed somebody to help people manage their money so they could be independent? I could do that. Not for all of them personally, but what if I organized a group of advisors from other investment companies to help out. Everyone gives a little, so no one has to give a lot."

"That's basically the same sort of thing I do, except I get them to show up here." It would be supremely ironic to be having this conversation with someone who turned out to be a lying swindler. It just couldn't be true.

"Pepe taught all of us growing up that we can't be just takers. We have to give back too, each one of us. He made us save part of our allowance to give to someone who needed it more, and told us to always try to be the kind of people we wanted as friends and neighbors."

So if Pepe was behind all this, how did he reconcile teaching children to be kind, and then turn around and steal from his clients? None of this was making sense.

"I lost sight of all that over the last few years. Delores and I used to joke about which one of us would be the first to make ten million dollars. Could anything be more trivial than that?" She sounded genuinely shameful.

Not that I could relate. "At the rate I'm going, I probably won't even crack my first million till I'm fifty."

"But you're happy. I know you have it pretty hard with your finances, but you don't let them rule your whole life. While I'm making ridiculous amounts of money moving paper around, you're doing something that matters. You're so good for me, Daphne. I want to get back to being the kind of person I should be…the kind of person I was raised to be."

There was so much melancholy in her voice I thought for a second she might actually be trying to confess. She'd already admitted the littering arrest was because she'd lost her cool and behaved rashly. These financial hijinks might be just another piece of it, something she'd pulled together to make a lot of money fast so she could rub it in Delores's face. What if she'd never intended to keep the money? Maybe her plan all along was to put it all back with interest once she bested Delores.

And maybe Fidel Castro could throw out the first pitch at a Marlins game.

I was convinced Pepe was behind this scam and keeping Mari totally in the dark. As much as I liked him, I'd been bothered by his overture to Gisela about investing the foundation's money. It was the act of a desperate man, someone who needed to raise money fast, maybe to pay dividends before someone got suspicious. That would also explain why he had taken Michael on as a client after initially snubbing him. Mari had seemed genuinely surprised by that.

The more I thought about it, the more sense it made that she couldn't be personally involved in any of this. This was all Pepe's doing, and he was dragging her down with him.

"Something wrong?"

I suddenly realized I'd stopped eating. "No…not a thing." Just like that, I'd figured everything out to a point where it all made sense.

"Hey, is that Nick Johnson?" she asked.

The policeman was walking toward us.

"You know Nick?"

"I'll say. He arrested me." Which made it bizarre when she greeted him with a hug and a slap on the back. "Nick's old partner was Delores's kid brother."

"And the biggest asshole on the force," Nick boomed. "How the hell are you, Mari?"

"Great, and staying out of trouble, thanks to my new girlfriend."

Nick looked at me and nodded his approval. "Good deal. You've come up in the world."

"I'll say. We were just talking about the devil herself a couple of minutes ago." Mari draped her arm around my neck and gave me a jostle. "If Delores is on one end of the decency spectrum, Daphne's on the other."

I loved Mari again. This was all a mistake. There was no way she was guilty of the things Agent Diaz said she'd done.

"She'll keep you in line, all right," he said. "She was out here earlier giving the feds what for."

Saint Peter's Polyps! Why did he have to go and say that?

"The feds?" Mari's cheery look faded for an instant. "What was that about?"

"Just part of their drug patrol. They always stop by and ask if we've seen anything in the neighborhood." I'd have to find a way to thank Bo for that cover story. In the meantime, a change of subject would be nice. "You guys need a hand with the roof? Mari's an old pro."

"She's not kidding," Mari answered, back to her jovial self. To my undying relief.

They chatted a couple more minutes and Nick headed back to the house.

Mari took my empty tray and dropped it in a plastic bag. "I'll dispose of this properly. Don't want any more trouble with the litter police. How about dinner tonight? There's a new Peruvian restaurant in the Design District."

I'd never be able to keep my secret, especially now that I'd figured out it was all a mistake. I wanted to blurt out everything and tell her to get as far away from Pepe as she could.

"I'm starting to feel a little sick, like I'm coming down with something." It couldn't be the stomach flu, not after I'd scarfed down a pound of Cuban rice. "Achy all over…probably just a bug."

"You should go home and take it easy."

"Yeah, I think so too. Can I get a rain check on dinner?"

"Rain check, nothing. I'll pick something up and bring it over about six."

Fabulous. At this rate I'd be locked up by midnight.

CHAPTER NINETEEN

Edith and Mordy's sliding glass door banged open the second the sun went down. Whatever they were arguing about, I hoped it wasn't Cubans, because Mari was stretched out on the chaise lounge beside me texting with Chacho about Talia's new boyfriend. I was pretending to nurse a headache, but a fight right now between Edith and Mordy could trigger a real one.

That the Osterhoffs were now a part of this investment scheme was surreal. If Pepe could use my neighbors that way, all my friends and co-workers were vulnerable. It was some comfort, however, to imagine ways I could entice him to drag Emily into his scheme as well.

"You should come out here, sweetie. It's nice and warm." Edith's voice had never sounded so sweet. Either her new anti-psychotic medication was working, or she'd finally offed Mordy and was talking to his bullet-ridden body. "Daphne, are you over there?"

"Yeah, I'm sitting here with Mari."

"That was Mari! I didn't even recognize her."

I lowered my voice so Edith couldn't hear. "They look through the peephole every time the elevator dings."

"You two should come over for some wine," Mordy called from behind the divider.

"Thanks, but I'm not feeling so hot. We're just going to hang out and take it easy." I whispered again, "They only drink Manischewitz. It's awful."

Mari smiled, flashing her adorable dimple. She had to be innocent. This person beside me—a woman who only today had talked about giving back to her community—wouldn't do what Agent Diaz said she'd done.

Not only that, I was having trouble believing the man who had taught her to be a good person would run a multimillion-dollar scam on his clients. But there weren't any other explanations, and Pepe had done some things lately that painted him as desperate for an influx of cash.

Poor Mari had no idea her world was about to come crashing down. It would break her heart to find out what Pepe had done. Their whole family would come apart. Hell, the whole city of Miami would be upended with a scandal like this one taking down one of the pillars of the Cuban community. People like Mordy would go on and on about how corrupt the Cubans were.

People like Mordy…

Only a few short weeks ago, I'd sat right out here on this very porch and taken his side in an argument with Edith over how the Cubans did business. I'd painted the whole lot of them as a network of patronage and nepotism, and railed at how they'd inflicted their culture and language on "real" Americans.

Mari was a real American and so was Pepe, at least in the values he'd taught his family. For that, I hoped the feds would show leniency.

The bigger question for me was if Mari would show understanding once she found out I'd helped set her up. I was no better than Delores, but they hadn't exactly given me a choice. Five years in prison for obstruction of justice was a formidable threat, though probably not as much as that conspiracy charge would have brought.

Wait a minute…

The conspiracy charge was no good. They knew that. The obstruction of justice was only if I tipped Mari off that they were closing in. That didn't mean they could force me to serve her up on a silver platter. It wasn't like I was breaking any laws by refusing to cooperate with their little sting at the Chamber meeting. I could just call in sick tomorrow and tell Agent Diaz she'd have to do it without me. Maybe by the time she figured out a new avenue into the investment fund, Pepe might have a change of heart and move all the money back around to where it was supposed to be.

Mari suddenly laughed. "Chacho's a riot. I asked what he wanted for his birthday and he said *cerveza* with a smiley face."

"He wants you to buy him beer?"

"Yeah, but he's only nineteen. Pepe would stuff me in a cardboard box and send me back to Cuba."

That didn't mesh at all with the kind of man who would bilk his investors. Everything I knew about Pepe—and Mari as well— ought to have both of them vying for sainthood.

"Mari, what's the worst thing you ever did?"

"You mean besides getting arrested for dumping trash behind Delores's car? I sneaked out once in high school and met my friends on South Beach. We were trying to get into a club with fake IDs and all of a sudden, Pepe's car stopped right there in front of us. He got out and opened the back door. That's all. He just stood there without saying a word. Needless to say, I got in, and I never tried it again."

"How did he even know?"

"The man has eyes and ears everywhere. He's like the unofficial godfather. People call him all the time about stuff so he'll use his influence to get others to do the right thing. He's always taken it seriously that he's considered one of the leaders in the Cuban community. I remember even as a kid him saying everything any of us did reflected on all of us."

She wasn't talking directly to me, but I heard her message just the same. I was guilty of blaming a whole ethnic community—the whole city even—when just a handful of people ran afoul of whatever I thought the proper standard ought to be. All the while, I never gave credit to the folks who stood up for their communities and families, who gave back the way Pepe and his family had, and who gave this place its character and verve.

Now that I understood, it was impossible to believe someone like Pepe would do what the IRS said he'd done. I just hoped he had eyes and ears all over this.

"Give this to Daphne," Mordy said to Edith. Then he yelled, "I'm sending over two glasses of wine."

I made a gagging gesture to Mari, who was already on her feet to take the glass Edith was handing around the divide.

"Oh! Wha—" Edith stammered. "No wonder I didn't recognize you. I could have sworn the woman I saw going into Daphne's had short hair."

Christ on a Crepe! Only one tall Hispanic with short hair would have let herself inside my apartment—Agent Diaz. She probably had it bugged and was listening to every word we said.

Mari didn't seem alarmed by the gaffe, but when she came back with the wine, she was definitely perplexed. "What was she talking about?" she whispered. "Short hair?"

"Who knows? She's on a new medication but I thought she was better."

It was beyond creepy to know Agent Diaz and her surfer-dude friend were spying on me. It was infuriating. If the three-hundred-feet rule was right, that meant they were...

Sure enough, their black SUV was parked directly below. What I wouldn't give to pee like a boy.

***

"You feeling any better?" Mari had practically hovered over me all evening, constantly refreshing my cold drink and bringing me pillows. Each time was punctuated with a kiss on my cheek or the top of my head.

I felt guilty for the charade, but damn, was it ever nice to get this kind of pampering. It wouldn't matter to me if Mari were an ax murderer. I was in love with her and there was no way I'd give her over to the feds. If Florida weren't such an oppressive state, I'd insist we march down to the courthouse and get married so we could assert spousal privilege to keep them from forcing me to work with them against her.

"My head still hurts a little."

Being spoiled by Mari this way made me want to lead her into the bedroom to see what else she could do to give me comfort. Still, I had to consider the possibility that Diaz had planted some sort of listening device in my apartment, so bedroom noises were out of the question. Blondie would have to get his Thrill of a Lifetime from someone else.

"Is everything else all right?"

"Of course." Except I truly hated myself. I hated the IRS even more. "Why wouldn't it be?"

"You just seem out of sorts." She touched a finger to my forehead. "And this little spot has been wrinkled all day like you're worried about something. It could be my imagination but it gets worse when you're quiet. Call me crazy, but that tells me you're thinking about things that bother you."

"I guess I've got a lot on my mind." If Diaz was listening, I hope she enjoyed the rest of this. "I've been thinking a lot about you over the last couple of days."

"That can't be too good if it makes you frown."

"It's all good, Mari. I'm just overwhelmed by how much I've grown since I've known you. I don't mean just the cultural stuff, like the fact I can now appreciate a good *arroz con pollo* and doing sixty-five in the emergency lane."

She chuckled and fell against me on the couch.

"You've always given me credit for the kind of work I do at the foundation, but I never took that job to help people. Sure, I say all those things when I go out and meet with businesses, but not because I'm a good person. I do it because it's my job. I love that you took it upon yourself to help Saraphine. That was a real inspiration, and it's always going to stay with me." No matter what else was true. "It makes me want to do good things too, and if there's a reason we're all here on this earth, that's it."

"Wow. That's a lot to live up to."

"You've already lived up to it, Mari. I love you for that." It was my turn to do the kissing, and I left my lips against her temple so we wouldn't be tempted to get carried away.

"I love you too. Who would have guessed I'd fall for my jailer?"

"Or I for a woman who grated on me the moment she stuck her finger up to shush me because she was jabbering in Spanish on her cell phone."

Mari laughed. "I remember that. Mima had gone into the hospital after her stroke and I was too ashamed to tell anybody in my family why I couldn't be there."

"Aw, now you're making me feel bad. I thought you were just being annoying."

"I was being annoying. But I had a pretty good reason."

I'd seen for myself the devotion of everyone in the family to Mima, so I knew what a big deal it was for Mari to miss being at her side at such an important time. It made me furious at Delores to think about all she'd put Mari through. There was no taking back any of the evil I'd inflicted on Mari at the jobsite, but I wasn't going to be part of doing it again. Starting right now, I was firmly on her side, regardless of what she'd done.

That meant taking sides against Agent Diaz and the IRS. If I could find a way to upend her investigation of Mari, I would. At the very least, I wouldn't be their stooge.

CHAPTER TWENTY

"...that's right, I'll have T-shirts and hats for everyone. So I'll see your crew on Saturday at seven thirty. Looking forward to it, Jerry."

Gisela loves it when I land big-name volunteer crews like Bacardi. They'll send a PR team with photographers, and then we'll get copies to use in our brochures and website. They like it. We like it. We'll talk it up this afternoon at the Chamber of Commerce cocktail party, not only to give them recognition, but to lure more businesses to our cause. Everyone wants to be in good company.

I'd come to work this morning with the blind hope Gisela would send me out on some sort of special assignment today, like schmoozing someone who needed a tax deduction before year's end. But no, few things are more important to the foundation than hobnobbing with our board members and the rest of the business community at the Chamber's social events.

My other blind hope—that something would come up for Mari—was dashed as well, since she'd texted me earlier to say she planned to be there around five. I hadn't seen her since Saturday night, when I talked her into going home so I could rest and sleep late to recover from my feigned headache. Then at my urging, she spent Sunday with her family, though we texted and talked on the phone a dozen times.

Maybe Mari would grasp right off the bat at the cocktail party that Diaz was a cop. I'd gotten that vibe about her the instant she stepped into the elevator—the strong hands, the serious slacks and blazer, and the stern look that was all business. If Mari got the vibe too, she and Pepe might realize the authorities were on to them. No way would they talk to her. And they'd hurry to dissolve the shell company, close my account and the one belonging to Edith and Mordy, put their clients' money in the right accounts and cover their tracks. No harm, no foul.

"Hey, Daphne." It was Rosa, the IT specialist. "You mind if I check something on your PC real quick?"

"Help yourself." I watched over her shoulder as she called up one of my system files and typed in a script. "I thought everything was networked."

"It is, but your machine's one of the old ones. It'll slow down unless I free up some of these processes." After a few more keystrokes, she took me back to my home screen. "By the way, have you had any more trouble with your phone?"

"No, it's okay now." I'd noticed all the things she'd told me about, how it lit up after every text or call while Diaz—actually, it was probably Henry, the surfer-dude technician—downloaded the e-mails, voice mails and texts. It also drained my battery, so I had to leave it plugged in nearly all the time I wasn't using it. "You know what, Rosa…"

I'd been thinking about what Henry said about background noise screwing up his recordings. I was pretty sure there were other ways to disrupt their plans, but I was too scared to research them on the Internet because either they were monitoring my web use, or they could reconstruct it later after they led me off in handcuffs for obstructing their version of justice.

"You were right. Someone has been hacking into my cell phone."

"I knew it!" She positively beamed, which I found disturbing in light of what I'd just told her. Techie types live in a world of their own.

"Is there any way I can stop it?"

"Oh." An earnest expression replaced her smile instantly. "Sure, call your provider and tell them someone's accessing your phone without authorization. They'll help you block them."

"And what if…it's official…and authorized?"

That certainly got her undivided attention.

"I haven't done anything wrong, Rosa. It's just that the authorities are using me to get to somebody else. I don't want to be in the middle of it." I looked back and forth between her and my phone hoping she'd take the hint. "I don't want to do anything illegal, but they're hanging one of my friends out to dry and I don't want to help. You can understand that, can't you?"

"Absolutely." She took my phone and played with the settings. "I just disabled your GPS and Bluetooth, but I don't think that's going to help for long because they probably have access to your settings. They'll just turn them back on."

"You're saying I can't stop them?"

She shrugged and tipped her head to one side. "Probably not, but you might be able to bother them a little. Voice files are all digitized these days, so they have to be decrypted. You can screw that up with a lot of background noise, but the problem with that is the person you're trying to talk to is going to have trouble understanding you too."

If I couldn't get through to warn Mari about what they were doing, at least I could try to make it harder for them to record what she said.

"Rosa, do you happen to know anything about wireless transmitters?"

"A little bit. What do you need?"

I shut the door, figuring a sensitive topic like this called for a little more privacy, especially since it probably amounted to obstruction of justice. I hadn't forgotten Diaz's threat of five years in prison.

"Let's say—in theory, that is—someone was wearing a wire in order to get a conversation on tape. All hypothetical."

"Of course." Except her twinkling eyes suggested she knew it wasn't hypothetical at all and wasn't the least bit put off by the possibility she was helping me commit a felony. By their nature, IT professionals rank a technical challenge above all else.

"Could someone potentially…do something that might… potentially disrupt that?"

"Wireless signals have been known to be unstable. In the first place, there's usually a limit to how far they can transmit."

"Right, like three hundred feet."

"Or even up to five hundred, but only in ideal conditions. If you've got something interfering with that signal, all bets are off."

"What kinds of things could cause interference like that?"

"Again, there's background noise. Other electronics could degrade the signal, especially cordless devices, like cell phones, Bluetooth headsets, two-way radios…that kind of stuff."

I could manage a cell phone and headset. "But I'd have to be talking on the phone, right?"

"Technically yes, but you could also be downloading stuff. Streaming video uses lots of bandwidth, and that could mess up anything else that was wireless. Hold on." She busied herself with installing an app on my phone. "Okay, here you go, one of my favorites. It's a website that streams twenty-four-seven—the 1998 Eastern Conference Finals, over and over. The Washington Caps beat the Buffalo Sabres in overtime, and I'm telling you, it was one of the greatest hockey games of all time."

A hockey game. I was going to bring down the IRS with a hockey game. "So I just…"

"Tap that app and drop it in your pocket. Joe Juneau and Olaf Kolzig will take it from there."

I'd have to take her word for it. "You think that might be enough?"

"Hard to say, but I think it's your best shot."

If Joe and Olaf let me down, at least I could tell Mari I tried. Let's hope I don't have to tap out that message on the bars of my prison cell.

***

Diaz's familiar four-wheel-drive ride was on the first level of the garage at the James L. Knight Center, which meant she and Henry were already somewhere setting up their sound equipment. She'd sent a text asking me to meet her before the event. Getting there before Mari helped her control the location, she said.

They weren't going to get as much of my cooperation as they hoped for. Even if I'd wanted to help, Gisela had other plans. She grabbed me after lunch to go over the list of names we needed to contact at this party. That meant I couldn't stand around all night waiting for Mari to work her way across the room to me. We had only a very short window to pull this off, and if Mari arrived thirty minutes late as usual, Diaz was on her own.

Except now that I had Joe and Olaf in my pocket, I didn't actually want to risk leaving Mari to deal with Diaz alone. Disrupting the recording was the critical piece to this meeting tonight, especially if Mari should happen to go into detail about the Iberican Fund.

I hadn't realized the cocktail party was slated for the Riverwalk, an outside terrace overlooking the Miami River and Brickell skyline. We'd have noise from the drawbridge and boat traffic, and even the hum of Interstate 395, which was only two blocks away. Henry wouldn't like that at all but I sure did.

Up until my chat with Rosa this morning, I'd been dreading this moment. Now I was eager for it to come so I could enjoy watching Diaz's frustration. With a last-minute stop in the ladies' room, I checked to make sure everything was working. I'd gone with my usual, a charcoal pantsuit with a paisley silk scarf, a look perfectly befitting the professional demeanor of someone soliciting corporate donations. Good thing I wasn't into cocktail dresses because they weren't suited to hiding gadgets. The pockets of my jacket were deep enough to conceal my cell phone, which was fully charged and ready to load the hockey game with a single touch. On the other side was my iPod, which I'd added for good measure.

The biggest problem was the Bluetooth earpiece. I didn't want it to be conspicuous, and there weren't many ways to hide it with hair as short as mine. I kept turning my head this way and—

"Daphne, you moronic imbecile."

I didn't have to listen to the stupid game. The earpiece was only for interference, and would be just as effective clipped to my knickers, as long as it was turned on.

The first thing I saw when I reached the terrace outside—to my utter delight—was a salsa band warming up. Even the Culture Gods of Miami were on my side tonight. We'd have to shout at one another to be heard over all that brass, which likely meant Diaz and Blondie would go home empty-handed.

I picked up a glass of white wine from the cash bar and perused the scene. Small cliques of people were gathered throughout the terrace but Diaz was nowhere in sight. The only woman standing alone was yet another one of those typical Latina model types—six feet tall in her three-inch pickle stabbers, a little black dress that put every curve on display and the sort of dangling diamond earrings you'd expect to see only on an heiress.

"Daphne?"

Great Versace's Ghost! It was Diaz in drag.

"Thanks for getting here early."

I was still too stunned to speak. She looked spectacular. Her hair was stylishly spiked and her eyes heavily lined and shadowed for a glamorous effect. As if it wasn't enough to hope Mari wouldn't incriminate herself, I now had to worry about these two running off to Bimini together.

"Here's my card. Elena Franco-Diaz. I recently sold my significant stake in Hart Paper Products, and moved to Miami from Virginia to be closer to my family in Puerto Rico."

I couldn't wait to burst her balloon. "Just so you know, Mari does a lot of research on her clients. She may not find out who you are, but she'll find out who you aren't."

"It's all covered. You'd be surprised how many of us work at Hart Paper Products."

In other words, they were all professional liars. Made me wonder how much of what she told me was true.

The terrace had begun to fill with new arrivals and we stepped away from the bar for more privacy.

"Daphne, I know this has been difficult. None of us like to believe bad things about our friends and loved ones, but the evidence we've gathered against Maribel and her uncle is rock solid. Using their clients' money to reap windfall profits for themselves is both illegal and unethical. And hiding that money in offshore accounts means they have to deal with me."

I had my own ideas about what was unethical. "By the way, I found your little bug on the back of my picture frame. I'm assuming that was included in your warrant."

She had the grace to look mildly embarrassed.

"My neighbor saw you through the peephole, so don't congratulate yourself too much on how good you all are at your jobs."

I spotted Gisela at the top of the stairs and waved.

"That's my boss. She's given me a long list of people to talk to at this event, so I'm not going to be able to stand here all night and serve as your bait." She didn't have to know I'd fall all over myself getting back to her side if I saw her moving in on Mari.

"That's fine. I'll watch for Maribel, and when I see her come in, I'll find you before she does."

As she walked away, I could still see her talking, which probably meant a sound check with Henry. I hadn't noticed an earpiece, so I wasn't too surprised when she pressed her heavy bracelet against her ear as she casually smoothed her hair. I was willing to bet the microphone was embedded in her necklace.

It was all I could do not to watch the door for Mari as I worked the room. As the party wore on, I grew hopeful she'd changed her mind about coming. I'd just wrapped up a chat with the woman in charge of community relations at Norwegian Cruise Lines when Diaz appeared suddenly at my side.

"She's here, Daphne. Remember, I'm new to Miami and came to the party to network with the business community." She threw her head back and laughed. "...and I decided I'd stick to the slow lane until I learned all the local traffic rules."

"Good idea," I said meekly, feeling Mari sidle up behind me.

"Hi, there." With one hand pressed into the small of my back, Mari extended the other to the agent. "I'm a friend of Daphne's, Mari Tirado."

As her hand lingered against my waist, I almost felt as if she was marking me as hers for the benefit of Diaz. I rather liked this possessive streak.

"Elena Franco," she answered. "I was just telling Daphne I haven't lived here long enough to figure out the driving rules."

Mari wore a bronze-colored sequined cocktail dress, its three-quarter sleeves slit from the shoulder to the elbow. I was one very lucky woman...as long as she stayed out of jail.

"The first few months are dangerous," Mari said. "If you live long enough, you'll catch on. Daphne did."

"Kill or be killed," I added sardonically. The glow from my pocket confirmed my phone was now streaming the hockey game, and I clicked the power button on my Bluetooth earpiece. "What else do I need to know about Miami?"

We bantered with senseless small talk until the inevitable swapping of business cards.

"Oh, you're an investment advisor. Just what I need."

Mari didn't exactly pounce on her, but she was clearly interested. "If I can help with anything..."

"Maybe you can. I sold my stake in a paper company last year and got out of the business. Right now that cash is sitting in a steady growth fund at Morgan Stanley, but I think it could be doing more. And now that I'm here in Miami, I want to work with someone local."

Diaz had definitely done her research on Mari, enough to know she'd love to steal a client from Delores's firm. Or more likely, Delores had suggested it.

"I'd be happy to talk with you. We've got several growth funds that are doing well and a few aggressive instruments too, if you don't mind the risk." The aggressive instrument was the Iberican Fund.

"I'm willing to take on some serious risk for the right return."

"Daphne, I've been looking for you." Gisela appeared behind me smiling and said a brief hello to Mari and Diaz. "I want you to come over and meet Fernando Rojas. He's our new HR contact with the county."

The band kicking off its set mitigated the horror of being dragged away from Mari by my boss. I'd never been so happy to hear salsa music.

Throughout my conversation with Rojas, I kept Mari in my line of sight. She was smiling and laughing, which I took as a good sign, since she wouldn't joke around about investments. It was obvious they had to talk loudly to be heard over the music.

Rojas politely excused himself, prompting Gisela to ask me for an update on the contacts I'd made so far. I'd just finished my rundown when she waved enthusiastically at someone behind me.

"It's Marco Padilla. Did I tell you he brought someone else to our board? Rob Jacobs, the CEO at Jacobs Building Supply. He's a perfect fit for the foundation."

"So, Gisela…that business about Mr. Padilla wanting to invest the foundation's funds. That blew over, right?"

"Oh, I meant to tell you about that. Our investment manager looked over the fund and thought it would be a good idea after all to move some of our assets into it. It truly was too good an opportunity to pass up. In fact, Jorge cashed in one of our mutual funds and gave it to Marco to invest too."

I almost spewed white wine in her face. Not only was the foundation going down the tubes, my boss and her husband were right behind it. When this blew up, their photos would appear in the *Miami Herald* among the prominent local victims, and I'd waltz away scot-free because I didn't have any money of my own to lose.

Now more miserable than ever, I worked my way across the room to see the last contact on my list, keeping an eye on Mari. Pepe was closing in on her and Diaz. The three of them chatted and laughed like old friends the entire time I was talking up Bacardi's volunteer day with their VP for public relations in front of the business writer for the *Herald*. By the time I worked myself free Diaz was gone.

"That was certainly worth getting dressed up for," Mari said as she slid an arm around my waist. "I'm about to steal nine million dollars out from under Morgan Stanley's nose. That calls for a daiquiri."

"You told her about the Iberican Fund?"

"We didn't get a chance to talk specifics. We could hardly hear each other, but then Pepe came over and I let him know she was a major prospect. He asked her to dinner on the yacht tomorrow night. You'll come, won't you?"

"Oh, I wouldn't miss it."

CHAPTER TWENTY-ONE

From my balcony, I could make out the lights of small boats passing underneath the MacArthur Causeway into the shallow waters along the Venetian Islands. The night was perfect for sailing unless, like me, you'd been praying for gale force winds and torrential rains. Unfortunately, it was too late in hurricane season for that kind of mayhem.

I'd come home early so I'd have plenty of time to obsess over what to wear. The casual boat pants I'd bought for last time were pretty much the only game in town, but they didn't have pockets to hide the electronics store I needed to disrupt Diaz's wireless signal. I first settled on a dark brown rayon shirt with breast pockets and sleeves I could roll up and tie off.

By the time I got everything tucked away, I felt like a shoplifter with aluminum breast implants. My Bluetooth earpiece hung from the drawstring inside my pants, my iPod was rolled up inside my left sleeve, and my cell phone occupied one of my breast pockets. The other pocket held a battery-operated ultrasonic emitter I kept under my kitchen sink to repel cockroaches. It didn't actually work on the bugs, but I thought it might give Henry an earful.

The problem was I looked ridiculous, which led me to my current ensemble—a thinner top with a lightweight denim jacket, stylishly faded yet not too ragged for the occasion. The best thing about the jacket was its four pockets, each perfect for concealing a potential signal buster.

The door suddenly slid open over at Edith and Mordy's.

"...and I'll take them all the way to the Supreme Court if I have to. It's a violation of my First Amendment rights to freedom of religion." Mordy was angrier than I'd ever heard him, and that said a lot. "Just because some dimwit catches her curtains on fire, they want to ban candles in the whole building. Not all of us are idiots."

I tiptoed toward my door so they wouldn't know I was outside.

"This memo says they recommend flameless candles that operate on a battery," Edith said. "We can't do that either."

"Don't they know the Sabbath means we can't turn those little suckers off and on? That's the problem with this place. Everybody thinks we all should do things the same way. They don't respect that people have their own customs."

I wondered if Mordy had any idea he'd come full circle on his own beliefs, or that he'd brought me with him. I had come to appreciate Miami's diversity in ways I never could have imagined a few short months ago. Where else could I work alongside an African-American foreman, share *Seudah Shlishit* with Jews on the Sabbath, and fall in love with a woman whose family was exiled from Cuba?

The truth is I'm quite crazy about this city now, quirks and all.

The moment I stepped inside and latched the door, my cell phone rang. Diaz.

"Glad I caught you, Daphne. Wanted to let you know how much we appreciate your help last night. It couldn't have worked out better because it gave us exactly what we wanted—dinner on the yacht." By her chummy tone, one would have thought we were best friends. "Now that it's all set up, you can feel free to skip this little boat ride tonight. You might not want to be anywhere around when this goes down."

"I told Mari I'd be there. Won't she get suspicious if I cancel at the last minute?" As if I would.

"I doubt it. These money types all have one thing in common. When you wave dollar signs in front of them, they don't see much of anything else."

"I see what you mean." You contemptible bitch. I didn't press it out of fear she might order me to stay clear, but I had no intention of missing dinner, especially since it meant I could watch Diaz pull her hair out as she tried to get her electronics to work.

With our days getting shorter, it was dark at a quarter past six. I parked next to Mari's Porsche in the garage at Bayside and strolled leisurely out to the marina. Diaz was already aboard and seemed genuinely stunned to see me.

Mari sprang from the sundeck, all smiles in brown tights and a pale orange linen tunic. "I was starting to think you weren't coming."

"And miss Benito's pork tenderloin? Not a chance."

The waiter emerged from the galley in his white jacket. "One mojito?"

"Thanks, Eddie. No one makes a mojito like you."

"You just made his day," Mari whispered as she guided me up the steep staircase.

"His mojito will make mine."

Lucia, dressed in a long floral jumpsuit and sandals, stood to greet me when we reached the upper level. "So glad you could join us again, Daphne."

"The thrill is mine, Lucia. It's such a lovely night, and I couldn't be in better company." I smiled formally at Diaz. "Nice to see you again, Elena. You're in for a wonderful treat tonight. The Padillas are such gracious hosts."

She should be ashamed of herself for taking advantage of their hospitality to set them up.

As we pulled out of the marina, I caught sight of Henry creeping along in the SUV on the overpass from the port. By the time we passed under the MacArthur Causeway, he had circled around to Watson Island, only a couple hundred feet away.

I nudged Mari and gestured toward my building. "I wonder if Mordy and Edith are out on their balcony. We should ride by there and wave."

"Are those the ones with the cat who jumped off the balcony? Mari told us all about that," Lucia asked.

"That was so amazing," Mari said. "Call them, Daphne. Tell them to come outside." She ducked below to tell the captain to swing close to the shore.

Diaz was practically grinding her teeth as she joined us in waving up at my neighbors on their balcony, all the while looking over her shoulder for Henry. When she ran a hand through her hair, I noticed the same bracelet she had worn the night before. "Where is this Star Island I've heard so much about? Is that the one with the celebrity mansions?"

"We'll go there now," Pepe said, nodding toward Mari to signal the captain.

"So we're turning around, I guess. It must be back near… what's that? The MacArthur? I haven't learned all my bridges yet."

Pepe named all the landmarks as we floated past, and I soon spotted Henry again driving parallel to us on the Venetian Causeway.

Diaz settled back with her glass of wine, which she'd barely touched. "So tell me about Padilla Financial. Have either of you had a chance to think about what type of investments you'd recommend for someone like me?"

I immediately tapped the hockey icon on my phone, which I'd been holding ever since my call to Edith. As I tucked it back into my pocket, I also turned on my bug emitter.

Mari took the lead in answering, leaning forward and gesturing with her hands as she spoke. "We've developed an international investment instrument called the Iberican Fund. Its main feature is—"

"Oh, my gosh! I just saw a dolphin." I scooted to the edge of the sundeck, only a couple of feet from Diaz. "At least I think it was a dolphin. Hard to tell at night. It might have been a shark."

"Probably a dolphin," Lucia said, peering over the side. "They love to run alongside the boat. They're so cute."

"Aren't they?" While everyone was looking into the water, I managed to activate my Bluetooth earpiece and iPod.

Diaz turned back around and leaned toward Mari, as if pushing the microphone necklace into her face. "So, you were saying something about a fund?"

"The Iberican Fund. It's a collection of manufacturing and distribution companies throughout Latin America that we believe are poised to experience exponential growth within the next couple of years, not because they're serving any particular industry, but because they're well managed and on the verge of taking off. We're capitalizing on that growth window by…"

As Mari talked, I began to hum. Not a tune, just a low monotone that I hoped would blend in with the yacht's purring engines. White noise, Henry had called it.

Diaz smoothed her hair for the hundredth time after Mari finished her explanation, and squinted with what I thought was overly dramatic confusion. "I'm not sure I caught all that. Would you mind terribly starting over at the beginning?"

What's the matter, Diaz? Are you finding out you're not as good at your job as you thought?

Pepe took over the presentation, and I realized with alarm his deep, booming voice might have a different effect on the recorder. I hummed louder, not so anyone else could hear, but enough to cause Diaz to frown in my direction.

Eddie suddenly appeared on the steps. "Dinner is prepared."

Lucia clapped her hands. "Wonderful! Let's see what surprise Benito has for us."

Diaz was frustrated. I could see it in her face, and when she grabbed my wrist before I started down the stairs, I expected the worst. "Watch out for dinner. Henry thinks our cook's preoccupied with a hockey game."

That was so perfect I wanted to clap.

Not so perfect were the seating arrangements at dinner. Pepe sat at the head of the table with Lucia on one side and Diaz on the other. Mari sat beside Diaz, while I sat across from Mari, as far from Diaz as I could be. I wasn't sure my electronics could cover that range, and humming was out of the question.

Pepe unknowingly saved the day with his pronouncement. "Lucia forbids talk of business at dinner, so we'll table our discussion of Iberican for now. Will you join us in saying grace?"

While heads were bowed, I managed to turn off my various devices to save power.

As a general rule, I have a lot of respect for people in law enforcement. Sure, there are guys like Delores's brother who get off on being macho jerks, but by and large, cops and other official government investigative types are the good guys. Even IRS agents, whom we all fear because our honest mistakes might turn out to be crimes, are necessary for justice and equality. I admire pretty much anyone who dedicates their life to public service, especially righting wrongs.

But I was having a lot of trouble with Diaz, not only because she was hell-bent on bringing charges against my friends, but also because she had used me to do it.

Mostly I hated that Pepe had put himself and Mari in this position. I was only buying him time. Even if Diaz went home tonight empty-handed, she wouldn't give up on her case. The only way out of this was for him to put everyone's money back so she couldn't make her case.

How many more times could Diaz put them through a drawn-out explanation of the Iberican Fund before they got suspicious? She'd done it twice already and still had nothing but spurts of a fifteen-year-old hockey game. Bless Rosa!

Dinner conversation began with small talk about where everyone was from, as Eddie served something called Camarones Benito, shrimp sautéed with tomatoes and peppers over saffron rice.

Pepe seemed especially interested in Diaz's Puerto Rican heritage. "Elena, do you think of yourself as an American?"

"Of course, but I was born in Washington, DC. My mother thinks of herself as Puerto Rican first, American second. I guess I'm like Mari. I grew up in a Spanish-speaking household, but my only taste of Puerto Rico is what my mother remembers, and what I've seen when I've visited."

"Except I've never visited Cuba," Mari said. "My only taste of Cuba is what I get when I go to Calle Ocho in Little Havana."

"Or from the stories Mima tells," Lucia added.

"And that's all that's left of the real Cuba," Pepe said. "This place, Miami"—he jabbed his finger on the table—"holds the true Cuban heart. But we are no longer Cubans. We are Americans. Cuban-Americans, yes, but Americans. I love this country. I may have been born in Havana, but America is my homeland."

I wondered if Diaz respected what it meant to be a Cuban exile. Thousands of people like Pepe rebuilt their lives here, nearly all of them starting over from the bottom of the heap. It wouldn't surprise me if she took special satisfaction from bringing down people like Pepe and Mari because it brought the whole Cuban community down a notch.

The *Herald* would run the story on the front page, and folks like Mordy would rail against the corrupt Cubans. One week later, all would be forgotten for everyone except Mari, Pepe and their family.

And me. I'd never forget I was the one who set them up.

"Benito makes the most delicious flan," I exclaimed as Eddie cleared the last of our dinner dishes.

Pepe gestured to the sundeck. "Please, let's go back upstairs and enjoy the view of our beautiful city lights. Eddie will serve dessert and *café con leche* there." He pulled out Lucia's chair and then hustled around the table to do the same for Diaz.

As they climbed the steps, I began the ritual of activating my electronics.

"Okay, who keeps calling you?" Mari suddenly asked. "I've seen you check that phone half a dozen times tonight. Should I be worried?"

"You should never be worried." I gave her a quick kiss when no one was looking. "My friend Rosa cleaned up some of the apps on my phone this morning and I'm just making sure it's working right."

It was working just fine, and once we reached the sundeck I practically leaped over Lucia to sit beside Diaz again. We had turned back toward the marina at Bayside, so I figured she'd be desperate for one more chance at getting a full description of Iberican on tape.

Right on cue she asked Pepe, "So where did we leave off? Never mind, I got so wrapped up in that wonderful dinner that I forgot every word you already told me. Why don't you just start over at the beginning?"

"I couldn't agree more," I said. "About dinner, that is. Everything Benito prepares is wonderful. You should have been here last time for the pork tenderloin. It absolutely melted in my mouth. And the flan! It's to die for."

This was called yammering, and every minute of nonsense was another minute she couldn't use to gather evidence. Eddie helped by bringing dessert, which was coconut rice pudding.

I moaned dramatically as I took my first taste. "This is exquisite! He's really outdone himself." I hate rice pudding. Nothing against any of the ingredients, just that a boy in my fourth-grade class told me it was maggots. Once that image got fixed in my head, it was all I could do to eat it without gagging.

After smoothing her hair several times, Diaz suddenly changed seats to sit between the two subjects of her probe. "So tell me about this fund. What sort of return would I be looking at?"

Pepe and Mari alternated pieces of the presentation, describing not only the general structure of the fund, but also specific details about the companies, one of which Diaz had told me didn't actually exist. If her recording device was working, she was now getting everything she needed to make her case against both of them.

"Like all investments, the Iberican Fund isn't without risk," Mari said. "Most of these are fledgling companies, but the funds are heavily managed. If any of the component businesses miss their key performance indicators, we reassess our capital commitment."

"Sounds like you earn your commissions." Diaz raised her bracelet hand to her head again. Only this time she smiled.

Son of a Priest.

"How much do you think I should invest?"

"This is a private fund," Pepe explained. "We've limited the number of investors in order to effectuate the largest returns."

Mari took over. "Our lowest investment increment for the fund is five million, which would allow you to diversify your remaining assets. Even though we believe in Iberican, we believe even more in sound investment practices."

That statement was all the proof I needed that neither Mari nor Pepe were the sleazebags Diaz made them out to be. Even if they'd done what she said, they weren't without a conscience. Had they been truly malevolent, they would have greedily gone for every dime they could get.

I'd lost hope in Diaz having a change of heart. The only chance Mari and Pepe had now was for a judge to see the good in them and grant leniency.

Apparently satisfied their pitch had been successful, Pepe rose and gestured toward the forward steps. "Let's go to the bow, shall we? It's a lovely view coming back into port."

Mari and I were the last ones down, and she stopped me on the sundeck for another kiss. "Thanks for bringing us a new client. I suppose you'll be looking for a referral fee."

A dagger straight to the heart. "I love you, Mari."

I couldn't tell which was more pronounced—her smile or her frown. It clearly was a puzzled look, not because of what I'd said, but the context.

"I love you too."

It was good to hear that, since it might be the last time.

When we reached the bow, I made no effort to position myself near Diaz, since she already had what she needed. It was surprising, then, when she left Pepe's side to stand beside me.

"I didn't realize you were a hockey fan, Daphne."

I experienced what's known as a Full Body Shudder, the kind you have upon learning a loved one was in an accident or that toilet paper is hanging from the back of your pants.

"I guess you forgot we were monitoring your phone."

My hand went immediately to my jacket pocket.

"Don't bother. Henry turned it off already." She sounded more disappointed than smug. "You understand you've committed obstruction, don't you?"

"Señor Padilla." It was Eddie. "Message for you on the bridge."

The bright lights of Bayside Marketplace glowed like a carnival, the starkest contrast imaginable to how I felt inside. I hardly cared that Diaz was threatening me with charges. The only thing that mattered was her case against Mari and Pepe, and the fact I had helped her bring them down.

Pepe returned to the bow and whispered something to Lucia before wrapping his arm around her waist and staring straight ahead. He looked like Washington crossing the Delaware—strong, defiant and resolute.

We arrived at the dock to a virtual parade of men and women in black Windbreakers and caps emblazoned in gold with various initials—FBI, IRS and even MDPD.

"What's going on?" Mari asked.

Pepe gave her a grim smile. "Do as they ask, *nena*, but do not speak. Everything will be all right."

Diaz moved behind Pepe and drew a pair of handcuffs from inside her waistband. "That's bad advice, Padilla. Don't you want your niece to save herself?"

"Save myself from what?"

"Do not speak," he repeated.

Several agents hopped onto the bow as we docked.

"This one," she said, pushing Pepe forward, "and these two," indicating Mari and me. "Keep them all separated."

CHAPTER TWENTY-TWO

I'd been left in a windowless room for over three hours, alone with three metal chairs and a veneer-topped table. At least I figured it had been that long. They had confiscated my wristwatch, purse, phone, iPod, Bluetooth earpiece and ultrasonic emitter. I was at the mercy of cockroaches. No one even cared that I had to pee, nor had they bothered to tell me what would happen next and when. That business about getting one phone call that you see on TV? Pure fiction.

Not that I had a clue who to call. The thought of seeing my calm, upstanding parents react to the news that I was in federal custody was almost worth the whole deal. My best bet was probably to call Edith, who would come down here with her gun

and demand my release. I knew only one lawyer—Emily Jenko—
and she was the last person on earth I wanted to see right now.

Near as I could tell, I was on one of the upper floors of the
Claude Pepper Federal Building downtown. I had no idea where
they'd taken Mari and Pepe but I couldn't imagine they were far
because I could hear Diaz shouting in the hallway from time to
time. Couldn't make out what she was saying, but she sounded
pissed. It would be awfully nice if that meant her devious little
sting had somehow failed. Maybe Henry forgot to push the Save
button.

My bladder was ready to burst when the door finally opened.
It was the man who had escorted Mari from the boat, which
made me think she was nearby.

"Let's go. You're being transferred to a holding cell."

I didn't care if they sent me to Guantanamo as long as they
let me pee first. "I have to go to the ladies' room."

"There's one on the detention floor."

"I can't wait."

He was younger than the other agents, which was probably
why he was given prisoner transfer duty while the others put the
screws to Mari and Pepe. His athletic build and baby face reminded
me of Nick Johnson, the friendly officer who had worked with
Delores's brother.

"Wait here," he said. "I'll have to get someone to escort you."

He left me standing in a long hallway, where the only open
door was more than thirty feet away. All of a sudden, Mari
emerged with her uncle Felix, the attorney, apparently having
been freed from custody. She was too far away for me to read her
expression but a chill ran all the way down my back when she
stopped and stared.

"Bathroom, Daphne." It was Diaz, and she was in a foul mood.

"What's happening?"

"I'm not at liberty to say."

"Does Mari know what I did? Did you tell her?"

Her only answer was a grunt and a mild shove in the direction
of the ladies' room.

Despite my rampant confusion, I was first and foremost
relieved to relieve myself. Once that was taken care of, I turned

my attention back to finding out everything I could about Mari and Pepe.

"What's going to happen to them now?"

"They're being released. You, on the other hand, are the only scalp I have to show for eleven months' work."

"What the fuck?" It felt good to say that. Fuckity fuck.

"She's done. Get her out of my sight."

I was the only one being charged. That had to mean my surreptitious plans had worked. Their recordings were unusable and they had to let Mari and Pepe go. I'd bought them time to clean it all up before the investigators could try again. I, Daphne Maddox, had saved the day.

Being impressed with myself didn't mean I was happy about spending the night in a cell, even though having a bed with a pillow and flimsy blanket was an improvement over metal chairs and a table. A better ending to all of this would have been me walking out with them.

I'd passed a clock on my way down and wasn't surprised to see it was nearly three in the morning. I was tired but there was no way I'd be able to fall asleep after a night like this one.

The next thing I remembered was a light turning on in my cell and the sound of the door sliding open. Felix Padilla was standing with Diaz.

"You're free to go, Ms. Maddox," she said through gritted teeth, handing me an envelope with my personal effects.

Free as in just for the time being? Or free as in she had calmed down and decided not to make this personal?

Not that it mattered. Free to go was free to go, and I wasn't going to stick around long enough for anyone to change their mind. Nor would I gloat to Diaz that she wasn't so good at her job after all, though it was tempting.

I waited until the elevator door closed. "What's going on, Felix?"

His only response was a finger to his lips.

It was still dark outside. A black limousine was parked at the curb and a driver in a suit and tie held the door for us.

"Am I going to be charged?"

"No."

"What about Mari and Pepe?"

"No, this is over for everyone. I know this is confusing for you, Daphne, but you don't need to worry about any of this. There is no record that you were taken into custody and held. It's as if it never happened, and the best thing you can do is treat it that way and not tell anyone—"

"But what about—"

"Nope." His finger went to his lips again. "That's it. I've said all I can."

Elena Diaz had said the same thing—she wasn't at liberty to tell me anything. Apparently, the price of my freedom was ignorance.

The real question was if that price also included Mari. There was no way to sugarcoat the fact I'd deceived her, even though I'd apparently dashed the IRS's plans for making their charges stick. Betrayal is one of those things you don't forget no matter how it turns out in the end.

When we reached my building, Javier met the limo, probably thinking he'd get a big tip from someone important enough to travel in style. His face fell when I got out, but then he gave me a look of approval, like I'd been out all night with the Prince of Monaco or something.

It was just after six a.m., too early even for Edith to catch me slipping in. The *Herald* lay at my doorstep, its headline proclaiming news of a body found stuffed inside a vending machine at a Metro rail station in South Dade. Even if our arrest had stood, it wasn't for certain we'd have made the papers, not in a news town like this one. We had neither bodies to hide nor novel places to stuff them, and financial fraud barely caused a blip on the radar around here, unless you used your ill-gotten gains to shower the local college teams with hookers and cocaine.

The sun was rising over Miami Beach when I entered my apartment. Since my likelihood of going to work today was below zero, I went out onto the balcony to savor the view and my freedom. It was too early to call Gisela, but once I did, I planned to sleep for hours on end.

Before anything else, though…I needed to text Mari to let her know I was sorry.

Moments later, my phone chimed with a reply: *Where r u?*

Home. Sorry wasn't enough. *I love u.*

"I love you too." The sound of her voice behind me nearly sent me flying over the railing.

"Jesus Jumping Rope, Mari! You scared the crap out of me."

"Sorry, I was sleeping in your bed when I got your text." She wore orange drawstring pants with the UM logo and a white ribbed tank top. Her hair was askew and she squinted against the light of day. "I told Felix he had to go back and get you out, and then I came over here to wait."

She loved me!

I threw myself into her arms as dramatically as I could without driving both of us onto the floor.

"I don't care what you did, or what Pepe did, or what anyone said you did. All that matters is what Felix said. It's over. It never happened." As long as Mari still loved me, I didn't need to know anything else.

"And I don't care what you did either, whatever it was."

"They didn't tell you?"

"Nobody told me anything. They kept asking me about the Iberican Fund but you heard Pepe. He said not to talk so I didn't. Then Elena told me if I didn't cooperate, you'd have to take the fall for everyone. That didn't make any sense at all. Felix said not to worry, that he'd get you out."

"She wanted to charge me with obstructing justice. She was trying all night to get you and Pepe to talk about the Iberican Fund so she could tape it, but I kept—"

Mari's jaw had dropped. "You were working with Elena?"

"No!" I closed the door in case Mordy and Edith came out, and led Mari to the couch. For the next twenty minutes, I walked her through the whole ugly mess as I knew it, including the fact that Delores was probably the one who had tipped off the feds, a tidbit that turned Mari so red with anger I thought she might have a stroke.

"*Pinche puta!*"

Whatever she just said sounded utterly venomous and I vowed to learn it. I finished my tale by saying I didn't care if any of it was true or not.

"Of course it wasn't true. You know I'd never do anything like that." Left unsaid was her growing suspicion that maybe Pepe had.

She abruptly rose. "I need to get dressed and go see Pepe. Are you coming?"

We showered separately but otherwise shared the bathroom like an old married couple—an image that was verbally descriptive but not visually desirable, since it conjured mental pictures of Mordy and Edith.

Mari drove so slowly on the way to Coral Gables, I wondered if she was having engine trouble. "Is something wrong with your car?"

"I guess I'm not in that big a hurry to find out what's going on. What if Pepe did those things? What if he was cheating our investors but got Felix to have it dismissed on some sort of technicality?"

I'd had longer to think about that question than Mari, and I knew the answer. "I had to ask myself the same thing over and over about you. That kind of disappointment in someone you love and admire is just off the scale. But even when I thought you were using me in your scheme, the thing that hurt most was thinking you didn't really love me. Once I realized you did, I would have found a way to forgive you, because I never want to lose that."

"You'd have stood by me even if you found out I was scamming my clients?"

"Yeah, but like I said, the disappointment would be pretty hard to deal with. I'd have to know you were genuinely sorry, and I'd expect you to make amends. That's the only way I'd know you were really the person I loved. It's like you told me about that Boston job I didn't take—it's about the future, not the past. If Pepe's done something wrong, what matters now is what he does next."

The grand house in the Gables gave off quite a different atmosphere from the night of Emilio's birthday party. Pepe's big Mercedes was the lone vehicle in the parking circle, the only sign anyone was home.

As we neared the steps, the front door swung open to reveal her beloved uncle, dressed casually in gray slacks, sandals with socks and a white Panama shirt.

"You don't seem surprised to see us," Mari said drily.

"I'm only surprised it took you so long," he answered, smiling with what looked like a combination of mischief and pride. "Good morning, Daphne."

We traded kisses as if getting arrested together was the most normal thing in the world.

Lucia made the moment even more surreal when she appeared in the foyer and did the same. "*Café con leche*," she told the housekeeper, along with a few words I didn't understand.

Nothing rejuvenated like strong Cuban coffee. Two shots of scalded espresso with four sugars and whole milk would have me awake until day after tomorrow.

Pepe led us all through a set of double doors off the living room that had been closed the night of the party. It obviously was his study, and it held a sofa, several leather chairs, bookcases and an enormous carved mahogany desk. We'd just gotten settled when Mima's caretaker rolled her into the room in her wheelchair.

It was sweet how they included Mima in all their important family discussions, as if to assure her that despite her age and declining health, she would always be their matriarch. Mari and I greeted her as the coffee was delivered, and the housekeeper closed both doors on her way out.

Pepe sipped his coffee and cleared his throat. "I should first apologize, especially to you, Daphne, for the events of last evening. In hindsight, we should have anticipated that our actions might trigger an investigation, but we had no inkling they would involve you."

So there was something. I could see Mari stiffen beside me on the couch, as though bracing herself for bad news.

"I was advised by my attorney, who happens to be my younger brother, to tell no one of the events of last evening, but I cannot leave those I love in such darkness. However, it is absolutely essential that what I'm about to tell you never leave this room. Is that understood?"

Mari and I both nodded eagerly. I'd promise anything if it meant someone would finally lift this veil of ignorance.

He leaned back in his leather chair, so far that I feared he would fall over. "Mari, the Iberican Fund is real. Several of our investors—and one of our companies—are not."

"Pepe, that's fraud!" Mari exploded from her seat and stomped across the room.

"*Siéntate*," Mima said firmly.

From the speed with which Mari returned to her seat, I took that to mean something like, "Sit down, you impudent child."

"It's more complicated than that, *nena*. There are things that are not strictly legal, yet must be done. When the Castro regime falls, America must fill the void. Not Russia, not China, not Venezuela. The companies that make up the Iberican Fund are a vital part of America's preparations for democracy in Cuba. We are poised to infuse an almost endless supply of building materials, along with agricultural equipment and mining machinery that will jump-start the Cuban economy and put the Cuban people back to work to rebuild their country. We cannot let America's enemies gain a toehold in that revitalization."

"But why is any of that illegal?"

"The complication is we don't know when Castro will fall. There has always been a plan for Cuba, but America's priorities and resources have shifted over the past decade to other fronts. Five years ago, I was asked by someone from the State Department in Washington to take up those preparations. They put me in touch with their CIA contact, someone inside Cuba who's building support for the transformation. I met with that person in the Caymans, and once I understood Cuba's needs, I set out to meet them—with your help, I should add— by pulling together those companies that form the Iberican Fund."

Mari shook her head. "I still don't see what the problem is, and why we've brought on bogus investors. The embargo applies only to Cuba, not to companies who might want to do business there after the old geezer croaks." She said something to Mima in Spanish that caused her to chuckle.

"The problem, as I said, is not knowing how long it will be before the fund takes off. It will ultimately be wildly successful. Of that, there is no doubt. But our investors want returns now, not, as you say, when the old geezer croaks. So in order to hold their investment, we must pay dividends. That's where our friends from the State Department come in. They invest a few million dollars in our shell company—which we pay out in dividends—in order to keep billions of investment dollars in place."

I could see from her fidgeting hands and feet that Mari wanted to get up and storm around the room again but didn't dare.

"You're telling me all the work I've done for the past three years on this fund has been bogus, that I've been lying to everyone about the financials and performance indicators. None of it ever mattered."

"Mari, before I ever agreed to this, I went to Mima for her blessing. I told her it could blow up in our faces, and might cost us everything if our work was discovered to be a front for a political cause not everyone cares about. She said yes, and she sold this house to Lucia and me so she could be the first to invest because of what it represented—a free Cuba. But she wanted you kept clean, so we agreed to set the investment bar out of your reach."

Commiserating with Mordy about how silly the Cubans were in their hatred of Castro seemed so foreign to me now. Even after fifty years, seeing the dictator fall was still the reason many of those in Miami's exile community got out of bed each day.

"If you wanted me clean, why did you let me sell it? You could have managed the fund on your own."

"I needed your help, because I knew that would guarantee the fund's success. But I also knew you'd never be dishonest with your investors, so I hid the details from you." Pepe smiled softly and looked at his mother. "And there was someone else who wanted you to be a part of this historic effort, and he helped convince Mima to let me bring you in."

I felt as if I'd been dropped into a spy novel, though for the life of me, I couldn't figure out what I had to do with any of this. But the shock and confusion in my head probably paled next to what had to be going on in Mari's.

"Mari, my CIA contact in Cuba is my older brother, Eduardo... your father."

Cue the kettle drums. Even I felt like standing up and waving the Cuban flag.

"He has been working secretly from within the country to advance the causes of freedom and democracy for the Cuban people. It is because of his work that those dreams will someday become reality."

If Mari was thrilled by the revelation, her twitching jaw hadn't gotten the news. She looked as angry as she had when I told her about Delores. "You expect me to believe after all these years that he's one of us? Not one word from him in thirty years, Pepe."

"He has made some bad decisions, and he doesn't expect your forgiveness. But his love for Cuba is genuine, as is his love for you. He's risking his life to make Cuba free. It is very dangerous for him, and would be even more so if he reached out to you. If his efforts are discovered, he will be thrown in prison or possibly worse. Therefore, we must commit ourselves to holding these secrets from all, as Castro has eyes and ears throughout the region, even here in the exile community."

Mima reached out a shaky hand to Mari, and spoke again to her in Spanish. I understood *hijo*—son—and the last words, which she spoke with tears in her eyes. *Te quiero también.* I love you too.

Lucia clasped her hands and blew out a satisfied sigh. "Very well. Mariana has prepared lunch for us all. Shall we?"

Even if Mari didn't fully accept the story of her father, I couldn't help but find it touching and noble. As difficult as it would be for her, I liked knowing that someday—

"Wait a minute." Before we all ran off to digest this startling news along with a few fried plantains, I needed answers too. "Did I have anything at all to do with this, or was the IRS just using me to get to Mari?"

Pepe looked truly baffled. "I believe you were approached because you accompanied us on the dinner cruise with Michael, whose money, by the way, we decided to accept after all when he became insistent. We couldn't afford to raise suspicions."

"Besides," Lucia added, "it pleased Pepe to know his investment allowed the firm to continue its support of things like your Miami Home Foundation, whether he approved of it or not."

"So the part about you guys setting up an account for me in the Caymans that held six million dollars was just…"

Pepe roared with laughter. "I am so sorry, Daphne. It is not true."

Figures. Diaz had lied to get me on board, and she'd undoubtedly added the bit about the Osterhoffs that day at the jobsite because she thought I was getting cold feet. "And you didn't pull any strings to get my mortgage principal reduced and the interest rate lowered."

His smile faded. "That went through?"

Holy Housing Bubble. "Diaz told me it did, but I haven't received official word."

"I would hold off on the official celebration, but it's possible it's true."

"You meddled in her mortgage affairs?" Mari asked, her dismay obvious.

"No, not directly. But I mentioned it to Juan that night we were out on the boat because the subject happened to come up. As you may recall, he's a bank executive, and he deals with these issues daily." He looked sheepishly at Mari and then at me. "Though it might appear unseemly, I assure you he would not have acted illegally."

Hooray! If my sweetheart deal turns out to be real, I get to keep it.

CHAPTER TWENTY-THREE

I took a deep breath and tried to remain calm as Mari blew warm air onto my still-crackling Lady Parts. After weeks of glorious practice, she had finally led me to the Promised Land of Second Orgasms, even though the process meant a momentary separation of body and brain. I'd discovered such disembodiment was necessary for only a few critical seconds while I passed from one ethereal level to another.

The problem we had at first was me getting reconnected when I got to the other side. Once I shut down my body's response in order to get past the tickling sensations, I found it difficult to recover my prior level of arousal. Mari decided that was a good thing because it meant she never had to stop, and sure enough, her torturous teasing eventually led to a follow-up frenzy.

From my current vantage point, which was peering down from a pile of fluffy pillows on my queen-sized bed, it didn't get any better than this. Mari's gorgeous naked self lay vividly exposed, her arms wrapped possessively around my thighs and her lips poised dangerously above that which put the nerves in central nervous system. As her mouth descended once again into Ground Zero, I sighed. She owned me.

The best part was I owned her too. We still hadn't talked much about what our relationship meant, but that was hardly necessary since we'd effortlessly folded our lives into one another's. I had as many clothes at her house as she had at mine, and I even had my own set of keys to her Porsche. If that wasn't commitment, what was?

We'd also talked some more about our financial differences. She insisted she didn't care if we sometimes did things on the cheap, but implored me to accept the gifts she lavished upon me. I relented but insisted we shop mostly at the discount stores. Last year's clothes had always been good enough for me, and that wasn't going to change because I now had an extravagant girlfriend. I was still behind on my credit cards, as usual. Despite the recommendation from the good folks at Banco Primero, my refinancing application was ultimately rejected by the Treasury Department—probably Elena Diaz's doing—which left me hoping for Christmas money from my parents to catch me up.

Mari and I barely spent a night apart. Felix and Robbie T kept us busy on the weekend nightclub circuit, and Mari sprang for her own set of box seats at the Arsht Center so we wouldn't miss a classical performance. For the New World Symphony, though, we stuck with the Wallcasts, making an evening of it with Mordy and Edith. I'd become a regular at Mima's for birthday celebrations, which were frequent in a family that large. Last week, we'd gone shopping for a winter coat so Mari wouldn't freeze to death over Christmas when she accompanied me back to New Hampshire.

It suddenly occurred to me why I had trouble staying aroused after my first climax—because I let my mind wander to practical things. There was Mari, eating her little heart out, so to speak, while I was thinking about box seats and winter coats. I should have been thinking about how her tongue felt as it rolled over my freshly waxed Brazilian playground.

Once I turned my attention back to what she doing, my numb nub became a buzzing button, making me wish I could moan in Spanish. My second orgasm was less intense than the first but longer, since I didn't have to pull away from overpowering sensations.

Mari crawled up to lie beside me and shared my essence with a kiss. "I love having breakfast in bed on Sunday mornings."

"And I love being breakfast in bed."

"I have a surprise for you, but first you have to make me a tomato omelet with crispy bacon."

I loved Mari's surprises, less so when they meant getting out of bed. Today's surprise apparently involved going somewhere to be with other people, because Mari insisted we both shower away the scent of several hours of sex.

"You don't need your purse, or your phone, or anything else," she said as we readied to leave. "Nope, not your sunglasses either."

The only time I ever went out the door with only my key was when I visited Edith and Mordy. That possibility vanished when Mari called the elevator.

"Where are we going?"

"You'll see."

I gave up trying to guess when we got on and she pressed the button for the fourteenth floor. Obviously, we were going to see the Garcías, but what that had to do with a surprise was beyond me.

Ronaldo greeted us warmly and invited us into the living room, where Tandra had already prepared a tray of *café con leche* and guava pastries.

I'd never been inside their apartment and couldn't resist looking around with envy. Though we had the same floor plan, the similarities ended there. Theirs was decorated in a style I could describe with only one word—tasteful. Whereas my place had all the standard features, they had oak floors, black granite kitchen counters and designer lighting throughout, and their furniture looked like something out of a décor showroom.

Judging by the presence of a baby monitor on the glass coffee table, Isabel was asleep in the other room. That took away my best way of communicating with the Garcías, so I'd have to rely on Mari as a go-between.

"Ronaldo and I were talking last week about the plans for his import business, which is growing," Mari said. "He wants to make his permanent home here in Miami, and would like to apply for US citizenship in three more years."

"We learn English," he said. "Little by little."

I couldn't resist sharing a bit of what Mari had taught me, that I was learning Spanish little by little as well. "*Aprendo español poco a poco también.*"

Except now I felt really stupid because the Garcías spoke Portuguese.

"*Pero no portugués.*"

"*Hablamos español,*" Tandra said.

In other words, everyone here spoke Spanish but me. If this was Mari's idea of a surprise, we needed to have a chat.

But it was nice to visit, as long as I had her to translate. I needed to do things like this more often. Not so long ago, I would have been intimidated at being surrounded by people who were so different from me, but I welcomed it now because it gave me insight into Mari's cultural world. She'd get a dose of mine in New Hampshire next week.

She and the Garcías chatted excitedly for a minute and then all eyes turned to me.

"Ronaldo wants to bring Tandra's mother from São Paulo to help take care of Isabel. They also want to have another baby soon."

That was very sweet. If Ronaldo would willingly bring his mother-in-law to live closer, it was further proof to me he was the Perfect Man.

"The problem is their apartment has only two bedrooms, and they'll need at least four. They like this building very much because it's close to where Ronaldo works, and Tandra has Brazilian friends who live here."

As far as I knew, there were a couple of three-bedroom units on each floor, but none with four.

"Daphne, Ronaldo talked to the building manager and learned others have bought adjacent units and joined them together. If you have the desire to sell your apartment, they'd be very interested in buying it. They'd add a staircase and make three of the bedrooms upstairs."

Was that a trick question? Of course I'd sell.

Except…

"I can't sell. I'd have to pay off my whole mortgage and my apartment isn't worth that much anymore. The bank would make me come up with the difference, probably a hundred thousand dollars."

She translated for the Garcías, and the three of them conversed for a couple of long minutes while I tried to catch a word here and there. *Banco* was bank…*barato* was cheap. That didn't bode well.

"He says they have the same problem as you because it's hard to sell anything right now. That's why he wants to buy yours instead of trying to sell his so he can buy something bigger. He wants to assume your mortgage."

If that was one of the conditions, this was going nowhere. "Good luck with that. I had to jump through a thousand flaming hoops to assume my own mortgage when Emily left. They wanted me to refinance."

"Ronaldo knows Juan. They'll work it out."

In other words, Ronaldo could work one of those Latin deals under the table, while I couldn't. I hate those shenanigans except when they work out well for me, and this did. In fact, it was the white knight rescue I'd thought was impossible. "And everything's on the up and up?"

Mari nodded. "You lose your initial investment, but you get to walk away. No more debt and your credit rating won't take a hit."

Walk away to where? It would mean I didn't own a home anymore. Sure, I could probably buy one just like mine on another floor for a hundred thousand less, but I had nothing for a down payment, and probably couldn't qualify for a new mortgage by myself anyway.

It was way too soon to think about moving in with Mari. I loved her and I even dreamed about growing old together, but we'd never talked about a life like that, not even once. Jumping into something after only three months of dating was crazy. I'd done that with Emily, and it had ended in disaster.

Besides, Mari hadn't exactly asked me to move in with her. The last woman she'd lived with burned her with a felony charge. As best I could tell, she was happy shuffling back and forth between my place and hers. It was safe, a way for both of us to have all the best things about a relationship with none of the pressure.

Not that I have anything against a little pressure. Marriage between two women is legal in New Hampshire. I could maybe drop an engagement ring into her Christmas stocking. No rush… just something to pencil in at a future date when we both realize how magnificently this is working out.

"Daphne?"

"I'm thinking."

I could rent something, maybe over on Brickell so we could be closer to each other. One-bedroom apartments were going for a third of what I'd been paying on my mortgage, so I'd have enough left over to have a life with fashionable clothes. And I wouldn't have to buy generic toilet paper anymore.

"Okay, what would I have to do?"

"Say yes and give Ronaldo a copy of your loan papers. He'll take it from there."

"Yes." The moment the word left my lips, it was if I'd broken the shackles and stepped free for the first time in three years. I found myself celebrating joyously right along with the Garcías, and Mari looked like she'd just negotiated world peace.

We ran back upstairs to make copies of the documents, and after delivering them to Ronaldo, returned to my place, where I walked from room to room as if saying goodbye to it already. A small apartment within easy walking distance of Mari's would be perfect.

"Daphne, with Juan's help, this paperwork could go through pretty fast, but I don't want you to feel rushed about anything. You can stay with me until you decide what to do."

Well, there you go. I guess that put us on the same page…not ready to live together, even though we hardly spent a night apart.

That said, what I really wanted was a commitment, not something as dramatic as a bent knee proposal, but something a little more promising than putting me up while I look for a place to live.

Not that I have anything against bent knee proposals.

"Though if you're planning to stay in Miami, it would be silly to move into my place for just a few weeks and then move out again. Just come live with me."

Hold that thought.

"What do you mean if I stay in Miami?"

She huffed softly and slumped onto the couch. "You're the one who talks about the big corporate job you missed out on because you came to Miami to be with Emily. Now you're free to go if a job in Boston is what you really want."

I hadn't thought about that job in weeks, or for that matter, leaving Miami. "Is that your way of telling me I shouldn't make the same mistake I did with Emily by staying here to be with you?"

"I didn't say that at all. I just don't want you to stay with me if it means you'll have regrets."

In the first place, it wasn't even relevant because there wasn't a job offer to consider. And in the second place, "Why would I even look for another job if I'm happy here?"

"Are you?" She patted the couch beside her and wrapped an arm around my shoulder when I sat down. "I remember when all you wanted was a way out of Miami."

"That was before I met you." And admittedly before I'd had the pleasure of watching the symphony from box seats, eating dinner aboard a private yacht, and skipping past the rope lines to get into the hottest clubs on South Beach. Miami really is the Magic City when you have access to money.

I wish I hadn't thought about money when I was trying to make a point about what a difference Mari had made in my outlook. The real changes had happened in my head and heart the moment I quit fighting the Latin culture and embraced it, especially once I understood why feelings about Cuba ran so deep. This was now home and I wanted to be here.

"How could I love you and not Miami? You're practically one and the same."

"Is that a good thing?"

"It's a great thing." I snuggled into her side and trailed my fingers lazily along her forearm, smiling to see goose bumps rise in the wake. "There's an old saying"—nothing as colorful as snoring mangos—"that happiness isn't getting what you want. It's wanting what you already have. That's where I am, Mari. I'm happy because I'm with you."

"That's nice...I like that."

"So where are you?" I wasn't looking for an ego-fortifying list of platitudes. I needed only to know that she thought what we had was special.

"We have a Cuban saying too. It won't sound as sweet as yours but it goes, *no hay mal que por bien no venga*. There is no bad that doesn't come to good. Delores meant to hurt me, and instead she gave me a beautiful gift because I met you."

Of all the things she'd ever said to me, that was far and away the most romantic. That and her statement that she loved me were probably the most I'd get. Plus her invitation to come live with her permanently. And her concern for my financial well-being and worries about my future regrets.

If all that wasn't Mari expressing herself, it was only because I hadn't been listening. One of us was holding back, but it wasn't her.

"I would like to live with you. And maybe someday we'll take an even bigger step than that." I was too chicken to look at her so I nuzzled my head under her chin. "I always hoped I'd get married one of these days."

She didn't answer me for a few seconds, which made me worry I'd gone too far. Then I felt her arm tighten around my shoulder and her lips press against my temple.

"I always say people should dream big."

Bella Books, Inc.

Women. Books. Even Better Together.

P.O. Box 10543

Tallahassee, FL 32302

Phone: 800-729-4992

www.bellabooks.com